MW01231459

TIGER WOMAN

A Novel

John W. Huffman

This book is based on true events, however the story is largely a work of fiction. People, places, events, and situations are the product of the author's imagination. Any resemblance to actual persons, living or dead, is purely coincidental.

No part of this book may be reproduced, stored in a retrieval system, or transmitted by any means without the written permission of the author.

Copyright © 2009 John W. Huffman
All rights reserved.

ISBN: 1-4348-5643-7
ISBN-13: 9781434856432

Visit www.booksurge.com to order additional copies.

ACKNOWLEDGMENTS

My deepest appreciation to Jerry Nealy, Jodi Nix, and Billy Sprouse for their invaluable time and input into my initial drafts of this story.

A special thank you to Anna Wood for her detailed, professional proofing of this work.

DEDICATION

To my wonderful wife, Misty, my youngest son, Westley, and my adorable daughter-in-law, Anna, whose encouragement made this novel a reality.

CHAPTER 1

Allen feared his imagination was getting the best of him, his mind playing tricks on him in the forbidding darkness. He swept the sandy mane of damp hair from his forehead with a brush of his hand, his eyes widening, trying to see through the murky haze, wishing he had blue eyes instead of brown. He had heard somewhere that blue eyes could see better in the dark. Kevin had blue eyes. He considered waking Kevin dozing restlessly beside him, as he imagined menacing shadows stealing towards him in the shapeless void smothering him. He held his breath, peering hard at the indistinguishable shapes, trying to convince himself it was only his psyche working overtime. Still, he considered waking Kevin with his blue eyes, as he glanced at the luminous glow of his watch to find fifteen minutes still left on his shift. If he woke Kevin early, he would probably only make a fool of himself again. He closed his eyes and lowered his chin to the stock of his rifle pointed out to his front, exhausted by the long day's grueling patrol in the ungodly heat and the arduous night march out to this hellish location, as he lay shivering in the damp, filmy nothingness, finding the chill night air almost as unbearable.

Mercifully, his equilibrium was stabilizing somewhat, though he was still weak and disorientated. Kevin, a veteran of five months in-country assigned by their squad leader to help get him squared away, said night ambushes were the worst part of combat. This, his own ninth day in-country and first day in a hostile environment, was proving to be the worst experience of his life. Though Kevin attempted to prepare him for what was to come, mere words alone could never have prepared him for this misery. He trembled under the unbearable tension, his heart thudding in his chest, his head pounding with the strain of listening to the deep hush, his attempts to force his heavy-lidded eyes open to peer into the void mostly futile as they quivered under the layers of numbing fatigue.

Huddled next to Kevin in the ambush site with their squad arrayed in two-man positions in the curved arc of a D formation and the remainder of the platoon strung out in a straight line behind them facing a road junction, they'd crouched here for four tedious hours waiting for unsuspecting prey to wander into their trap. After the harrowing, groping, stop and go movement through this alien world surrounded by lethal shadows, he was now alternating one-hour guard shifts with Kevin as mosquitoes swirled about him in droves, leaving whelps on any exposed patch of skin, even biting through his jungle fatigues to devour his blood in greedy droughts. Tiny creatures crawled under his shirt in hot, irritating patches of discomfort, but he dared not move or swat at the annoying insects in the suffocating quiet. All seemed evil in this ominous setting, filling him with dreadful trepidation. He breathed in shallow pulls, fretful that expanding his chest would make an accidental rustle in the leaves where he lay facing the sinister blankness to his front. Tears trickled down his cheeks, softening the coating of camouflage paint on his face, as he considered the year stretching before him.

He had joined the Third Platoon the previous day, after attending the mandatory weeklong combat orientation classes staged for new replacements. The horror began this morning, when Sergeant Davis got their squad up and moving early to cross the five strands of concertina wire surrounding their base camp out into this no-man's land with the rest of their platoon on what was supposed to be a routine search and destroy mission. He drank all of the water in his three canteens by noon in the oppressive heat and humidity. By early afternoon, dizzy from dehydration, he was merely stumbling along in a heat-induced fog, trying to stay online with the rest of the platoon, as they broke out of some scrub brush and slogged through knee-deep water across a rice paddy several hundred yards wide. A sharp *Crack! Crack! Crack!* sent a drove of hornets swarming around his ears. He gaped in surprise for a startled instant, as those around him lunged for cover before belatedly plunging headlong into the brackish water in panic when he realized someone was trying to harm him. He wallowed to the safety of an earthen berm dividing the paddy into squares and cowered there, his nose inches from the filthy water, as the men on each side of him returned fire in a jarring roar.

"Get your head out of your ass, Hayes!" Sergeant Davis yelled at him in the ensuing chaos. "Return fire, goddamn it!"

Until that moment, he had not even considered firing back at the antagonists shooting at them—his only interest being survival. When he sheepishly raised his head, a harsh slap across his face snapped his head back. He dropped his rifle into the tepid water and clutched at his eyes with the thundering weapons around him even more terrifying in his unseeing state, thinking himself seriously wounded. He staggered up and turned in a confused circle to find safety, to seek help, to…

3

"Allen! Get down!" Kevin screamed in the disorder before colliding with him and knocking him back down into the mud. "Stay down, man! You'll get killed running around like that!"

"*I-I can't see!*" he whimpered in the uproar.

When the firefight ended as abruptly as it started, and the enemy disappeared back into the hedgerows, Kevin propped him against the berm to assess the damage as Sergeant Davis sloshed over to them.

"Do we need a medevac here, Kev?"

"Naw, he's okay, Sarge," Kevin replied, as he scooped water from the rice paddy with his cupped palms and washed Allen's face. "Just caught an eye full of mud from a ricochet is all."

"Goddamn you, Hayes, you ever turn tail on me in a firefight again, I'll fuckin' shoot your stupid ass myself! You got that, dip-shit?"

"I-I thought…"

"You *weren't* thinking! You were freakin' the fuck out! Get this Fuckin' New Guy shaped the fuck up, Kev, before I have to order a fuckin' body bag to ship his dumb-ass back home to his mother in!"

"I-I wasn't trying to run, Kevin, honest," Allen mumbled as Sergeant Davis stalked off. "I-I thought I…"

Kevin fished his M-16 out of the paddy and thrust it at him. "Aw, don't worry about it, man. You'll eventually catch on to what's going down around here, if you last long enough."

Allen fell back into the squad behind Kevin in shame as Sergeant Davis got them up and moving again. He followed up this debacle by collapsing from heat stress as the afternoon wore on. Again, Sergeant Davis stormed over to where he lay gasping, his mind revolving in dizzying circles.

"You fuckin' pussy! You drank all your water, didn't you? I swear to fuck, they don't teach you Fuckin' New Guys shit in those orientation classes. *Not shit!* Kev, get him a few ounces of water from the rest of the squad and distribute his rifle and gear around to them, or leave him to fuck here, it don't matter a shit which to me!"

Allen could not remember ever being so humiliated as when he staggered along afterwards in the 110-degree heat trying to recover his wits, unable to carry his own load, fighting waves of nausea, trying desperately to maintain his balance as objects swirled at crazy angles in his reeling, heat-crazed mind.

He had never failed at anything in his life, but he was a failure as a soldier. He couldn't help it. No one had ever told him it would be this bad, this inhumane. Somewhere lurking out there in this god-awful place men waited to hurt him. He did not want to hurt anybody; but they wanted to kill him and he didn't even understand why. He longed for the comfort of his bed back home, or even for the safety of the wretchedness of their primitive base camp back at Cu Chi. If only he had enlisted he could have chosen to become a clerk or a cook or qualified for any number of other safe jobs in the rear. Anything was better than being in the infantry, even serving three years as a volunteer instead of two as a draftee. He could not take twelve months of this. He would crack up first. He would disgrace himself and his family if he did not find a way out of this living hell.

He jerked his head up and forced his eyes wide in alarm, willing his dulled senses to yield something comprehensible as a twig snapped. *Damn, one of the shadows moved!* He was certain of it. No, maybe not. He forced himself to look off to the side, as they had taught him in basic training, instead of staring directly at the blacker orb in the overall darkness.

There! It *was* moving—straight at him! His heart pounded in earnest as terror surged through his body. He reached a tremulous hand over to grasp Kevin's arm, as leaves crunched to his front.

"*Kevin! Something's out there!*" he yelped.

An orange blossom spouted almost in his face. A numbing blow slammed into his arm. A roar of automatic weapons fire deafened him. Running shadows swarmed over them as strange voices screamed abruptly in the mayhem. He rose to his knees, not even bothering to pull his rifle up. Something hard slammed against his head.

All noise faded as he succumbed to the welcoming tranquility of oblivion.

CHAPTER 2

"*Sergeant Adkins!*" a voice yelled, as the beam of a flashlight swept back and forth between the twin rows of cots lining each side of the narrow aisle in the noncommissioned officers' hooch.

Adkins' eyes snapped open, bringing him to full awareness without preliminary grogginess, as was his custom in awakening.

"*Sergeant Adkins!*"

"Last bunk on the right, goddamn it!" an irritable voice growled from somewhere in the center of the hooch.

Adkins swung his bare legs over the side of the cot and sat up as the man shined his light in his face. "Sergeant Adkins?"

"Get that fucking light out of my face, jackass," Adkins ordered, shielding the beam with his palm.

The man jerked his flashlight upwards to the green tarp ceiling, the vertical glow revealing a wide-eyed young replacement. "Top says to tell you to get over to the Orderly Room pronto! Says to get your platoon together and combat loaded!"

Adkins glanced at the glowing dial of his watch: 0215 hours in the morning. "Why?"

"Top didn't say why, Sergeant. He just said to do it," the soldier explained breathlessly.

Adkins sighed and stood up. "Go over to the First Platoon hooches and wake my Squad Leaders. Tell them to get the men saddled up."

The private rushed out of the hooch, anxious to leave this cauldron of irritable NCOs behind before someone nailed his hide to the wall, slamming the screen door in his haste, causing several sleeping men to groan and curse in the restored darkness.

Adkins stretched, peeled his underwear off, and tossed them on his bunk, leaving him naked except for his dog tags hanging around his neck. Dead tired after fourteen straight days in the field, he'd relished the prospect of bringing his platoon to the rear for a much-needed rest and retrofit. After choppering in the evening before with the rest of the company, his fifty-man platoon was physically and mentally exhausted, in an ill mood, and badly in need of downtime. They'd enjoyed their first shower and hot meal in two weeks before spending the evening drinking cold beer in the Wolf's Den, their squalid battalion beer joint, to unwind after their taxing mission into the Boi Loi Woods.

He cursed as he slipped on his fresh jungle fatigues and shoved his bare feet into the new canvas jungle boots he had exchange earlier for his worn out rags and boots with the wheezing alcoholic who posed as their supply sergeant. He purposely omitted underwear, undershirt, and socks due to the humidity that clung to those garments in the 100-degree plus heat of Southeast Asia, fostering trench foot and jungle rot. He despairingly strapped on his web gear, jammed his helmet on his head, grabbed his M-16 from its place above the head of his cot, and eased out the back door, pausing to light his first cigarette of the day before threading his way through the narrow opening in the waist-high row of sandbags surrounding the hooch. He inhaled deeply, using the harsh sting of nicotine to shock his system to full alert, as he assessed First Sergeant Vickers sitting at his desk inside the squalid wood and screen walled hooch of the orderly room, which differed from the others in the unit area only by its rusty tin top. Captain James stood near him talking on the field phone. Adkins thumped his cigarette away and slipped through the sandbag wall, climbed the rickety steps, pushed through the screen door, and headed for the coffee pot.

"Morning, Captain," he greeted his commander cordially before glaring at First Sergeant Vickers. "Top, I *assume* you need some asshole killed to get me up this early in the morning. Just point the son of a bitch out and I'll go shoot him so I can get back to bed!" he growled, as he filled a cup from the tap at the bottom of the large pot.

"My-my, aren't we in a lovely mood this morning?" Vickers allowed, twirling his ever-present fat cigar between his thumb and forefinger.

Adkins grimaced, as he sniffed at his cup. "Actually, my mood sucks, and so does your coffee. What did you mix with this mud, cow shit?"

"You ain't got time for coffee. The 5th Mechanized Ready Reaction Force is rolling towards us now. They've requested a platoon of infantry as reinforcements."

Adkins cut his eyes at him. "Who's getting their ass kicked?"

"Our goddamned Third Platoon got hit twenty minutes ago. It doesn't look good."

Captain James hung up his field phone and turned to them. "Lieutenant Bryant screamed over his radio they were being overrun and called for all preplanned supporting fires. That was his only transmission. Battalion says there's only scattered fighting in the area now, according to the gunships circling overhead. We need somebody out there on the ground to tell us what's going on."

Adkins slammed his cup down and turned to the door, his gut clenching. "Shit! I assume they're on our company freq?"

"They were until they stopped responding to our calls!" First Sergeant Vickers yelled after him.

Adkins rushed to his platoon of bleary-eyed men assembling in front of their hooch as the armored personnel carriers churned towards them, his thoughts on his best friend, Kevin, a member of the Third Platoon. "Okay, listen up, you shits! Our Third Platoon is in deep *do-do* out there. All radio contact with them has been lost. We're the designated Reaction Force. We'll be riding out to their fucking rescue with the Mech. Squad Leaders! Give me two men from each squad for my track! Let's move it!"

He turned and trotted towards the APCs rolling to a stop on the gravel road beside them and scrambled up the back ramp of the lead track as eight men peeled off and ran in behind him, with the remainder of the four squads filing into the other four vehicles.

The lieutenant commanding the tracks leaned down from his turret housing the .50-caliber machine gun. "Are you the Platoon Leader?"

"I'm Sergeant Adkins, the Acting Platoon Leader," Adkins yelled back over the throbbing diesel engine. "Let's roll these monsters!"

The lieutenant swung back up to his turret and pressed the transmit button on his radio headset as they rumbled towards the Charlie Company exit through the fifth wire.

CHAPTER 3

Allen grew conscious of ringing in his ears. Feeling returned with raw pounding in his head. He rolled sluggishly over onto his back and moaned as sharp pain lanced his left arm. A Vietnamese voice growled something in the yellow wavering light. He tried to focus on a flare floating overhead casting artificial dark patterns about him as it drifted high in the sky, becoming cognizant of tight cords binding his hands behind him, cutting into his wrists. The sharp odor of cordite assailed his nostrils as he licked at the corroded salt on his lips and gagged when he realized it was blood. As his vision cleared, he lifted his head groggily to look around.

A Vietnamese man with an AK-47 automatic rifle prodded him in his side with the muzzle. "You no move! You stay. No move!"

His heartbeat increased rapidly with the abrupt realization that he was a prisoner. Sticky blood oozed down his left arm from a throbbing wound just below his shoulder. The left side of his aching head seemed to have a large growth on it. He dimly recalled someone bashing his skull in during the sudden onslaught. He turned his head and saw Kevin crumpled next to him.

"No! *Please, no! Don't oww aiiiiiiiiiii!*" an American voice wailed from his left, out of his range of vision.

A female laughed harshly and barked something in Vietnamese. The man next to Allen grabbed a handful of his hair, jerked him up into a kneeling position, and forced him around to face the rest of the ambush site. Bodies lay scattered about. A large group of Vietnamese men and women armed with rifles stood in a half circle around two American soldiers kneeling with their hands tied behind their backs in front of a petite woman with short hair dressed in green jungle fatigues with yellow slashes. A third American soldier lay moaning at her feet with his pants pulled down. The woman lifted her bloody fist triumphantly above her head as the soldier on the ground whimpered. Black blood spewed from his groin area. Allen gasped in horror as the tiny woman stooped and stuffed the man's testicles into his mouth as he squirmed. She inserted the point of her knife into his stomach just below the ribcage and sliced him down to his bloody groin as he jerked in agony. She then reached into his stomach, grabbed a fistful of his guts, and flipped the mass into the man's face to muffle his screams.

The little pixie laughed as she kicked the writhing man in the ribs. "You pig. *American* pig! You beg to die, pig! You *beg* like dog!"

Sergeant Patterson from First Squad, one of the two kneeling men, squirmed, his face contorted in rage. "You fucking bitch!"

The little woman turned to Sergeant Patterson. "You no like? You no enjoy?"

She spoke something in Vietnamese. Two men rushed forward to grab Patterson's head. She dug her thumb into his eye, gouging his eyeball out, leaving it dangling down his cheek. As he screamed, she swiftly dug the other eye out of its socket, then grabbed his jaw with one hand and sliced his tongue off with the knife she held in the other, leaving him gurgling in his own blood. She quickly sliced off his ears in two quick strokes and sliced his stomach from side to side, spilling his intestines out onto the ground in front of him.

"I fuckin' bitch now?" she taunted, as the two men released him to collapse quivering onto the ground before her.

The remaining soldier, Private Slocomb from Second Squad, wept as she moved in front of him and grasped his chin, forcing his terror-filled eyes to look up into her face in the flickering light.

"Please, Ma'am, don't hurt me. Please ..."

Her bloody hand caressed his cheek. "You pretty boy. You want to fucky fucky with me, pretty boy?" She sliced his belt and pants, which sagged to his bended knees, and grabbed a handful of his bare genitals as he sobbed. "Why you not big for me, pretty boy? You can no fucky fucky me with noodle." She squeezed as Slocomb shuddered. "If no use to me, no use to you!" In one motion, she cut his penis off and plopped it in his mouth to stifle his choking screams. "Can no fucky fucky me now, pretty boy," she insisted, as she slashed his stomach and hacked his ears off before placing her foot in his chest and shoving him over backward with his intestines trailing after him.

She stiffened and turned to listen intently to a growing rumble in the distance, then barked orders sharply in Vietnamese. The man beside Allen jerked him to his feet as the woman reached into the pouch slung at her side, pulled out an eight-by-ten glossy black-and-white photograph, and pinned it to a stake with her bloody knife. As the guard drug him past, Allen saw the picture depicted the woman dressed in her green jungle fatigues with the yellow stripes staring into the camera, smiling maliciously as a group of men and women brandished AK-47s in the background in a mocking jeer.

The man tugged at his elbow. "You move! You keep up or you die!"

Allen struggled along in a half stumble as a ripping roar of carbines and AKs erupted behind them. His guard prodded him along as an angry volley of M-16s answered, interspaced with the thumping of heavy caliber machine guns.

They quickly splintered into smaller groups moving in different directions until there was only his guard and one other man remaining with him. The two men jerked him into a heavy bamboo thicket, where one of the men pulled up a leaf-covered top to a hole in the ground and motioned to him. Allen slid his six-foot frame down to sit on the edge of hole and swung his legs into the small opening, as the other man untied his hands and shoved him downward. He worked his body awkwardly into the narrow opening, his insides jelly, his mind feverish, fearing that at any moment the little Vietnamese woman would materialize out of the night with knife in hand.

A second tunnel at the bottom led off to the side of the vertical shaft, delineated by a dim light at the end. He crawled on his hands and knees into the cramped space, as his wounded arm protested, traversing through the narrow, descending channel to his front. The dark passageway led to a larger, faintly lit area thirty yards in front of him, where the stooped head of another Vietnamese man watched his progress as the two men behind him prodded him along. The man at the end of the burrow grabbed him by his shoulders, jerked him into the larger carved out room, threw him onto the dirt floor, and began cursing him in Vietnamese as he kicked wildly at his face. Allen cowered and covered his head with his arms as the other two men crawled out and tried to pull the first man away from him. The first man pushed them aside and kicked him in the groin for emphasis, sending blinding pain shooting up through the pit of his stomach.

"You no big man now, American dog!"

Allen curled into a fetal position grasping his groin, gagging in his own vomit, as the two men who brought him here pulled the other man back.

One of his benefactors bent over him. "You move! On hands and knees, or maybe I let him kill you, American pig!"

Allen rolled over onto his stomach and struggled up onto his hands and knees to crawl in the indicated direction into another narrow passageway approximately two meters in height leading away from the small cavern. As he crawled past, the first man rushed forward and kicked him in the buttocks, dumping him onto his face in the dirt, as he laughed.

Allen struggled up and crawled for an indefinite time, passing through several larger, dimly lit rooms two meters high and ten meters wide, each separated by the narrow earthen-connecting tunnels. The Vietnamese occupants in the larger rooms stared at him curiously as he crawled by, but no one spoke to or attempted to injure him. He gasped for oxygen in the damp, foul air, as he struggled along with the man behind him prodding him, indicating the different routes in the semi-darkness. Eventually he crawled into a large, two-meter high, thirty-meter square, oil lamp-lit room containing cots with Vietnamese men wearing bloody bandages lying on them.

A Vietnamese man bandaged his arm without speaking, and then superficially inspected his facial cuts and bruises before pointing to an empty cot, where he collapsed in gratitude as he succumbed to the pain and exhaustion racking his battered mind and body, praying silently that this was all just a nightmare.

CHAPTER 4

Sergeant Adkins clung to the high sides of the armored personnel carrier as it lurched through the rubber trees towards the flare lit sky and circling red lights of the gunships. Low hanging branches scraped the steel sides, forcing him to dodge as the limbs slapped at his exposed head. The night was disorientating in their onward rush as he looked out from the open top, the churning diesel engine drowning out all other sound, as the giant vehicle twisted and turned without warning, the unexpected jolts slinging him against the inside walls.

A multitude of AK-47 automatic weapons and carbines opened fire on them from the darkness to their left front, the bullets clanking against the steel sides of the APCs and zinging away in piercing ricochets. His men rose up as the tracks came to a halt, returning fire at the sprouting muzzle flashes, the big .50-caliber machine guns of the five APCs thumping in earnest along with them. The enemy firing ended abruptly. They lurched forward again, and immediately encountered a second volley of gunfire. The APC's again halted and his men returned fire into the shadows.

Adkins ducked down and snatched at the pants leg of the track commander up in the turret. "Lieutenant, this is just a delaying action! They're trying to slow us down.

The next time they fire on us, have two of your tracks stop and engage them. We and the other two tracks need to charge on through. We'll be all night getting to our Third Platoon at this pace."

"You want me to split my force, Sergeant?" the lieutenant yelled as he leaned down from the turret. "Are you crazy? We don't know what the hell's out there in front of us. We could be running into an ambush ourselves!"

"Whatever the fuck's out there is more afraid of us than we are of them, Lieutenant!" Adkins yelled back. "That's why this group is trying to hold us up. Just charge on through, god damn it! We're in five fucking steel fortresses with .50-caliber machine guns and a platoon of pissed-off Infantry. We're the bad asses out here and they know it!"

The lieutenant returned to his turret and they lurched off again. Almost immediately, the gloom to their front erupted into sprouts of yellow-tinged gunfire. The two tracks on the left stopped and lay down a wall of fire as their command track and the two on the right continued charging forward. The surprised VC broke ranks and fled into the night before the onslaught. Within minutes, they approached the ambush site and paused for the two tracks left behind to catch up before moving forward cautiously to draw up before the indistinguishable, strewn bodies of the Third Platoon backlit by the flares overhead.

"Lieutenant, space your tracks around this place facing out for security," Adkins directed. "We'll dismount. Have the artillery fire more flares for visibility."

The APCs lurched forward to space themselves around the Third Platoon position in a rough circle. Adkins motioned for his men to dismount and sent the squad leaders and their men into positions between the tracks for further security as he looked the area over carefully.

A dirt road was to their front. The Third Platoon had set up with that as their kill zone. A large thicket was to their rear. It was a good ambush site, he approved, as he led his eight-man group and Doc, the platoon medic, to the scattered shapes lying around in a rough circle. They were inside the former perimeter of the platoon itself before they could clearly see the bodies in the artificial light of the flares.

"Oh my god!" Doc moaned, kneeling beside one of the bodies. "Oh my god ... what happened here?"

One of the men near Doc fell to his knees vomiting. Another turned away, his face ashen. "Man, I can't take this shit," another moaned, his voice quivering.

"Check them all," Adkins ordered grimly. "See if anyone is still alive." He knew in his heart none were as the pungent smell of blood, death, and torn, leaking intestines waffled over them in a nauseating wave. Near the rear of the position, he found Kevin. He stood over him fighting the bile rising in his throat as tears welled up in his eyes. He turned and stumbled away from the gruesome sight, only to draw up abruptly in front of the bloodstained picture pinned to the stake in the middle of the ambush site. He squinted hard at the woman with the striped fatigues surrounded by her jeering comrades. His stomach clutched. A profound, dark, bottomless rage welled up within him as the woman in the picture stared back at him with a faint, mocking grin. Ice-cold apprehension gripped him and his teeth gritted until his jaw ached. He had on occasion known fear born of circumstance, but until this moment, he had never feared any one person in his life.

He looked into the eyes of the woman as tremors coursed through him. "You bitch!" he spat at her mocking picture. "I'll kill you for this. I'll hunt you down and kill you like the fucking animal you are." He glanced back over his shoulder at Kevin's mutilated, crumpled form lying in a pool of bloody gore. "I promise you, man, I'll fucking kill this crazy bitch for you." He stretched out his arm to his radioman. "Carl, bring my fucking radio."

The RTO stumbled over and handed him the handset with a trembling hand, tears trickling down his cheeks, his eyes wide in shock.

Adkins cleared his constricted throat and keyed the transmitter. "Mustang Alpha Six, Mustang Alpha One. Over."

"Mustang Alpha One, this is Mustang Alpha Seven," First Sergeant Vickers answered. "Mustang Alpha Six is at Hotel Quebec. Over," he responded, informing Adkins that the commander was at the battalion headquarters.

"Roger, Seven, relay a message to Alpha Six. Over."

"Roger, Alpha One, send your message. Over."

"I need Alpha Six out here at first light. Over."

"Are there any survivors? Over," Vickers asked.

"None that we've found so far. I've never seen anything like this. Over."

"Roger. I'll pass your request for Alpha Six up the line. Over," Vickers confirmed.

"Roger, Seven. Request that he expedite. Over."

"Roger, Seven. Out."

"Alpha One, out." Adkins handed the handset back to the RTO and brushed at the tears staining his cheeks.

CHAPTER 5

Tran Thi Cai slipped into the tiny room carved out of the earth deep below the surface that had served as her home for the last two years and pulled the cloth door covering closed behind her, disdainful of the damp quarters, which held only a narrow canvas cot and one small, hand fabricated bamboo table. She stripped her fatigues off with trembling hands, almost giddy, as she stood naked in the iridescent candlelight and washed the dried blood from her fingers in the small pan of water, basking in the glorious victory she had achieved. After weeks of recruiting and training, her soldiers performed flawlessly in their first operation. The American imperialists put up only a token resistance. None of her marvelous soldiers incurred an injury in the abrupt attack. They exercised admirable discipline and restraint in the capture of the enemy soldiers as well. They were a great credit in serving a poignant message from the People's Liberation Army upon the imperialistic dogs occupying their country.

She shuddered pleasurably as she bathed, closing her eyes in rapture as she recalled the prisoners they had taken groveling before her. She had waited for months for that moment. It was unfortunate time did not permit her to service the wounded one they had captured, but she was content with the fact that the cadre would ship him north as further proof of her imposing victory.

She assuaged this single regret with the reminiscence of her group stumbling upon two more of the American dogs during their hasty withdrawal who were cowering in a bush without their weapons after having run away in panic during her initial assault. She made quick work of them, taking just enough time to savor their desperation and ensure they suffered as much as possible before their unworthy essence faded into obscurity. She imagined again the feel of their warm blood splashing across her hands. As she dipped her cloth into the pail and washed her small, delicate body, a rustle of cloth introduced another presence into the room behind her.

"Cai," a voice spoke in a commanding fashion.

She stiffened at the intrusion on her delicious revelry and reluctantly turned, casting her eyes downward, standing naked before him, suppressing the familiar jolt of revulsion.

He moved to her and placed his hands on each side of her bowed head. "Cai," Colonel Nguyen Van Chien, fifty-five years old and thirty years her senior, repeated softly as he gently stroked her hair.

She stood submissive, his to use as he wished. Though she loathed his exploitation of her body, she preferred his singular attentions to the constant barrage of solicitations she received from other men before him. It was a small price to pay for his pulling her from the lowly transport service and eventually placing her in the Liberation Forces, where she rose rapidly in rank to command her own elite unit.

"Cai," he spoke her name again with the familiar huskiness of need in his tone.

Her name meant simply "female." She was resigned to the fact that men found her attractive, in spite of her efforts to appear plain, such as wearing her hair uncharacteristically short for Asian women. However, she could not disguise her perfect nose or pouting, sensuous lips below large, almond eyes, slightly slanted due to the touch of Chinese in her heritage, which gave them an inviting, wicked countenance men found irresistible. As a child, her father often proudly remarked that she would choose from many that would attempt to woo her. As a woman, with small breasts perfectly proportioned for her tiny body and full, curvaceous hips, many found her striking, even beautiful; but she only resented the unwanted attention her physical attributes brought her.

Chien, her sole lover for the past two years, placed his hands on her shoulders and pressed her down onto her knees. She had long reconciled herself to the depraved satisfaction he took from her body and impatiently anticipated the day he would eventually tire of her and take up with a younger woman.

"We had a great victory tonight," she whispered, as she unbuttoned his pants.

"You have brought us great honor," he agreed as his hands grasped her hair and his breath quickened. "Your victory will not go unnoticed by our comrades in the North. They will sing your praise throughout the land."

CHAPTER 6

Lieutenant Colonel Moore stepped from the helicopter followed by several of his aides and hurried past without pausing. Captain James turned and followed the Wolfhound Battalion Commander and his entourage, resisting the urge to salute, as would be the custom in base camp, cognizant of the fact that in the field snipers were always on the alert for officers and a salute would be an invitation to make his commander a target.

Colonel Moore drew up short of the strewn circle of bodies. "Sweet mother of Jesus!" He turned to Captain James, who had flown in a half hour earlier at first light. "What the fuck happened here, Captain?"

Captain James averted his eyes from the site. "Sir, it's the worst thing I've ever seen. As near as we can piece together, they hit my Third Platoon around 0200 hours this morning. It appears they caught them unawares and overran their position. The few M-16 shell casings indicate they didn't have much of a chance to put up a fight. It looks like they disfigured most of the men after death, Sir, with the exception of these three over here with their hands tied behind their backs. They were definitely alive when they were... *butchered...*"

Colonel Moore stared at the three men lying at his feet. "Are all of the men in the platoon accounted for?"

"There were eight men missing when the Reaction Force arrived, Sir. Five men have since been located alive. They wandered back into our perimeter during the night. They're in shock and can't tell us much. All they know is that the bastards were all over them without warning. According to them, everything was quiet one moment, and the next all hell broke loose. They've been medevacked out to the hospital. Two more were found strung upside down in a tree and slaughtered in the same fashion as these three about a half-mile from here. There's still one man missing and unaccounted for."

Colonel Moore turned back to survey the gory carnage. "What kind of fucking animals would do this sort of thing?"

"This kind of animal, Sir." He indicated the stake with the picture of the alluring woman in tiger fatigues and her grinning companions pinned to it by the knife covered in dried blood.

"Sweet mother of Jesus!" Colonel Moore swore as he moved closer to the picture. "What the fuck are we dealing with here, Captain?"

"Damned if I know, Sir, but this isn't war according to the Geneva Conventions."

"That's a good point. This is definitely a war crime. I want this whole scene photographed from every angle. I'm certain the Commanding General will want to see this first-hand. As of now, this incident is classified. Who has seen this mess up to this point?"

"Sir, currently the First Platoon from my Alpha Company and the Mechanized Platoon from the Reaction Force have viewed the site. Outside of you and your staff, that's all that's seen this ungodly mess."

"I want your First Platoon and the Mech Platoon informed they will not discuss what they have seen here with anyone outside of their immediate detachment. Keep them together and keep the others isolated from this position until we get this mess cleaned up. I want as few men as possible to see this debacle. Is that understood, Captain?"

"Yes, Sir. It is done, Sir." He turned to the shade of a tree and motioned to Sergeant Adkins standing off to the side watching them as he pressed a handkerchief over his nose to ward off the stench from the bloated corpses blackening in the rising temperature of the noon sun.

Sergeant Adkins moved over to him, swatting at the hoards of green flies buzzing around them drawn by the congealing pools of blood. "Captain?"

"Sergeant, a chopper is inbound with body bags," he advised, his voice muffled by the handkerchief covering his mouth. "Have your platoon place these... *men*... in them and load them on the birds as they come in."

Adkins looked over his shoulder at the site. "My men... are not trained to handle something like this, Captain."

"This site is classified, Sergeant. Your men have already seen it. You and your men will not discuss what you have seen here with anyone outside of your immediate platoon. Is that clear?"

Adkins nodded. "Your order is clear, Captain,"

"I know this task is normally one the graves registration personnel perform... but I'm sure your men will manage, Sergeant," Captain James continued.

"I'm sure they will, Captain," Adkins swore under his breath, as he turned to the outside of their small perimeter

manned by his platoon and the five tracks from the 5th Mech, which was now inside a larger circle of soldiers from the battalion forming a protective circle around them. Beyond that ring were hundreds more soldiers searching for the missing man of the Third Platoon as gunships lurked overhead looking for targets of opportunity. "*Squad Leaders, post!*" he shouted, and waited for his squad leaders to gather around him. "I don't want to hear no bitching, because I've already bitched for you. You shits got that?" The squad leaders nodded in unison, eyeing Captain James behind him warily. "A chopper is inbound with body bags. Form your men into teams and get these poor sons of bitches zipped up and on the choppers."

"You gotta be shitting me, Sarge!" Sergeant Gonzales, the second squad leader, groaned.

Adkins glowered at him. "I said no fucking bitching, Gonzales—now just get it done!"

"Yeah, but, Sarge," Sergeant Fielding from third squad moaned, "these guys are cut all to pieces. Their guts are hanging out and everything. There's body parts laying everywhere."

"Borrow some shovels from the Mech to scoop up the remains with, Fielding," Adkins ordered. "Do your best to get the right parts with the right body."

"You heard the man," Sergeant Handler from first squad encouraged. "All we're gonna do now is get our ass chewed for whining. Let's get the shit done so we can get the fuck out of here already."

"You're a real kiss ass, Handler," Sergeant Brooks from fourth squad retorted. "I'd rather do this sick shit myself than make my men do it."

"You're right, Sergeant Brooks," Adkins said, turning to Kevin's swollen body near the rear of the ambush site. "We never ask our men to do something we're unwilling to do ourselves. Me and the rest of you fucking prima donnas will pitch in and help them."

"Aw shit, Brooks, you big mouthed shit-head!" Gonzales moaned from behind him.

"I agree with Sarge," Handler said, turning to his squad. "As bad as this shit's gonna be, we need to help pull the load."

"Aw shit, Handler, I bet you're gonna re-up for twenty and be a fucking *Lifer* just like Sarge," Gonzales swore, turning to his squad.

Captain James stood in his patch of shade watching the men of his First Platoon as they and their NCOs began the grim task of stuffing the residue of the men of his Third Platoon into the body bags, focusing on Sergeant Adkins working alongside them. Adkins was a real enigma to him.

When he first met with First Sergeant Vickers the month before following his assignment as the new unit commander for Alpha Company, they sat at the small conference table in his office reviewing the personnel roster.

Vickers drew a line under Adkins' name on the sheet. "Sir, we lost our First Platoon Sergeant a couple of days ago. I recommend we move Sergeant Adkins from his squad leader position in the Third Platoon to that spot."

"I normally consider the noncommissioned officer assignments your area, First Sergeant, but I have some reservations in this instance. Adkins is only a sergeant. The platoon sergeant slot calls for a Sergeant First Class E-7."

Vickers nodded. "I know, Sir, but we've got a serious leadership crisis in our NCO ranks. We lost practically every non-commissioned officer we had in Attleboro. That adds to the already existing problem of casualties suffered over the last year of sustained combat operations and the rotation of our noncoms who've served their twelve months in-country. Army wide, the few NCOs we've got left are in our training programs stateside. In the six months Adkins has been over here, he's risen from private to sergeant based purely on his demonstrated leadership merits. He's very capable."

"I'm well aware of our noncom situation, First Sergeant, but the S-1 doubts we'll get a new lieutenant in for several weeks yet," he argued. "The commissioned officer problem is as acute as the noncommissioned one. The Officer Candidate Schools are cranking up to full capacity, but the graduates haven't made it into the replacement pipeline yet. That, along with General Westmoreland's policy of officers spending six months in staff assignments and six months in the field, has put a severe strain on the system. Under the circumstances, to place a Sergeant E-5 in charge of a platoon without even a commissioned officer is unthinkable."

Vickers nodded. "I fully understand your reservations, Sir, but there's really no other choice: Sergeant Adkins is one of the few still around who has combat experience. If it will ease your mind, Sir, I was his platoon sergeant from the day he got here. I can personally vouch for the fact that he's one of the best combat soldiers around. He has natural instincts and an eerie ability to feel the enemy and sense looming trouble. He's quick and decisive under fire, reads the battlefield better than anyone I've ever known, and never loses his cool. Most of the survivors of Attleboro report his leadership alone held the line as our normal chain of command fell around them like flies during the battle. From their reports, Adkins was everywhere during the encounter, mustering the men, distributing ammo, adjusting avenues of fire and, in general, taking charge as the situation dictated."

"Can we promote him to Staff Sergeant?"

Vickers shook his head. "Unfortunately, Sir, he received his promotion to sergeant just last month. He doesn't have the time in service or time in grade to qualify for another promotion. The best we can do is to hang blood stripes on him."

"*Acting* Staff Sergeant?" he asked, referring to the field expedient temporary rank recognized only as long as the man was in the unit and held the specified leadership position.

Vickers nodded, "Yes, Sir. He won't receive any additional pay, but at least he'll be afforded all other benefits of the rank."

"So we're to have a one-month-in grade Buck-Sergeant, Acting-Staff-Sergeant serving as a Sergeant First Class Platoon Sergeant without even the benefit of a Platoon Leader? I can't imagine a better formula for disaster. What are we coming to, First Sergeant?"

"Our ruin if we don't get some leadership in soon, Sir; but Adkins will do fine. He's a natural leader."

He nodded grimly. "Then see to it, First Sergeant. This ought to make his day. We're putting a hell of a load on this young man. He's going to need every bit of self-confidence he can muster."

Vickers grinned. "Unfortunately, in that regard, you'll find he's the most arrogant son of a bitch you've ever met... in fact, back in base camp, he's a pure pain in the ass. He's egotistical, opinionated, and possesses a disdainful attitude towards authority. That'll keep him from having a long-term successful military career, but for now, his combat talents far outweigh those character flaws."

Adkins, indeed, had proven quite capable of handling the platoon without a commissioned officer during the last few weeks. On the operation into the Boi Loi Woods, his

31

platoon racked up a body count of twenty-seven confirmed kills, higher than the rest of the battalion combined. Now, as he stood watching Adkins and his men perform their current odious task, it was obvious his men revered him. He was proving to be a loner by nature and a leader by instinct, with a well-honed ability to bring effective firepower to the most vulnerable point of an enemy concentration in order to exploit their weaknesses to the fullest extent possible. Thus far, the results were devastating to the enemy forces they faced, and his status with the command group was rising rapidly with each operation he conducted.

When the last body bag was loaded, Sergeant Adkins approached. "All finished, Captain."

Captain James nodded. "My apologies to you and your men, Sergeant. I regret the next task I'm required to assign you as well. Instead of returning to base camp, you are to remain with the Mechanized Platoon to continue the search for our missing man. I know how worn out your platoon is, but we need every available man in the field until we've exhausted every option to locate him."

Adkins nodded. "We're about physically done for, Captain, but I reckon the men will understand. If it were one of us out there, we'd want every effort made to find us. At least we can ride. That'll help some."

"You're doing a fine job with these men, Sergeant. I appreciate your dedication."

Adkins nodded curtly. "I'll get them loaded up so we can go hunt down the crazy bitch who done this."

"Good hunting, Sergeant."

CHAPTER 7

Cai climbed out of the stream as rivulets of water clung to her skin and donned the baggy, black-silk, pajama-style pants and shirt to hide the contours of her supple body. She placed a conical straw hat on her head to conceal her compelling dark eyes and short-cropped black hair, slipped crude rubber sandals onto her dainty feet, and subtlety transformed into one of the hundreds of undernourished peasant women dotting the countryside. She picked up a rusty hoe and slung it over her shoulder to enhance her costume as she ambled along, seemingly in no hurry and without care.

Refreshed from her bath, her spirit soared as she watched the many American troops in the distance rushing around under their umbrella of helicopters in the sky, thrilled with the knowledge that they were all looking for her, running in circles like rabbits, the exact effect she wished to achieve. Just beyond the far tree line lay the bodies of the men she had slain the night before. Her stomach fluttered as she recalled the prisoners they had taken, again savoring the ecstasy as they begged for their unworthy lives, and the feel of their warm blood nourishing her skin, intoxicating her like nothing she had ever experienced before. Not even Chien's punishing exploitation of her body afterward could erase that delicious sensation. She eagerly anticipated the next opportunity to deploy her soldiers against their enemy. Perhaps they could capture even more of the imperialists alive. The thought of this brought a smile to her lips.

When she chose her soldiers, she looked for those who displayed weak wills, those who lacked confidence, and those who had received little formal training. She searched for the meek and the mild, without regard to sex or age, seeking dumb, unpretentious peasants she could mold into her own persona and infuse with her own creed. She did not desire to waste time un-training them, or to take the time to destroy their own existing high self-esteem in order to mold them to her doctrine. She sought robots that would react to what she taught without question. They were not to be simply soldiers she commanded, but warriors imbued with her wisdom that followed her concepts of warfare without the taint of inferior tactics, inept training, or pious notions of individual self-worth. They would know her way and no other. They would obey without question. Their loyalty would be to her and no other.

She then isolated and impatiently trained them to perfection by her own stringent standards, infusing them with her own unwavering confidence to make them aggressive and bold. Her only weak link was Lieutenant Le Loi and his allegiance to Colonel Chien. She would eventually win him over... or dispose of him.

She froze as an American patrol appeared out of the bushes to her front, her eyes narrowing as the soldiers approached her. It was foolish of her to insist on bathing so soon, but she had felt the need to wash the unpleasant smell of Chien from her body. One of the men drew up before her as several of the others passed her by to take up security positions behind her. The American dog before her propped his rifle on his hip, muzzle pointing to the sky, as she lowered her eyes in a submissive posture.

"Hey, *Girly-san*, we look for VC, you *bic*?"

She shook her head. "No *bic*, no *bic*!"

"Yeah, sure you don't understand, *Gorgeous-san*. You're a cute little bitch. You're probably VC yourself. You *boom-boom girl*? You fucky-fucky G.I. for piaster?"

She fleetingly recalled another group of imperialists in an armored car who called out to her and a friend on their way home from school, offering them fruit, beckoning to them as they strolled by. An involuntary shudder coursed through her.

"No *bic*! No *bic*!"

Another soldier moved up to them, scowling, "Leave the little girl alone, Riley. You're scaring her to death, man."

"Aw shit, Sarge, I'm just trying to ask her if she's seen any VC today."

"Yeah, like she'd tell you if she had," the sergeant grunted. "Let's get on down the road. I wanna get back for a cold one before dark and we've still got a lot of ground to cover."

The first man shifted his load. "Bye, Cutie-pie. You tell your VC boyfriend I was looking for him, ya hear? You *bic*?"

"No *bic*, no *bic*," she repeated.

The patrol moved around her and off into the brush as she fought to keep the sardonic smile from her lips.

American boys were so naïve and stupid!

CHAPTER 8

Captain Christopher Christen stopped stiffly in front of the commanding general's desk and saluted. "Sir, Captain Christen reporting as ordered."

The general snapped a quick salute back. "How are you, Chris?"

"Just fine, Sir."

"How are Peggy and the kids?"

"Great, Sir. Thank you for inquiring."

The general moved to a conference table situated before a huge map covering the back wall depicting the 25th Infantry Division's area of operations with the various unit emblems pinned to it signifying ongoing missions. "Sit down, Chris," he directed as he filled two cups of coffee from his pot.

Christen seated himself at the conference table absently studying the familiar terrain features of their III Corps area of operations. The topography was the most diverse in Vietnam, encompassing the Cu Chi district's lush rice paddies and thick hedgerows in the center, dipping south into the swamps of the Mekong Delta, circling west through the trackless triple-canopy jungle on the Cambodian border, swinging north through the thickets of the Iron Triangle, and dropping back east to Saigon on the coast.

"Cream or sugar?" the general offered.

"Plain, Sir, thank you."

The general placed a cup before Christen and dumped two heaping spoons of sugar into his own cup before sitting down. "Chris, I have a very sensitive mission for you. I have directed the G-2 to reassign all of your current duties to others in order to allow you to concentrate on this one task until it is complete. Is that a problem for you?"

"No, Sir, not at all. I'm honored you selected me."

The general sipped from his cup, his steel-blue eyes watching him from under his bushy eyebrows. "I assume you've heard about the platoon that was attacked last night?"

"I've heard bits and pieces, Sir: mostly rumor and speculation."

"Here's the file on the incident." The general slid a folder in front of him. "I think what you find in there will be unsettling, to say the least."

Christen's blue eyes widened in surprise as he scanned the carnage depicted in the photos, his right hand lifting to brush at his thin, frizzled red hair as his heavily freckled face darken. He held the bloodstained picture of the diminutive woman while he read the brief after-action report carefully, and then stared grimly into the engaging, taunting eyes of the grinning woman in tiger-striped fatigues once again.

"Her personal calling card, Chris," the general explained as he cleared his throat and pushed his cup away. "*Vengeance is mine, sayeth the Lord.* Your mission is to form a small task force and gather all the information you can on this creature to help bring her to justice. You will report directly to me. Do you have any questions?"

"No, Sir," Christen replied, ashen faced, his minions of freckles standing out in severe contrast to the whiteness of his features. "I'll get started right away." He stood, snapped a quick salute to the general, and hurried out.

He stopped just outside the entrance to the headquarters bunker to lean against it with an outstretched arm to heave up his lunch in shuddering gasps as he clutched the file of repulsive photographs in his other clammy hand. He stood on trembling legs in the simmering heat waves, drawing deep breaths of muggy air, staring unseeing at the ménage of tents, sandbagged bunkers, and thin black strands of drooping communication wires hanging from every structure affording an advantage in height. The dismal base camp resembled a miner's turn-of-the-century ghetto, stretching for over a mile in circumference, filled with half-dressed men moving about in the dizzying heat performing impervious tasks in the confusing chaos of the 25,000-man encampment located on the outskirts of the small village of Cu Chi located twenty-five miles northwest of Saigon. This was his fourth month in-country of his twelve-month tour. Returning home to his wife and two kids still seemed an eternity away. He collected himself and strode forcibly across the short distance to the G-2 Intelligence bunker.

"Sergeant Pierce!" he barked as he stalked through the cramped operation's section.

Master Sergeant Pierce, a short, bull-necked, all-pro linebacker type with a shaved head and small black eyes, followed him to his small, cluttered office. "What's up, Cap'n?"

"Close the door. As of now, we have a new mission. We will report to the Division Commander directly. Is that understood?"

Sergeant Pierce nodded. "Yes, Sir. What's doing, Cap'n?"

Christen eased his six foot frame into his chair behind his desk and tossed Sergeant Pierce the folder. "You are now part of a special task force to gather intelligence on the most evil woman on the face of the earth, Sergeant. Our mission is to hunt her down and eliminate her."

Sergeant Pierce opened the folder. "Cool, Cap'n. What is this wicked little lady's name?"

Christen glanced at the photo of the woman with her unique tiger-stripped fatigues. "We'll code name her *Tiger Woman*!"

Chapter 9

Five miles north of where Master Sergeant Pierce stood studying the classified file with Captain Christen, Lieutenant Le Loi paced in his small underground quarters indecisively, a most uncharacteristic state for him. Short in statue and slim of build, with a mop of black hair and almond eyes, he stood erect and missed little around him, while holding his opinions to himself unless called upon to voice them. He sought to do so then only with well-formulated reasoning and solid tactical thinking. As the executive officer of Captain Cai's force, his imminent distress was the appalling spectacle he had witnessed the night before after their successful attack upon the American ambush position.

Some five weeks before, Captain Cai had slipped into the small room carved out of the earth deep below the surface and stood in front of the table in the yellow lamplight where he sat with Colonel Nguyen Van Chien and his staff. Having just returned from her six-month journey to North Vietnam for specialized training in guerrilla warfare, where she received a promotion to Captain upon completing her schooling, every member of the command knew Chien was her lover, though he acted as if she were merely one of his many subordinates.

"It is good you have returned safe from your perilous journey," Colonel Chien greeted, tapping a file before him on the table. "You have excelled in your schooling. You have brought distinction to my command."

Cai bowed her head in deference. "I am honored that you approve of my performance of my duties."

Colonel Chien inclined his head back to her. "You will be assigned to my personal tactical operations staff, where your valuable training can be put to the best use."

Cai drew herself up stiffly. "I feel my specialized training can best be put to use in the field instead of a staff position, my Colonel," she challenged.

In the heavy silence that ensued, Colonel Chien nodded cautiously, obviously caught off guard by her reproachful stance, acutely aware that he must not show favoritism. Advanced graduates from the North routinely receive their own command upon their return. He would lose face if he withheld this privilege from her. Still, he must find some way to protect her without being obvious. "Your... position has merit, Captain. I will reassign Lieutenant Le Loi from my staff to serve as your executive officer. You will select a cadre from within to form the basis of your new command and recruit your unit from the Liberation Forces in the district."

Cai inclined her head. "As you command, my Colonel."

After Chien dismissed Cai and his staff, he turned to Le Loi. "You are not pleased with your assignment to Captain Cai as her second in command?"

Le Loi swallowed his bitter disappointment. Though technically it was a promotion for him, his imminent desire was to continue serving as Chien's personal aide, a most coveted position within the command structure. "I am only displeased to leave you, my Colonel."

"You have served me well, Lieutenant. I trust I can rely on your support to Captain Cai in the same admirable fashion?"

"You do me honor to place such faith in me, my Colonel."

"You will... look after Captain Cai's... *personal safety*..."

"I understand, my Colonel," he acknowledged, knowing full well the reason for this strange directive. "You may rely on me to do so at the expense of my own life."

Colonel Chien took him by the shoulders. "I have no son. If I had one, I would want him to be like you."

Taken by surprise with this bold statement, he was unsure of how to respond. He nodded awkwardly. "Yes, my Colonel. I am flattered."

Afterwards, he stood silently by observing in his quiet fashion as Captain Cai selected their cadre of ten NCOs allocated to them by Colonel Chien. Though dumbfounded by her selections, he offered no opinion unless called upon, which was rare, and never entailed a request for his judgment on the soldiers she chose. He was far too subservient to challenge her decisions—though, for the most part, he disagreed with the recruits she picked. Although all were battle hardened, most had little or no experience in leading actual troops. They appeared marginally capable, in his opinion... definitely not the elite of the potential candidates with which to build their force around.

He then escorted Captain Cai as she traveled throughout the district meeting with the scattered guerrilla forces of the People's Liberation Army. She walked the rows of assembled men and women in each location, observing their mannerisms as she looked each soldier in the eye and spoke brusquely. If they stared back at her, she rejected them out-right. If they stood too proud or showed the slightest hint of defiance, she moved on to the next potential recruit. If they had acquired rank or been in the service for any length of time, she passed them over.

"What are you seeking in these soldiers, my Captain," he had finally inquired, puzzled by her strange selection process.

"I seek soldiers of merit," she replied harshly.

Thereafter, he held his curiosity in check as he followed his erratic captain on her rounds. At the end of the sixth day, he again politely approached her. "My Captain, we now have the fifty soldiers and ten NCOs allocated by our Colonel for our unit."

She bristled. "Most of these recruits will not complete my training requirements. We will select eighty soldiers and narrow them down to the fifty authorized. You will prepare the logistics needed to move our contingent to Nui Ba Den for the training phase."

Stunned by this directive, he performed the assigned mundane task with competence, if not enthusiasm, as she completed her selection process. He reported to Colonel Chien on each stage of their recruitment, but the colonel made no comment or asked for his candid assessments. If anything, the good colonel seemed dismayed that they were far ahead of their timetable, seeming to resent the efficiency displayed in carrying out his order to form a new company. This also confused him, as he stoically carried out his duties to the best of his ability.

Captain Cai moved their new force west to the triple-canopy jungle near Tay Ninh in groups of twos and threes dressed as farmers and merchants, while ox carts and three-wheeled Lambrettas transported their equipment and supplies to the region. When reassembled, she moved them deep into the dense jungle between the sacred mountain of Nui Ba Den and the Cambodian border. There, she set them to building straw hooches to sleep in, an open-sided classroom for tactical instruction, an outdoor kitchen for cooking the meager ration of rice allocated to each soldier on a daily basis, and the digging of slit trenches for their body waste disposal. She then divided the assembled men and women into two detachments: thirty under his control and fifty under her personal command.

Their training consisted of grueling patrols by day and night. Cai shifted soldiers back and forth between the two elements searching for the right blend, though Le Loi had no idea of what combination she was looking for. They spent endless hours slipping through the jungle, each force opposing the other in war games. She was relentless in her demand for stealth in their movements. The slightest noise or light infraction brought her wrath down onto the culprit who made an unwitting mistake. By the end of the first week, she had set the thirty men in his section and the fifty in her section to her satisfaction. She then sent his element out on night marches and had them set up in a precise manner. Afterwards, she would settle her force into position around them and launch vicious simulated assaults against them. The next day in the improvised classroom, she critiqued her fifty-man force—while his slept—modifying and strengthening their tactics and strategy.

She drove them with relentless determination, demanding Le Loi's force do everything possible, within the latitude she gave him, to detect and defeat her force. Their maneuvers became grueling cat–and–mouse games between them. Night after night, he moved his force through the darkness, using every means of deception he could conceive. Night after night, while they lay in their defensive positions, her force slid in around them and struck with paralyzing swiftness. It was unnerving to him, almost as if ghosts materialized from nowhere to swarm over them in a teeming horde, running through their defenses at will. He gradually gained respect for her, as she outmaneuvered and outfought him on each occasion. He began to detect a certain pride in her element, a decided swagger in their walk, a glimmer of defiance in their eyes, a quiet confidence in their bearing.

The last week of training, Captain Cai took small contingents of her detachment and fought light-running battles with the American patrols in and around Tay Ninh in order to test her troops under fire and to build their confidence. At her direction, he disbanded his thirty-man element and sent them back to their original units in small groups. When he rejoined her force, he could contain his curiosity no longer.

"For what are we training, my Captain?"

"We will destroy the ambushes our enemy employs at night to limit our troop movements and resupply efforts," she replied.

Upon his return to her unit to complete their training, he began to grasp the tactics she intended to use against the small, dangerous forces the Americans strung out around their base camps at night. He came to understand how her force defeated his repeatedly by pinpointing his precise location and troop placements, and grasped her demands that they move without sound and strike with crushing velocity. With each arduous training exercise, his esteem for his new commander grew and his anticipation for what was to come heightened.

When they moved their well-trained, lethal force back to the Iron Triangle for the impending attacks against the unsuspecting Americans, that enthusiasm culminated in the very successful attack they had sprung on the enemy the night before.

The aftermath was what he had not expected or been prepared for. He drew himself up, summoning his courage, resolving to approach Colonel Chien on the matter.

CHAPTER 10

Allen struggled through the heavy layers of fatigue weighing him down, as the tantalizing aroma of his mother's sizzling eggs, bacon, and hot biscuits tickled his senses and fueled his ravenous appetite. It was time to get up and get ready for school. Bret Baldwin, the first team running back, was injured. They had a big game that night and it was to be his first start.

Sharp pains lanced up his left arm. He opened his eyes to find a Vietnamese man prodding his shoulder, drawing him from his delirious daze. With growing awareness, a deep, throbbing ache encased his body. Gripping fear pitted his empty stomach. Renewed futility eroded his soul. With the fading visions of home and food too painful to endure, he focused his hazy thoughts on the squalor of the olive drab, sandbag covered structures of his former base camp at Cu Chi, embarrassed by the despair he experienced the first day he arrived there. On this side of hell, it seemed luxurious now by comparison, and he longed for its primitive comforts.

As a prisoner of war, he did not know what the next minute held, but from what he had experienced thus far, he expected none of it would be good. He sat up groggily, dressed in his fatigue pants only. They had taken his shirt and boots from him sometime the day before. Maybe it was two days before, or even three. He had lost track of time in this underground cavern, and could only recall long periods of emptiness, where he dozed and ached from his various injuries. No one talked to him. He could not leave his cot. The medical personnel came and went, but disregarded him for the most part as well, other than for re-bandaging his arm twice with coarse cotton dressings, during which they applied no medication or antiseptic to his wound. The various wounded Vietnamese men in the room with him either ignored him or stared at him with hostile eyes. In his undeterminable time here, they had provided him with two bowls of yellow rice and a few cups of brackish water when he begged for something to eat or drink. The guard positioned near his cot displayed a keen sense of aggravation each time he requested to go to the toilet, which was a large pot on the floor in a smaller room off to the side of the hospital ward, to relieve his severe case of diarrhea. He had no toilet paper with which to cleanse himself after his bowel movements, and suffered through his own odious stench due to his awkward lack of personal hygiene.

"You come now!" The VC prodded him on his wounded shoulder, eliciting sharp pains from his arm. "You come now. You stink like pig!" The VC held his nose as the other men around them laughed. Allen swung his bare feet to the floor and stood up on quaking legs.

"No! You must to crawl like dog!" The man punched him in the stomach, grabbed him by the back of his neck as he folded over gasping, and shoved him down onto his hands and knees. "Come quickly!" the man ordered, indicating the opening to a corridor leading from the hospital room.

He crawled in the indicated direction as the man shuffled along behind him for over a hundred yards on his protesting knees and aching arm, passing through several of the larger rooms before entering one with four Vietnamese men and the woman he had seen at the ambush site sitting behind a table. He watched the woman furtively as he was prodded before them and made to squat barefoot in front of the table as the group studied him impassively, but she seemed bored and uninterested in him or the proceedings.

"What your name?" the older Vietnamese man in the center of the table demanded.

His mind flashed back to basic training as he tried to remember what he could tell them in accordance with the Geneva Conventions. *Name*, *rank*, and *serial number*, flashed into his weakened mind. "Private First Class Allen Hayes, Sir."

"I am Colonel Nguyen Van Chien. You are my prisoner. You will be tried for crimes against the Viet people."

He cringed. "But, Sir, I haven't committed any crimes against the Vietnamese people."

"That not for you to say. That for me to say. What your unit?"

"I-I'm not supposed to tell you that, Sir. I can only give you my name, rank, and my serial number."

Chien inclined his head at the man standing behind Allen, who stepped forward and whacked him across his bare back with a bamboo cane in a sharp, stinging blow as he cowered and gasped.

"What your unit?" Chien demanded in the same monotone.

"Private First Class Allen Hayes, Sir. My serial number is US 16542199."

Chien nodded. The man again stepped forward and beat him across the back with his cane until he collapsed onto the floor crying out in pain as he withered on the ground.

"What your unit?" Chien asked stoically as the man stepped back.

"*Please, Colonel, I can't…*"

The man methodically beat him again as he whimpered and cowered on the dirt floor. He was vaguely aware of his bowels turning loose and soiling his pants in a warm gush before sinking into welcoming oblivion.

CHAPTER 11

Colonel Nguyen Van Chien, above average in height for an oriental, with a softening, portly physique, and a thick, well-groomed mast of graying black hair, prepared to make his routine rounds through the vast tunnel complex after his interrogation of the American prisoner.

Although the ultra secret caverns of the Iron Triangle were ideally suited to their guerrilla warfare tactics and afforded them unprecedented hidden protection from which to launch their attacks on the jugular of Saigon, life in the tunnel complex was anything but pleasant. There were only four entrances to the cavernous compound, each camouflaged and protected. The floor, walls, and ceilings were exposed raw earth, fortified in scattered locations with sandbags and reinforcing timber. The air was damp and putrid, the earth sodden and spongy, the oil and candle lighting gloomy with no indication of day or night. Noise of any kind was a distant muffle. The temperature stayed at a constant, disagreeable 65 degrees.

After extended periods underground in this depressing atmosphere, he often dreamed of the balmy brightness of sunlight to soothe the strain of the smothering dimness and warm his chilled body. He longed to hear the music of chirping birds to assuage his muted eardrums; to feel the crackle of dry leaves underfoot to supplant the damp sponginess of his step; and most fondly, to embrace the comfort of a stirring breeze to tickle his skin and ruffle his hair as it supplied agreeable fresh oxygen to his congested lungs.

He considered himself a fair but stern commander, and a better than average tactician. He served against the Japanese during their occupation in the Second World War, and afterwards, with the Viet Minh against the French in the colonial days, earning a solid reputation as a cunning, fearless warrior. Though not a staunch socialist, he was an ardent supporter of the communist cause to oust all foreigners from his beloved country and reunite the northern and southern providences back into one people. He suspected his less than whole-hearted embrace of the party was the primary reason he had not risen above the rank of Colonel in his twenty-six years in the People's Liberation Army, in spite of his untarnished war record. However, this was of no great concern to him, for he had little ambition beyond his sworn duty to defeat their current enemy.

His command was part of the vast tunnel network located in the Iron Triangle, just north of the village of Cu Chi and the 25th Infantry Division base camp. The complex consisted of one of six separate underground systems spanning some thirty miles, housing subterranean hospitals, storage rooms, and troop billeting space. His particular compound was composed of an intricate amalgam spanning almost three miles of stacked layers of access tunnels and troop depots, as well as the second largest hospital in the southern district. He had twelve-hundred soldiers under his command, with five-hundred of them housed in the tunnel network itself. The remaining seven-hundred were above ground in far-flung locations saturating the countryside.

His command performed support, courier, and combat missions. The vast majority of his forces were devoted to intelligence gathering services and the medical field, but he also had four hundred liberation fighters whose primary mission was to harass the enemy at every opportunity by direct and indirect warfare. The direct combat consisted of springing ambushes, harassing sniper fire, and the occasional full-scale attack on an outnumbered and isolated enemy patrol or post. The indirect conflict consisted of laying minefields, digging and maintaining punji pits, and stringing the feared booby traps across likely avenues of enemy advance.

The tunnel complex he commanded had existed for over 25 years, dating back to when they fought the occupying Japanese, and was virtually unknown outside of a select few for reasons of security. The Americans, like the Japanese and French before them, patrolled overhead without ever suspecting what lay under their feet. Protecting the secret of this enormous staging area was of paramount importance. If discovered, the enemy could trap them underground and destroy their entire Southern Vietcong infrastructure, which encompassed an area covering a third of the whole of South Vietnam. Their primary mission was to capture the heart of the country itself—Saigon—the decadent capital city of the South Vietnamese government, located thirty miles to the southeast.

In addition to his strategic duties, he was required to be ever vigilant to the continuing maintenance needs of the tunnel system itself. Diligence was required to keep the weak ceilings and walls shored up against cave-ins, to maintain the imperfect air supply piped in through hollow bamboo stakes hidden in thickets of covering vegetation, in pumping water from the caverns in the heavy rains of the monsoon season, and in maintaining light and noise discipline amongst his crouching troops. With one year left in his assignment to this command, he counted the days to when he could return to the North and settle down to devote the rest of his life to raising a new family in the sweet air above.

Twice married and widowed, after a French artillery barrage killed his first wife just prior to Dien Bien Phu, and an American air strike killed his second wife and a child in their modest home on the outskirts of Hanoi, he harbored hopes of remarrying and having additional children. He longed to retire after his current assignment and live a quiet life of relative comfort in his ancestral village of Mount-La in the providence of Son La, 45 kilometers northwest of Hanoi, which he had not seen in years, but for which he still harbored fond memories.

Less than pleased over the last few weeks, he made his rounds on this day with a light heart. In the time Cai had been back from the North, he had seen little of her. He had not anticipated her many absences from the underground complex for such extended periods. He had managed to visit her in her quarters only twice since her return, much to his dismay. He now recognized he had made a mistake in allowing her to expand her horizons from a meek servant to that of a keen warrior.

As he made his daily rounds to inspect his underground fortress, his former adjutant, Lieutenant Le Loi, approached him.

"My Colonel, may I speak with you?"

"You have brought us a great victory," he praised. "I have not had the opportunity to congratulate you."

He in fact was not pleased with the merits of their accomplishment. He had not expected them to recruit and complete their training in the short time they had. Nor had he expected them to succeed so grandly in their first venture against the enemy. He would have much preferred Cai remain anonymous and unrecognized.

In spite of his better judgment, he had agreed, in a moment of amorous weakness the year before, to allow her to transfer from her junior staff position within his command to the Liberation Forces. To his surprise, she excelled as a freedom fighter. Due to her escalating battlefield prowess, he hoped her selection by the cadre to attend advanced training in the North would dampen her increasing enthusiasm for combat. There she again exceeded his expectations by graduating at the top of her class. He much preferred the total domination he once exercised over her when she served as one of the nameless, faceless thousands of humble supply couriers in the logistics corps on the Ho Chi Ming Trail from which he plucked her. Over the preceding months, her budding self-confidence was becoming troublesome to him due to her growing, disconcerting independence.

Le Loi's expression grew strained. "It is on this matter that I seek your counsel, my Colonel."

"Walk with me on my rounds," Chien directed, turning into one of the narrow connecting passageways between the larger rooms that made up their multifaceted, intricate complex, absently inspecting for loose soil and undue dampness that would indicate an imminent failure in the earthen structure. "You are still displeased with my assigning you to Captain Cai?"

When he belatedly directed Captain Cai to recruit and train a new company from the infrastructure within the district, his hasty reassignment of Lieutenant Le Loi from his staff to be her second in command was a calculated move on his part. He selected Le Loi from the ranks of the Vietcong the year before—a promising young soldier with demonstrated bravery and a solid determination to rid their country of the foreign devils—and placed him on his personal staff for further development. Though Le Loi was devout to their cause, time had proven him not to be the brightest star under his command; but he was loyal without fault, and followed orders without question, which was crucial in his resolve to restore Cai's subservience to him. He expected Le Loi would serve him well in this capacity.

Cai's insistence on serving in a combat assignment upon her return in lieu of a staff position within his headquarters group had taken him by surprise. To give her a token cadre of hardcore NCOs and one junior officer, who was well known for his devotion to him personally, and further directed to recruit and train a nonexistent unit from unmotivated peasants instead of assuming an existing operational command, was a deliberate ruse on his part. Though surely this was an affront to her, she merely inclined her head in acquiescence, no doubt suppressing her disappointment. He had concealed a smile of satisfaction at the time, thinking the task would occupy her for many weeks to come and keep her out of harm's way.

He had not anticipated she would so quickly overcome the obstacles in her path, accomplishing in a week what he anticipated would require a month or more in recruiting her force. She surprised him again by requesting to move them to the thick jungle near the Cambodian border for specialized training.

"Is this specialized training really necessary, Captain?" he had challenged indulgently.

"There, we will be shielded far from the dangers in our current heavily patrolled region. I will have the freedom to conduct exercises and the security to assemble and teach without fear of blundering into enemy patrols."

He searched his mind for grounds to deny her this move, the thought of her further absence from his arms almost unbearable after her long journey to the North, but tactically it was sound judgment on her part, and he could find no reason to deny her.

"Colonel ...?"

He turned back to Le Loi. "Yes, Lieutenant?" he replied vaguely "Speak your mind."

"Over the last few weeks I have been torn between my allegiance to my Captain and my devotion to you."

"You are troubled by this, Lieutenant?" he asked.

"Yes, my Colonel. Last night we... did things I do not understand. I do not know how to approach you on this matter. Some of our soldiers are... disturbed."

"Speak of this matter directly, Lieutenant," he ordered impatiently.

"We... tortured and killed five American soldiers we captured. We also disfigured the dead."

He stared at Le Loi for a stunned moment. "You... were directed to do these things by your Captain?"

"Yes, my Colonel... except the torture and killing of the prisoners. My Captain did that on her own... it was very distressing to our soldiers. It is for them that I speak."

"Let us continue," Chien directed, unsettled. His mood darkened as he made his rounds through the vast tunnel complex. He must discuss this most disconcerting facet of their glorious victory with Cai. It was paramount that she do nothing to bring disgrace upon herself to impair his plans for their future together.

He turned abruptly to Le Loi. "You did right to bring this to my attention. You will speak of it to no one else."

Le Loi stiffened. "Yes, my Colonel. I must attend to my duties now."

Colonel Chien stared after him, greatly troubled, as he departed.

CHAPTER 12

"Got a minute, Captain?" Specialist Robert Howell inquired from the doorway.

Captain Christen looked up from the report he was reading and motioned him in. Howell, a colorful man five-feet, nine-inches tall, weighing a slim 150-well-distributed pounds, wore a floppy boonie hat with camouflaged markings and a silk camouflaged scarf around his neck. Dark complexioned, with well-groomed black hair and soft brown eyes, he spoke perfect Vietnamese and had a quick, keen mind, which was the main reason Christen handpicked him for this project.

"What've you got?"

"Don't know for sure, Captain, but one of the outlying ARVN posts says they have a Kit Carson scout that can identify this Tiger Woman bitch."

Christen frowned. Kit Carson scouts, former Vietcong soldiers who supposedly had switched sides and now supported the South Vietnamese government, were notoriously unreliable. Most would do anything to avoid prisoner of war camps or outright execution by the South Vietnamese government when captured. No one on either side trusted them. They were literally men without a country who swore allegiance to whoever had the current upper hand.

"He identified her by the picture you had blown up and sent out, Captain," Howell continued.

He had taken the picture of the woman with the intriguing eyes to the lab and had it enlarged and the background faded out, giving them a grainy, but clear picture of her alone. He then dispatched the photograph out to the surrounding ARVN outposts with the offer of a reward for information on her. "Dispatch a chopper to pick him up."

Howell smiled. "Already did that, Sir. Chopper's inbound now. Where do you want me to interrogate him?"

"Here, in my office."

Howell grimaced. "I guess that means there won't be any blood spilled then." He flashed a sardonic grin, tossed a two-finger salute, and shuffled out.

When Pierce and Howell ushered the Vietnamese man into his office, Christen sized up the small-framed individual in his mid thirties with a jagged scar across the left side of his face and dark eyes filled with mistrustful apprehension. The man wore new ARVN fatigues with a yellow silk scarf at his throat and a wide black leather belt supporting a holstered nine-millimeter pistol on his hip.

"I'm Captain Christen, special project officer to the Commanding General of the 25th Infantry Division," he introduced, extending his hand. "This is Master Sergeant Pierce and Specialist 5th Class Howell, my assistants."

"So good to meet you, *Di Wee*," the man replied in remarkably good English, using the Vietnamese word for "captain."

Christen handed the scout the modified picture of Tiger Woman. "I understand you can identify this woman?"

The scout glanced at the picture without taking it. "Yes, it is so. You are offering reward for this information I give you?"

"That is correct. What is your name?"

"Ly Cam, *Di Wee*, but my American name is 'Billy.'"

Christen seated himself across from the scout. "Okay, Billy, what can you tell us about this woman?"

Billy shrugged. "Many things, *Di Wee*. Some fact, some rumor. How much you pay?"

"The reward you refer to is based on the amount of information you have to give—and our verification of that information," he replied, masking his irritation.

Billy did not blink. "I want ten-thousand piaster for this information, *Di Wee*. And I want to work for Americans now, not ARVNs."

Christen whistled softly, quickly calculating that the average Vietnamese worker made approximately one hundred and fifty piaster a week. "That's a lot of money, Billy."

Billy nodded. "Yes. I wish to leave this country someday. To go to America."

"Your information would have to be strong for that kind of money," Christen bargained.

"You must be judge if my information is *beaucoup* useful, *Di Wee*."

"Give me a minute." Christen motioned Pierce and Howell out into the hall and closed the door behind them. "What do you think?"

Howell smirked. "Give me a pair of pliers and fifteen minutes with him and I'll save you ten-thousand piaster, Captain."

"That's only about six hundred dollars, American," Pierce counseled. "If his information is any good, I'd pay that much out of my own pocket to get at that bitch. We sure as hell haven't come up with anything else to go on in the last five days."

"I'd still prefer the pliers and the fifteen minutes," Howell argued.

Christen led them back into the room. "Providing your information is accurate and of use to us, we agree to pay your price."

"Very good. And to work for you Americans now, as well?"

"I believe we can arrange that on a temporary basis as well," Christen acknowledged.

"Very good, *Di Wee*. I tell you everything now."

CHAPTER 13

Cai lay restlessly on her cot in her darkened underground quarters, estimating it to be early afternoon. In a few short hours, they could start the hunt. The anticipation elevated her heart to a rapid rhythm. It had been five long days since they struck at the American imperialists and she was eager to renew the offensive.

She imagined her scouts stationed at various locations around the vast enemy base camp awaiting the enemy patrols who would soon cross their barbed wire entanglements and enter into her domain, each waiting to slip along with them and watch as they set up in their ambush positions. The scouts would then glide away in the darkness to meet her main force at a prearranged location at midnight to brief her on the different target areas. She would select one, finalize the plan of attack, and the scout would lead them back to the chosen American site. She visualized them staging silently to the rear of the American position, the weakest link in their perimeter, and striking viciously out of the shadows. It was almost too easy. The Americans were such babies at warfare, and even more helpless when the night hampered their ability to maneuver. She had trained her soldiers and modified her tactics to exploit their weaknesses. She expected to take many prisoners. The anticipation kept her awake, the expectation building to a crescendo within her.

She forced her mind to drift in an effort to control her rising fervor, and unwittingly found herself in a place she rarely dwelled upon—her previous life as the only child of adoring parents. The unexpected memory haunted her. She had slipped into a cold, apathetic existence after the hated French imperialist visited their village, a murky cerebral place to which she did not care to return to, and from which she had never really escaped.

As she attempted to calm the pounding in her chest, Colonel Chien entered her room. She stiffened, fearing he desired to be intimate with her. He had been especially forceful with her on the occasions he visited her in the last few days. He seemed displeased as he stood over her, his eyes startling her with their burning intensity.

"Cai, I must speak to you on a matter that has come to my attention. It is of grave concern to me. I have been negligent in not discussing this issue with you before now."

She slid from her bed to stand before him. "Yes, my Colonel?"

"You error in your treatment of the American prisoners you take and the atrocities you commit upon their slain. Your methods serve no purpose but to inflame our enemy and strengthen his resolve. Your hatred of them is blinding you and corrupting your soul."

"Lieutenant Le Loi has done a disservice in speaking with you on this matter," she replied coldly, resolving to chastise him for his indiscretions.

"He is only concerned for your welfare. Disagreeable things will come if you persist in these actions. You must not continue this course."

"Of what disagreeable things do you speak, my Colonel? Surely my desire to strike at the Americans and chase them from our land is not displeasing?"

"It would sadden me to see you harmed by the Americans—or by our own comrades if you continue to disregard the noble ideology of our struggle."

She turned from him fretfully. "I do not fear the Americans, nor am I aware of debasing our principles, my Colonel."

"You must not defile the dead or torture the living again. This goes beyond the duties of a soldier. It brings discredit on your valiant efforts in the service of our cause."

"My Colonel, the only alternative to the occupation of our land by the imperialistic foreign dogs is to serve death and dishonor upon them in order to weaken their spirit and dilute their resolve. In the North, they taught me to instill fear in our enemy as a way to make them vulnerable. My actions are only intended to terrorize them in order to achieve this end."

"Your soldiers are disturbed by your actions. Our superiors will question your judgment if they become aware of this. You must hear me on this issue. You must obey my wishes."

She sank down on her cot as her knees weakened with anxiety. What he was asking of her was unimaginable. He was attempting to rob her of her only enjoyment in life. Surely, her soldiers and her superiors did not share his views where the despicable Americans were concerned. To give up the tactics she employed against them would be an injustice to their cause—and deprive her of the indescribable sense of fulfillment she derived from the acts. The fact that she took such pleasure from this was only a verification of the zeal with which she supported their cause, a confirmation of the righteousness of her methods. Chien was wrong. He was weak in his attempt to control her. His only desire was to keep her docile in order to extract his pleasure from her body.

"Please forgive me, my Colonel," she replied tersely. "I must rest now."

He stared at her for a long moment before turning and stalking from the room.

She sighed despondently. She must not alienate him. She vowed to conduct herself in a more disciplined manner to appease him. She shivered in anticipation, attempting to calm the renewed tremors pulsating within her as she reached an inner compromise.

She would only amuse herself with some of the prisoners, not all.

CHAPTER 14

Adkins limped down from the back of the command track after the APCs drew up in a line and dropped their rear ramps on the gravel road beside the unit area. He paused as the dust settled over him, watching the exhausted members of his platoon straggle by, deliberately ignoring First Sergeant Vickers seated at his desk staring at him through the screen siding of the orderly room. They had fought six engagements in the last five days and accumulated another even dozen confirmed enemy dead, without finding a trace of their missing man.

He took in the scattering of dilapidated half-tent, half-wood structures behind the sign reading:

A Company
1/27 Infantry
The Wolfhounds

The decaying unit area contained a double row of canvas-topped structures facing each other across a twenty-foot common area with waist-high rows of sandbags surrounding them to protect the occupants from exploding mortar fragments. Rubber trees spaced ten feet apart strung out in perfect lines along the front and rear of each hooch. To his right, a screen-sided board structure with a tin roof housed the mess hall. Beside it, another tin-topped building held the supply room. Running in a line beside the supply room were four canvas-topped billets, which housed the First and Second Platoons. The orderly room was in a tin-roofed shack to his left. Next to this were the NCO hooch and another row of canvas-topped billets for the Third Platoon and the Heavy Weapons Platoons. Behind the orderly room stood a wood-and-screen building with a thatched roof, which provided quarters for the officers. Next to this were separate latrine and shower facilities for the officers and enlisted men of the company. Across the road, a heavy screen of brush hid the bunkers encircling the perimeter of the base camp from view.

He sighed as he made his way unhurried to the orderly room. This dismal place had been his home for six months. He wished nothing more than to never see it again. It had once nurtured his naïve illusions on the glories of combat and housed his brothers in arms as they faced a common adversary. Now it held nothing but bitter memories of lost innocence and disenchanted dreams. These things had not slipped away from him over time. The 9th North Vietnamese Army Regiment wrenched them from his former idealistic mindset in the recent confrontation in War Zone C, now referred to as the battle of Attleboro. The savage encounter decimated their whole unit after their previous commander maneuvered them deep into the triple-canopy jungle near Tay Ninh, in hopes of closing the door on the only escape route for the surrounded enemy regiment. However, Bravo Company lagged to their rear due to heavy sniper activity and failed to move on-line with them, leaving a gaping hole in their left flank. As the assembled American forces around them squeezed in from all sides, the trapped men of the Ghost Regiment sought the weakest point in the encircling columns—their Alpha Company. Over the next thirty-one grueling hours, the desperate enemy regiment hit them with five human wave attacks. Out of ammo, medical supplies, water, and hope, the last charge swept over them as they hung on with little more than courage in the ensuing hand-to-hand combat. The wounded men of the company were in a shallow area to the rear when the enemy soldiers breached their defenses. The NVA ran through the improvised aid station, killing the wounded in a grisly massacre that forever left its mark on his mind, erasing any empathy he had ever held for the enemy.

Now his best friend Kevin, who had survived Attleboro with him, was gone. Killed outright and then disfigured in the most gruesome fashion he could have ever imagined. He had sworn personal vengeance against the crazy woman brazen enough to leave a picture of herself mocking his corpse. He meant to keep that promise.

Three times wounded, he was eligible for transfer to a rear echelon position by the commanding general's two-wound decree, which ensured him a safe position in the rear for the remainder of his tour. He refused a transfer and signed a waiver to stay in a combat assignment, holding rear echelon soldiers in contempt. If he was going to serve, he was going to do so in a fighting unit. Anything less was unacceptable.

First Sergeant Vickers sent him to the Leadership Academy two months before, where they taught him the mechanics of how to use the vast array of weapons at his disposal—the artillery, helicopter gunships, and Air Force fast-movers with their loads of bombs and napalm in a close air support capacity. Vickers promoted him to sergeant upon his graduation from the academy. In seven days, he went from being a private first class common soldier with no responsibilities other than day-to-day survival and following the last order given, to being a squad leader, where his every decision could be the last undertaking for himself and his men if it were a poor one. The month before, Vickers had promoted him to acting staff sergeant and moved him into the platoon sergeant position over the First Platoon. The bastard. But for that, Kevin might be alive today.

He dropped his helmet and web gear on the sandbag wall, laid his rifle on top, and mounted the steps to the orderly room. He continued to ignore Vickers sitting at his desk glaring at him with the proverbial cup of coffee in one hand and the stinking stogie in the other, smugly aware that it would annoy him to the point of distraction, as he entered and made a beeline for the coffee urn.

He trusted Vickers more than any man alive, but couldn't say that he liked the bastard. During the months Vickers served as his platoon sergeant, prior to his own promotion to the unit first sergeant slot just before Attleboro, they endured some hard times together. He had never known Vickers to be wrong. He also knew him to be an un-mitigating asshole. He was undoubtedly the meanest son of a bitch alive... and the best combat leader that ever lived.

Vickers clenched his cigar in the corner of his mouth and nodded at a chair beside his desk. "I see your scraggly ass finally managed to find its way back home."

Adkins settled his lean, medium-height frame down in the chair beside Vickers's desk and raked his fingers through his black, curly hair in need of a trim. "I damned sure didn't see any reason to hurry back for a cup of this shit." He grimaced as he sniffed at his cup, knowing Vickers' tendency to add water and coffee grounds on top of the old as needed.

Vickers smirked. "It'll make a man of you."

"Only if it don't kill my ass first."

Vickers blew a blue cloud of foul smoke into his face.
"How was the hunt?"

Adkins shrugged. "Killed a few stragglers, but didn't get
a sniff of our missing man."

Vickers sighed. "The poor bastard. What happened out
there? I'm hearing all kinds of crazy rumors, but the brass
has put a tight lid on everything concerning the incident."

Adkins looked over his shoulder to the two clerks at their
desks across the room. "You shits take a hike." He waited
until they snatched their hats and hurried out of the room.
"I don't really know for sure, Top, and what I do know is
classified, but off the record, they cut most of the bodies to
pieces and butchered some of the men while they were still
alive. Apparently, a woman runs the group. I'm going to kill
the bitch when I find her."

Vickers arched his eyebrows. "And how do you intend to
find her when the whole damned Division is running all over
hell's half acre looking for her?"

"That's the easy part: she'll find me if I make myself
readily available."

Vickers frowned. "Do you want to elaborate on that?"

"She'll strike again. She's not going away until someone
kills her. What she did to our men, dead and alive, doesn't
make sense. She's deranged and out of control. She'll make
a mistake. I'll be waiting for her when she does."

Vickers' eyes narrowed. "You sound like you're taking
this personal. Your fucked up mind-set doesn't have anything
to do with your good buddy, Corporal Ward, does it?"

"Leave Kevin out of this, Top," Adkins warned. "If you
saw what I saw, you'd take it personal too. Look, don't take
this as a slight on your sunny personality or anything, but
I've really got better things to do than to sit around here

jawing with you all day. I need to get my men rested and healed up. They're in bad shape."

"Don't lose your perspective," Vickers advised. "Otherwise, this place will make you *dinky-dou*. Keep your professional distance."

"Professional distance, my ass: I remember you taking things pretty personal a time or two out there, Top—before you quit soldiering and became just another rear echelon Desk Winnie shuffling paper, that is."

"You're out of line, Sergeant. Get your shit together."

"You taught me everything I know, Top, remember?"

Vickers glowered. "Well it sure as hell doesn't look like I taught you much! You can't let this shit get to you. It'll destroy you."

Adkins grinned. "Are you afraid I might fuck up and make you look bad?"

"I put a big load on you," Vickers snapped. "So far, you've proven me right, but I'm still holding my fucking breath."

"It ain't nothing but a *thing*, Top, and *things* don't fucking matter." He dumped his coffee into the trashcan beside Vickers' desk. "Anything else, or can I go to the infirmary now and get this poison pumped out of my stomach?"

"Remember what I said, Hotshot," Vickers growled. "Keep your emotions locked away. Do your job and then forget it. If you start harboring vendettas, it'll get you killed."

Adkins smirked. "Yes, Daddy."

"I say that for the good of your men as well," Vickers insisted. "In the end, they're the only thing that counts. Now take my fucking advice and don't let this fucking woman get in your fucking head."

Adkins set his cup on the edge of the desk. "Sorry, but I'm not up to speeches at the moment, Top, I'm fuckin' tired. *Toodely-fucking-loo now*."

Vickers glared at him. "Get your head out of your ass! I don't want to hear no more bullshit about you wanting to kill this woman in a personal fucking way. Got it? Now get your smelly ass out of my orderly room and go get your platoon squared away. I've got better things to do myself than sit around here all day listening to your whining, pompous ass."

Adkins limped out of the orderly room with his left boot sole flapping and turned into the NCO hooch next to it. He stumped down the sagging plywood floor stained and marred in numerous places to his corner at the end of the double row of cots and hung his rifle on a nail below the canvas drooping between the two-by-four beams supporting the top. He hung his web gear on a nail in the board siding, limped outside to the low shelf running around the outside of the hooch for storage of personal gear, opened his cooler, and drew a can of warm beer from the brackish water within.

He was near exhaustion, but opened the beer and went back inside to clean his weapon. He opened a second beer on his way to the shower point to scrub the layers of crud off that had accumulated over the last five days, and opened a third on his way to the supply room with his towel wrapped around his waist to draw new jungle fatigues and boots. When he returned, he collapsed onto his bunk, still with his towel around his waist, and was asleep within minutes, dreaming of the smug woman with the compelling slanted eyes as she chased him through the night jabbing at him with her knife. He awoke in late evening covered with a chilling film of sweat, dressed, gobbled down a hurried hot meal in the mess hall, and then settled in at the Wolf's Den for a hefty load of well-deserved bourbon.

The next morning, he was dismayed to learn that the evil woman had struck again while he lay drunk in his bed.

CHAPTER 15

Kim-Ly slipped from her pallet beside her husband, taking care not to disturb his sleeping form. He was home on one of his frequent visits from his ranger battalion, which was assigned to the ARVN outpost two kilometers from their small hooch, and fortunately able to visit with her and their two sons often now due to his recent promotion to sergeant. With the exception of his military duties, they lived a simple life blessed with much happiness. Her husband was a good man, accepting of her plain features and gentle, unassuming manner. His parents lived in the same village as they. Her parents lived in the adjoining village and visited often. They owned a small rice paddy, and though the planting and harvesting fell mostly on her shoulders due to his military duties, he helped where he could. His meager army wages allowed them to purchase a water buffalo to till the rice, and they planned to purchase a second paddy. They owned one of the finer hooches in the village, with cement floors instead of dirt, stucco walls instead of mud, and red tiles on the roof above instead of thatched grass, with matching shutters for the windows. They were saving to educate their children in the Catholic school, and could afford a doctor if they became ill. Though considered by many to be on the higher end of middle class, life at this level was still difficult.

What disturbed her sleep was the troubling picture her husband brought home in his knapsack and carelessly showed to her. It sent her pulse racing, though she hid that from him at the time. Now she slipped the photo from the pouch and moved closer to a dim oil lamp to study the image with trembling hands. There was no doubt in her mind she was staring at her long ago friend, Tran Thi Cai. Though she had matured, her exquisite nose and mouth were unique and unmistakable, though the leering grin and hard eyes were unknown to her. She knew Cai as a quiet, withdrawn girl. The image she studied now almost belied that distant memory.

The story her husband told her of this vicious communist leader was implausible to her and required her to study the photograph to ensure she was not mistaken. Her mind flashed back to the terrible event Cai had experienced, and in which she had almost suffered through herself if not for her shyness. They placed Cai in a hospital for many weeks afterwards and later put her in an orphanage upon her release. When she visited Cai there afterwards, Cai treated her with indifference. After several of the inane visits, she stopped going and they lost contact with each other. Seeing her old friend now after these many years brought conflicting emotions fluctuating inside her, as she considered the reward her husband told her the Americans were offering for information on Cai. If true, the money would purchase the ox cart her husband wanted. That would add further to the comfort of their lives. She knew she should not feel empathy for this woman who was now thought to be an enemy of her country, and as such, a danger to her husband, but Cai had been her most devout friend before suffering greatly at the hands of the Frenchmen. A tear crept from the corner of her eye to trickle down her cheek as she placed the photo of the grinning woman back into her husband's knapsack.

She quietly returned to her husband's side, filled with the uncertainties of conflicting loyalties.

CHAPTER 16

"Good morning, Sir," Lieutenant Colonel Moore greeted the general as he strode briskly from the chopper with his half-dozen aides scurrying to catch up. He resisted the urge to salute the general, though they were more than secure in the middle of a large, far-flung perimeter of troops surrounding the site of the second massacre of an American ambush patrol in five days. The general nodded and stalked by him without a word as he continued towards the strewn, mutilated bodies. Colonel Moore hurried after the general, drawing abreast as he stopped abruptly with his nostrils twitching at the sickly-sweet smell of blood and death to take in the scene slowly, his bushy eyebrows drawing together in a scowl.

The general exhaled, seeming to wither from his six-foot two-inch frame and collapse inward on himself. "This is an outrage."

Moore nodded to the stake in the ground with the woman's portrait pinned to it. "Yes, Sir. This is the work of that fucking she-devil."

"Don't be crude on this hallowed ground, Colonel."

Lieutenant Colonel Moor flushed. "Sorry, Sir."

"Chris?" the general called without taking his eyes from the tragedy before him.

Christen hurried up to him. "Yes, General?"

"Get your team started on the documentation. I want these poor boys in body bags as quickly as possible and out of here."

"Yes, Sir." Christen turned to Pierce, Howell, and Billy hovering behind them. "Get your cameras and let's get going!" He pulled a handkerchief from his pocket to cover his mouth and nose as he led them forward grimly.

The general swatted irritably at the droves of green flies attracted to the gore. "Give me the particulars, Colonel."

"General, these men were from my Second Platoon, Bravo Company. There were forty men total on the mission. Twenty-eight are accounted for here. Five of these have their hands bound behind their backs, indicating they were tortured to death. The rest were... hacked up after death. Ten men were located during the night hiding in the surrounding brush, six of them wounded. Two men are still MIA. Sir... I uh, hope you don't think that just because these men and the other platoon were from my Battalion…"

"Let's take care of the business at hand, Colonel Moore," the general interrupted. "I find no fault at present with your leadership in this or the other instance."

Moore exhaled. "Yes, Sir. Sorry, Sir."

CHAPTER 17

Allen lay on his cot in a half-conscious state, licking ineffectively at his cracked lips and gasping at the putrid, nauseating cloud of defecation clinging to his pants. He moaned and drew his knees up into a fetal position as racking pain tore at his midsection. His half-lidded eyes took in the streaks on his arms and chest from the beating he received from the bamboo canes, as his feverish mind attempted to analyze his desperate situation. Through the haze of sweat clinging to his eyelashes, he saw a guard looming over him, scowling as he pinched his nose with his thumb and forefinger.

"You get up now, pig! You stink! You must to bathe!"

He tried to muster the strength to move and was appalled to find himself stuck to the soiled sheets by the clotted blood of his wounds. The guard rapped him painfully across his shins to get his attention as he fought to stay cognizant. He focused on the Vietnamese standing over him brandishing the cane as the man whacked him across his shins again. He groaned as he rolled off the cot, fell face down onto the dirt floor, and struggled up onto his quivering hands and knees with his head drooping.

The man whacked him across the buttocks. "You crawl now. You stink. Must to hurry!"

Allen clutched at the earth with his trembling hands and lurched along in a daze, his body racked with pain. The guard held his nose, prodding him with the tip of the cane as he wobbled in the indicated direction. In his near-delirium, he imagined he saw another American on his hands and knees crawling along in front of him with a second VC urging him along. They entered a moderate-sized cavern with several large barrels. He crawled onto a low wooden platform and stood up unsteadily, leaning his chest and head against the dirt wall as he fought to stay conscious, half-aware of some-one stumbling up beside him, as he struggled to maintain his balance.

"Easy, Bo, let me help you," an American voice soothed as he pulled Allen's soiled trousers down. "You're a mess, pal, but I'll get you cleaned up. My god, what've these assholes done to you?"

"You no talk! You wash!"

"*Yeah and fuck you too, you slope-eyed piece of shit,*" the American voice growled in a low hiss. "Hey, jackass, you wanna do this?" he demanded in a louder tone. "I gotta give the man directions so I can clean him up. So fuck you, slope, you *bic*?"

"You hurry! You wash!"

"*Fuck off, Charlie-san.* Hey fellow, this's probably gonna hurt a little. Hang on for me, okay?"

Fire spread over Allen's body as he cried out and clutched at the wall, gasping for breath as the man poured liquid over his head and across his back, the fluid eating into his cuts and scrapes.

"Sorry, Bo, there's no easy way to do this. I've got to get you cleaned up or you're gonna die of infection. Go ahead, big guy, hate me for it, but I'm only doin' this 'cause I gotta help you. Can you hear me? Do you understand why I'm hurting you?"

Allen choked back his tears. "Yes... thank you..."

"That's the spirit, Bo, just be tough for me. Now, I gotta use some soap to scrub you. I gotta get all the shit cleaned out of these cuts and sores. You cry if you need to, Bo. I'll do this as quick as I can, but I gotta do it right. Okay, big guy?"

Allen nodded, clenching his teeth as more liquid fire covered him from head to foot. A harsh cloth raked at him, scrubbing at his inflamed skin as a low, involuntary wail erupted from his throat.

"Just a little more, Bo," the American voice reassured him as he worked. "I promise you, I'm gonna kill one of these little fuckers for doin' this to you. You just pick one of 'em out for me. I'm gonna rip his head off and shit down his neck for you. Just for you, big guy. You pick any one of these little yellow, slant-eyed fuckers out you want to, and I'll nail him for you. Hang on now, Bo, don't pass out on me, hang on, just a little bit more now. I'm gonna shift you around, Bo. I gotta clean your front. We're halfway there, big guy. Where you from, Bo?"

"Ohio..."

"Me, I'm from Georgia, Bo. We got the prettiest little girls in the world down in Georgia. Little Georgia Peaches is what we call 'em. Ever had you a Georgia girl, Bo?"

"*Nooo...*"

"Ain't no other girl will ever do after you had you a Georgia peach, Bo. They'll ruin you for all the other women in the world. I got me one named Beth. I sure miss that little gal, Bo. What's your girl's name?"

"Shirley ..."

"That's a beautiful name, Bo. Bet she's a beauty, too. Now I'm gonna have to pour more water on you to rinse you off. Can you handle it, Bo? That's my man. My name's Robert Andrews, but everybody calls me Bubba except my mother. She calls me Bobby. What's your name, Bo? Here it comes now, hang on."

"*Awwwww, Allen, awwww, Hayes, ohooooooo. Please, I can't take anymore …*"

"This is the last one, Allen. Hold on, man, I'm almost through now. That's a good fellow. Go ahead, yell and let it out. Now I'm gonna put some drawers on you, Allen. That's all I've got, just these here boxer drawers. Lift your leg for me, Allen. Here, let me lift it for you. Now I'll just slip them up to your waist. There we go, Allen. Now put your arm around my shoulder and I'll walk you back to your cot."

"You must to crawl like dog! No walk!" the VC guard ordered.

"Aw fuck you, Dopey-san! He can't even walk, much less crawl. Save your bullshit for another time. Come on, Allen. Just put one foot in front of the other for me. Lean on me, buddy. Now that I'm here to take care of you, Bo, you're gonna be just fine!"

CHAPTER 18

The general cleared his throat and all talk ceased from the gathered staff in his small conference room. "Gentlemen, this is Captain Christen, my special project officer out of the G-2 Intelligence section. Captain Christen is in charge of assimilating information on the female he has code-named 'Tiger Woman.' Chris, give us what you've got."

Christen moved to the podium in front of the conference table and shuffled his notes as he viewed the division headquarters staff assembled around the table. "Thank you, Sir. I'll try to be brief. First, we may have a break on the identity of the woman. Yesterday, in response to some pictures and the offer of a reward I sent out to the ARVNs, a Kit Carson scout came forward with some information concerning her possible identity."

The chief of staff harrumphed. "A Kit Carson? How reliable do you think that is?"

"Generally, not very, Sir," Christen acknowledged. "But we'll be checking it out for accuracy. In the next couple of days, we should know whether we're on the right track or not. Essentially, the scout reports that this woman recruited him several weeks back. She commands a sixty-man unit. He states that she trained them in specialized tactics. Specifically, it sounds like they were training to attack small elements at night, such as our night ambush patrols manned by platoon-sized elements."

"And how did this Kit Carson end up on our side of the fence?" the G-I Personnel Officer inquired.

"He turned himself in to the ARVNs two weeks ago under some sort of an amnesty program they've got going on. He agreed to serve the South Vietnamese government on a fee basis. The scout states that the woman's name is Tran Thi Cai. It is rumored Colonel Nguyen Van Chien, the reported Vietcong Commander for this district, is her lover. It is also rumored the North Vietnamese Army trained her in her tactics and authorized her to recruit her own guerrilla force locally. According to what the Kit Carson says, it sounds like she taught her soldiers that psychological warfare is important in achieving battlefield victories."

"So this Kit Carson defected from her organization?" the G-1 asked.

"No, Sir," Christen corrected. "Apparently he trained with her force for a time, but eventually he was sent back to his regular unit after she deemed him unworthy of further training."

The G-1 smirked. "Great. We get her rejects. And what is his price for assisting us?"

"He wants ten thousand piaster and to work for us instead of the ARVNs, Sir," Christen advised.

"Hell, it sounds like he's playing to the highest bidder," the G-3 Operations Officer observed as those around the table nodded. "Did he give you the location of her base, or does that cost extra?"

"Unfortunately, he doesn't know that, Sir. The training he went through with her was near the Cambodian border. He was released before she moved back into this AO."

"So he claims the mutilation of our soldiers, dead and alive, is some sort of psychological warfare, Captain?" the G-2 inquired.

"Apparently she feels like it is, Sir. Having personally viewed her second attack site this morning, I'll admit that she makes my blood run cold. It's one thing to die honorably for my country and quite another to be strung up and butchered alive like a hog."

"That's enough, Chris," the general ordered. "Let's not desecrate our dead."

"My apologies, Sir. That was not my intent. In any case, psychological warfare seems to be the most logical explanation for her actions. The other alternative is too far out to even consider."

"And what would that other possibility be, Captain?" the G-1 asked.

"That she's a psychopath, Sir; a genuinely crazy person who inflicts pain for the pleasure of it."

"And now she's trained a whole specialized unit of psychopaths as well?" the G-3 asked.

"Not necessarily, Sir. She could merely use them to foster her own madness, if that were the case. Her soldiers wouldn't necessarily have to be as crazy as she is."

"Gentlemen, this sort of speculation serves no purpose," the general interrupted. "Chris, get out there and get me more information on this woman. I don't want to view another tragedy like I did this morning."

"Yes, Sir." Christen picked up his notes and departed the conference room feeling as though he had disappointed the general. Pierce, Howell, and Billy followed him into his office as he flopped into his chair and tossed his notes on his desk.

"Didn't go well, Cap'n?" Pierce inquired.

"We need to accelerate our efforts, gentlemen, unless we want to spend the rest of our tour walking through the bloody gore of this bitch's leavings like we did this morning."

"Billy and I've been talking, Sir," Howell offered. "We're convinced her base is not more than a few miles from us."

"So where the hell is she?" Christen demanded. "She seems to disappear into thin air after she strikes. We've had troops all over the area in ever widening patterns after each attack and found nothing. It's as if she crawls into a hole in the ground."

"The big question now is, where and when will she strike again?" Pierce added in the silence. "I recommend Billy and I get on a chopper and fly to every ARVN outpost in this sector and talk to the Commanders there to have them canvas their troops for any information concerning this woman known as Tran Thi Cai."

Christen nodded. "Let's get off our asses and find something useful!"

CHAPTER 19

"Hey, Allen, wake up, man. I've got some rice for you." Allen opened his eyes to find Bubba standing over him holding a bowl. "How you feeling, Bo?"

"Better... I think." Allen groaned as he shifted and attempted to sit up.

Bubba helped prop him back against the earthen wall next to his cot as he clutched at the bowl, using his fingers to scoop the chunky rice into his mouth, pausing only once to sip some lukewarm water in a tin cup that Bubba offered to him.

"You're half starved, Bo. I'll take better care of you from here on out."

"I'd eat a can of ham and lima beans right now," Allen swore, savoring the thought of the least desirable C-ration meal he normally shunned. He handed Bubba the empty bowl. "How're you faring?"

"Not bad, Bo: living in a hole in the ground ain't exactly the Ritz, but it'll do until I can figure us a way outta here."

"Why haven't they beat you like they did me?"

"'Cause, Bo, I told the little slant-eyed fuckers everything they wanted to know."

"You can't do that, Bubba! You'll get court-martialed."

"Fuck it, Bo, we're probably gonna die down here any-way, and I don't know nothin' worth a shit knowin' no-how. But just in case we do make it, everythin' I told 'em was bullshit. Stuff I made up on the spur of the moment. You need to do the same, Bo. Just be careful to keep your lies straight. They get pissed off if they catch you in a lie. An-other man was beaten worse than you 'cause they tripped him up and caught him lying."

"There are other prisoners down here with us?"

"One more that I know of; maybe more. A man from my platoon named Callahan, but I didn't know him all that well. I've got some salve for you, Bo. Don't know what the shit is or nothin', but one of the medics gave it to me."

"What unit are you from, Bubba?"

"Bravo Company, First Wolfhounds, but don't tell no-body. I told the slopes I was a payroll clerk in the Brigade Headquarters Section. I said they sent me out on patrol 'cause my commander was pissed off at me 'cause he thought I was a sorry soldier. I told 'em he thought some combat exposure might help straighten me out. I told 'em I didn't know nothin' about nothin' 'cause I'm just a dumb private who just got in-country a few weeks ago. The silly shits bought it. They're dumber than a rock, Bo. They think I'm harmless."

"I'm from the First Hounds, too. Alpha Company."

"Hell, I know that, Bo. We ran around looking for you night and day after you guys got your ass busted. Then we got our ass busted and I found you. That's one crazy little fuckin' cunt that runs this group, Bo. I was next up on the choppin' block when the Mech came roaring up and inter-rupted her. They saved my ass. She'd done carved up the rest of the prisoners. I was shittin' my britches, Bo. I mean it."

Allen shuddered. "I saw her kill three of our men in cold blood with their hands tied behind their back. It was the most god-awful thing I've ever seen. How long have you been here, Bubba?"

"I don't know for sure. Time down here gets confusing, but I got here about a week after you did. It's been about two or three days, I'd guess, maybe longer. Can you believe this setup, Bo? We've been runnin' around like chickens with our heads cut off lookin' for these sons bitches everywhere and all the time they were right under our nose in these fuckin' tunnels. We've gotta get outta here and report this shit, Bo. I'm gonna personally lead the whole fuckin' Wolfhound Battalion down into this snake pit to kick some slope ass. Know what I mean, Bo? There, that oughta fix you up, if it don't kill you." Bubba put the top back on the jar of salve.

"How do you get away with talking to them the way you do, Bubba? And why do they let you move around?"

"It's a delicate balance, Bo, but basically they're just like our own fucked-up army. You gotta know when to bluff and when to fold. Some of these little jerks you can intimidate and push around if you don't go too far. The higher rankin' pukes you gotta kiss a little ass with and do a lot of stoopin' and bowin' to. It's how all military systems work, Bo. But dinks are naturally subservient, so they're easier to intimidate than our own guys are."

"Where is the other man kept?"

"Ain't rightly sure, Bo. You and I are in the hospital 'cause we're wounded. I saw the other one when we were being interrogated together, but they wouldn't let us talk to each other."

"Where are you wounded?"

"My ass, Bo. Took a round through my left cheek, but it didn't do a lot of damage. Weren't much more than a grazing shot really, but I've been playin' it to the hilt. Hurt like a son of a bitch though. You don't wanna go gettin' shot in the ass, Bo, I'm here tellin' you."

"Do you really think we can escape?"

"I'm working' on it, Bo. But I need you to get healthy for me. When we go, we're gonna need to be haulin' ass, for sure."

CHAPTER 20

Nguyen Van Chien watched Cai with misgivings as she prepared herself for the coming operation. His trepidation increased as she slipped on the tiger fatigues and took up her AK-47 automatic rifle, which appeared too large for her small frame, sensing her boundless desire to engage their enemy. If he would allow it, she would seek battle with them every night.

Her unremitting torture of her captives troubled him deeply, her need to do those things beyond his ability to comprehend. She had virtually ignored his wishes in this matter the last time she took her force out. He had taken extra care to reprimand her strongly on the issue when Le Loi reported this to him. He had no love for the American occupation forces, but the descriptions of her method in dealing with them were unnatural. There had been talk within his command that was sure to reach his superiors, who much preferred to use the captured Americans as propaganda tools. To kill them without reason in any fashion deprived them of that opportunity. They would be very unappreciative of this, regardless of how they viewed her methods of disposing of them. He would have to monitor her very closely in the future. He could not allow his superiors to discipline her, and was even fearful of his own chastisement if he did not contain her excesses.

"Cai?" He spoke in a commanding voice, determined to reinforce his position on the matter. "You will remember what I have said. You will bring the captives here to face the People's Court. Do you understand?"

She tucked her head in tact submission. "Yes, my Colonel."

"If you persist in these deplorable acts, I will have no choice but to remove you from command and place you back on my administrative staff."

Her eyes flashed up. "You would take my soldiers from me, my Colonel?"

The hostility in her tone perturbed him. "I will have no choice. You must stop these unspeakable atrocities against the prisoners you take."

"Do you not agree that my soldiers have brought us two great victories, my Colonel? Do you wish for them to show our enemy compassion?"

"It is not of your soldiers I speak. I insist you conduct yourself in an honorable manner befitting a worthy warrior. I will not speak of this to you again. Do you understand me, Cai?"

She turned from him abruptly. "You have made your position clear, my Colonel."

"Cai, you must understand—"

She strapped on her ammo pouches. "I must go now!"

Chien softened his tone. "I... will be waiting for you when you return."

She turned to the cloth covering the entrance to her tiny room, snatched it aside, and disappeared into the corridor, leaving the cloth swaying and his emotions in a disagreeable jumble.

Pangs of anxiety stabbed at him. What if she did not return? What if the Americans killed or captured her?

Perhaps he should have stopped her before she departed. Perhaps he should call her back, cancel her mission on this night until he could reason with her. He should never have allowed her to join the Liberation Forces where she was in danger in the first place—and where she was now ever so subtlety slipping from his grasp. That had been a blunder on his part, but at the time, he could not have imagined his docile little Cai turning into the fearful predator she had become. This too was disturbing.

CHAPTER 21

"*That's what the fuck I'm looking for!*" Adkins shouted into the night when the first volley of frantic gunfire broke out less than a mile from where they lay hidden in their night ambush position. "*Saddle the fuck up! We're going after that fucking bitch here and now!*"

He felt cheated after the woman hit the Bravo Company Platoon the very night they returned to base camp after searching for their MIA. With his men exhausted at the time from spending almost nineteen straight days in the field and unable to participate in the second all out manhunt that followed, he sat on the bunker line for the next six days while his platoon recuperated and watched the activities from the sidelines. He intentionally timed their return to combat to coincide with the termination of the new search for the missing men of the second ambush, convinced it was not fate when she struck on the very night the first search ended. He judged she waited for the hundreds of soldiers rushing around the countryside to give up and return to their base camp, deeming it too risky to operate with so many American soldiers in such close proximity, all looking for her. He figured she deliberately waited for them to thin out so she could strike again with the same paralyzing results as with the first ambush she destroyed.

Helpless to do anything on her second strike, he rested his men and waited until the brass called off the second search. When that occurred this morning, he approached Captain James with a request for an ambush patrol in their sector, anticipating she would again strike on this night. The raging fight in the distance proved him right. The bitch might be cunning, but she was also predictable. Now he meant to give her a taste of American tactical ingenuity.

He had spent the last six days planning for this event and formulating an unorthodox plan of action. That afternoon he sketched the location of each ambush in the division on his map, some eleven different sites in all. Now he quickly pulled his squad leader's heads under a poncho with him and illuminated his map with a red filtered flashlight while his men scrambled to retrieve their claymore mines and strap on their gear.

"That's the location of an element of the 2-14 Infantry Golden Dragons," he explained, taking a quick compass reading and matching it against their location on the map. "There's sparse, open scrub brush on the other side of the rice paddy they're set up in. That will be the most logical route of departure when our Reaction Force charges out to the rescue. If we move fast enough, we can cut across that avenue of escape and jump her when she attempts to withdraw."

Sergeant Brooks grinned. "I'm game! Let's bust that bitch's ass!"

"We're wasting fucking time!" Sergeant Handler chorused.

"This is the craziest fucking thing I've ever heard of, but it just might work!" Gonzales allowed.

"This is nuts, but count me in!" Fielding agreed.

100

"Let's move it!" Adkins ordered as he threw the poncho back. Within two minutes, he had them moving at a fast trot, throwing caution to the wind. He led them rapidly across fields and through knee-deep paddies in open abandon, indifferent to the noise they made, which was muffled by the distant firefight in any case, and uncaring of any enemy force they might encounter, believing their foe was focused on the attack on the Golden Dragons. In any case, he figured that if he guessed wrong, they would soon have hundreds of troops swarming around to pull their ass out of the fire. He led them not to the raging fight, but slightly away from it, angling towards the thick growth of the most logical escape corridor, intent on reaching that area before her force did. It took fifteen minutes of hard, headlong flight before he drew up on the edge of the dark vegetation that bordered the paddy area.

"Give me... a headcount..." he panted, bending over to hold his legs as his lungs fought for oxygen.

"First... Squad... accounted... for..." Handler gasped.

"Second... here..." Gonzales confirmed.

"Third... accounted for..." Fielding wheezed.

"Fourth... is all... here..." Brooks choked.

"Give me... a line across... the front of... this shit," Adkins gasped. "Get some claymores out. Move it!"

The squad leaders led the gasping men forward, grimly placing them in position. They quickly set their claymores out to their front and concealed themselves in the fringe of the trees, as Adkins placed himself in the center of the line, his eye glued to the starlight scope, which gave him four-hundred meters of green-hazed visibility across the area to their front.

There he hunched, face streaming sweat, hopeful heart pounding, nerves taunt, eyes peering into the darkness, ears strained to catch the faintest sound... and his mind wondering if he was as crazy as a loon for pulling such a dubious stunt as this.

When he spotted a large contingent of black shapes hurrying towards them in his starlight scope, he made quick adjustments in their line. When the first man in the group was fifteen meters to their front, he opened fire on full automatic, knocking the first three men backward into their comrades behind them. His whole platoon opened fire with a crescendo of orange billowing muzzle flashes and yellow exploding claymores in a furious onslaught of devastating firepower, as the dark mass of men in front of them scattered frantically in all directions in the face of the unexpected onslaught.

"Hold your fire!" a hysterical voice screamed from their front. *"We're Americans! Don't shoot! We're American!"*

Adkins' heart clutched. *"Cease fire! Cease fire, goddamn it!"*

"Fuck! We've ambushed our own guys!" another voice cried.

"Cease fire! Cease fire!" others took up the call. *"They're friendlies! We're firing on friendlies, goddamn it!"*

CHAPTER 22

"Captain, wake up, Sir!"

"What the hell?" Christen struggled to find his bearings as Specialist Howell shook his shoulder.

"It's Tiger Woman, Sir! Another one of our ambushes just got hit!"

"*What*?"

"I've got a chopper standing by, Captain. Pierce and Billy will meet us at the helipad."

"Son of a bitch! What time is it?"

"0200 hours, Sir. The Reaction Force is en route and gunships are flying over the site as we speak. It doesn't look good for them, Captain. We've lost radio contact with the platoon under attack and the gunships are having a hard time picking out friend from foe. The 5th Mech is almost at their location now."

Christen sat up and pulled on his trousers as Howell stepped back. "Son of a bitch! Let's go!"

Thirty minutes later, Christen stared out of the wide cargo door of the command and control helicopter as they circled some three thousand feet up in the air. Below them, flares drifted and helicopter gunships circled looking for targets. No enemy contact had occurred since they arrived on the scene ten minutes before, although there were reports of fierce fighting just prior to their arrival between unknown forces to the north of the ambush site.

In the half-light provided by the flares, Christen could see the personnel carriers from the Mech with their high steel sides churning up clods of dirt from their tank treads as they maneuvered. Though he monitored the command frequency of the ground troops with a headset, he was powerless to do anything else but watch.

"Can you set us down near the ambush site?" he inquired of the pilot over the aircraft intercom.

"Roger that, Captain. We can drop you off, but we can't stay on the ground and wait for you."

"Contact one of the APCs and set us down near them. You can return to the helipad and we'll call when we're ready to be extracted."

"Roger, Captain. I'll coordinate a pickup zone."

"Thanks." Christen pulled off the headset and leaned toward Pierce, Howell, and Billy seated beside him. "We're going down there!"

They gave him a thumb's up in acknowledgement. Moments later, they followed him through the swirling grass thrown up by the rotor wash to an armored personnel carrier as the chopper lifted off behind them. A lieutenant stepped out of the back of the APC as they approached.

"I'm Captain Christen, Special Investigating Officer for the CG." He held out his hand and shook with the platoon leader.

"Lieutenant Groves, Captain. How can I help you?"

"We want to get to the ambush site as quickly as possible, Lieutenant."

"Climb aboard, gentlemen. I hope you brought your barf bags. It's not a pretty sight."

They climbed into the back of the personnel carrier, the hydraulic door lifted, and they rumbled off through the light brush, twisting and turning to avoid the larger trees. Five minutes later, they lurched to a halt in a lightly wooded, smoke-filled area with flares floating overhead.

The lieutenant leaned down from his turret to shout above the throbbing of his diesel engine as the rear ramp dropped. "Directly to your front, Captain. I'll be here in the track if you need me—I've got a weak stomach."

"Thanks!" Christen called as he led his staff down the ramp of the APC and circled to the front.

The flares floating overhead provided adequate, if somewhat distorted, light. Fifty feet in front of the track, Christen saw scattered bodies strung about and moved towards the area dreading what they would find. He paused on the edge of the third massacre site as Pierce, Howell, and Billy drew up beside him, and counted nineteen bodies, each mutilated in one or more ways.

"How many men were on the patrol?" Christen asked softly.

"Forty one, Cap'n," Pierce answered.

Christen sighed. "Twenty-two are unaccounted for then."

Howell nodded grimly. "Some have been located by the Reaction Forces, but we don't have a complete accounting yet."

Billy turned away from the carnage. "Maybe I keep working for ARVNs. Not pay as much, but better working conditions."

Pierce scowled. "You were almost part of this, you jackass."

"I think maybe I not ever be part of this sick shit!" Billy retorted.

Christen led them through the battlefield, stepping around the congealing pools of blood, looking closely at the disfigured corpses, as the others fanned out and shadowed his movements. On the far side, they drew together to stare back at the site in horror.

"Did you notice none of them were tied up this time, Captain?" Howell asked in a subdued voice.

"Maybe the Reaction Force got here so fast she didn't have time to torture them," Christen suggested. "There are still a lot of men missing."

"Maybe, maybe not," Howell argued. "Come over here, Captain, and look at this man."

"What am I looking at?" Christen asked as he edged closer. "He's mutilated just like the others."

"No, Captain," Howell insisted. "Not like the others. Look at the trail of entrails behind him. He crawled on his hands and knees with his intestines dragging along behind him before he died. He's also been shot in the shoulder."

"So?"

"So he was wounded and then his stomach was sliced open," Howell pointed out. "He wasn't tied up. And look at this one over here, Captain. It appears he initially suffered an arm wound before they cut off his ears and tongue. Once again, he crawled away. And this one here as well. Shot in the upper chest before they gouged his eyes out. See what I mean?"

Christen looked closer at the bodies. "So she's still butchering them, but she's not tying them up. What's the difference?"

"That's the interesting part, Captain," Howell pointed out grimly. "There's not a single man here who wasn't wounded before she tortured him to death. In the other two sites, they tied the prisoners up and tortured them to death. She didn't do that this time. I think she took the unwounded prisoners with her instead of torturing them."

"But what does it mean?" Christen demanded.

"Damn if I know, Captain. But for whatever reason, she's changed her MO."

"What M-O mean?" Billy asked.

"Mode of Operation," Howell answered. "How she does things."

"You mean because she torture and kill only wounded men this time, not all the prisoners she take?"

Howell nodded. "That appears to be the situation. She just cut the wounded up and allowed them to crawl off to die."

"So fucking what?" Pierce demanded. "She's still a psycho."

"That's not the point, Sarge," Howell insisted. "The point is: she apparently kept the healthy prisoners this time."

"Does that make her more humane?" Pierce retorted.

"No, but it does mean she's doing things differently," Howell argued. "*Why* she's doing things different may mean something."

"And may not," Pierce argued.

"There other differences," Billy observed, as he eased around the site. "I think this time American patrol surprise her. There many more American cartridges expended than other time. They put up good fight this time. Maybe many escape. Also she not leave picture of herself like before."

"He's right," Howell concurred.

"Maybe this was another enemy force that attacked them and not Tiger Woman," Pierce offered.

"No, it was definitely Tiger Woman," Howell insisted. "But she did things differently, and we need to figure out why."

"Let's get pictures of everything and get the hell out of here," Christen ordered. "I want us back at the base as soon as possible. We've *got* to develop some new leads to help put an end to this madness!"

CHAPTER 23

Chien watched Cai bathe in her quarters with some anxiety, her eyes glinting in the candlelight, noticeably filled with anger as she scrubbed at her skin in furious circles with the bar of yellow soap. When he attempted to question her earlier, she fled to her quarters without comment. Her obvious keen displeasure made him hesitant to approach her in an ardent manner, which he had anticipated since her departure the previous evening. It seemed with every mission she grew more intolerant of his needs and became less compliant with his demands on her, versus the previous indifference his attentions elicited from her. The open hostility she exuded dampened his desire and he resented her cold disposition.

He must be tolerant of her on this occasion, he reasoned. Le Loi reported the preceding engagement had been less than successful as compared to the others. The Americans discovered them creeping up on them and blew their devastating claymore devices in their faces before the signal to attack was given. Things then degenerated into a series of running skirmishes as the Americans fled the trap and fought savagely, as part of her force attempted to pursue them. In the ensuing mêlée, she lost two men killed and five wounded.

Even more poignant, as they regrouped and fled from the encroaching enemy reaction forces, she lost another nine killed and twelve wounded in a surprise ambush. Le Loi swore they thoroughly cleared the area beforehand, and that it contained no American forces. Where the unknown patrol came from, and how they got there, was a mystery to them. Luckily, Cai and the prisoners they had taken were at the rear of the formation and Cai was able to make her escape from the unexpected confrontation, as what remained of her force scattered into the night to make their way back as best they could. Out of necessity, they were required to abandon the prisoners in the confusion. Overall, it was a dismal defeat for her in both instances, with fully half of her command lost in the two encounters.

Obviously, she blamed herself for the failure. He must help her understand things did not always go as planned in battle. He must provide her comfort and give her the benefit of his wisdom and experience. He would show his compassion by limiting his personal demands on her in this instance. His empathy would help assuage her disappointment.

"Cai?" he commanded huskily as he moved towards her. He stopped, startled to see her eyes flash up to meet his, defying him to approach her. A shiver of fear waffled through him. Her eyes spoke death. What he saw in them confused him. He stepped forward again and she withdrew, turning away. He hesitated.

"*Cai!*" he commanded, ordering her to turn back to face him. Her shoulders stiffened, as she remained with her back to him in an ultimate insult to his authority. He trembled in near rage and drew his hand up to cuff her head.

He slowly lowered his palm, turned and stormed out of her little room, snatching the cloth door covering down and flinging it aside in his haste to get away from her before he lost complete control of his dignity.

CHAPTER 24

Kim-Ly stepped down from the American helicopter and stooped as she ran through the swirling wind behind her husband, her long black hair thrashing about her head as her heart beat wildly. Having never ridden on an aircraft before, she had been fraught with fear as she watched the paddies flash by below them at incredible speeds. She clutched her husband's arm as the aircraft banked to land at the huge American base at Cu Chi, terrified of falling out, but he, and the Americans on each side of her staring out from behind their machine guns with their dark visors pulled down to hide their face, seemed unconcerned.

She deeply regretted telling her husband about Tran Thi Cai and their childhood friendship this morning. It had been hard for her to do so since he considered Cai his enemy. After much anguish, her loyalty to her husband mandated she be disloyal to her friend.

Her husband became excited with her revelation and summoned his parents to care for their sons before hurrying her to his ARVN outpost to send a radio message to the Americans. They immediately dispatched the helicopter to pick them up and fly them here. She was filled with consternation for all of the excitement generated over her knowing a schoolgirl from her past. Surely she had nothing of value to offer, and would only bring shame on her husband and her parents.

The Americans alarmed her. They were so big and curt in spite of their youth. The time they passed through her village, she gathered her children at her feet and squatted before them as they searched her house. They spoke in quick, harsh tones, which she did not understand, and they seemed angry when she peeped at them from her lowered eyes. When one of them gave a bar of chocolate to her eldest son, she had been terrified it was poison. The unexpected gift delighted her child, and thereafter, he followed his soldier benefactor around, to her dismay, as they searched the rest of the village. Though they treated the adults gruffly, they seemed to love the kids. They handed out fruits and candy to them, and sat them on their laps, as they rested in the shade to eat meals from cans before they left her village. Now she was in the middle of their ugly, squalid city made of bags of sand.

She stood to the rear with her eyes lowered, as a tall American with red hair and many freckles greeted her husband in English. When her husband directed her into the back of a jeep, the American took her elbow to help her up into the vehicle, his hands firm, but gentle. She was shocked that he touched her, and fearful of her husband's disapproval, but he only seemed amused by the American's assistance to her.

She wanted only to return to her village and her children, to get as far away from this bewildering, unpleasant experience as possible.

CHAPTER 25

Cai listened to Colonel Chien rush from her quarters with smug satisfaction. If he so desired to deprive her of her gratification, she would deprive him of his. The resolution helped assuage the hollowness deep inside her, the emptiness that was robbing her of satisfaction. Torturing only the wounded frustrated her. Most were in shock and barely acknowledged her or her knife. Only one begged for his life, and weakly at that. By comparison, the four prisoners they took assumed they were her next victims, and immediately fell to begging for their miserable lives the instant she started on the wounded. She trembled with desire, longing to get at them. But Le Loi cautioned her sternly when she turned to them, thirsting for gratification. She stood shuddering with the unrequited craving consuming her as Le Loi moved to place himself between her and the kneeling prisoners. She considered killing him, but he was a devoted executive officer, even if he did report to Chien outside of her operational control and most likely was merely following Chien's orders to prevent her from harming the unwounded prisoners. She turned away in revulsion, allowing them to live with great reluctance, so enraged, she refused to leave the photograph of herself to mock their enemy.

She restored the cloth covering to her entrance and stripped off her tiger fatigues. On an impulse, she turned to the cloth and drew it aside. A passing soldier of low stature within the headquarters staff caught her eye. She beckoned him inside as others watched her with unease. She drew the cloth closed behind him and lowered her eyes in submission as she stood naked before him. She would punish Chien for his denial of her pleasure in a way that would bring him as much anguish as he brought upon her. The peasant before her stepped back nervously and turned to the cloth door to leave.

"You will stay!" she ordered. He hesitated and turned back to her. She lay back on her cot and opened her thighs. He stumbled towards her.

As she laid under his cautious, course machinations, oblivious to his growing enthusiasm, she let her mind drift back to the sudden appearance of the mysterious enemy force across her path. Where had they come from? Their positioning did not fit any known enemy ambush site she had ever studied. Their presence at such an improbable location made no sense. The enemy she knew did not fight in that manner. Le Loi had cleared the route earlier with his scouts. It unnerved her to have them appear out of nowhere like that to nearly destroy her entire force. What had she missed? Who were they? Where did they come from? What could she expect of them next?

The most excruciating sting was that her prisoners had escaped in the confusion of the attack. This only proved that Chien was wrong to constrict her. If not for him, none of the despised dogs would have survived to escape.

She abruptly shoved the squirming, grunting man on top of her onto the earthen floor beside her cot.

"Did I do something wrong, my Captain?" he whimpered as he stared up at her in surprise.

"Get out," she hissed.

"But…"

"Leave me," she ordered, pulling her knife from its scabbard beside her bed.

The man leapt up, grabbed his clothes to his chest, and rushed from the room.

CHAPTER 26

Captain Christen led Specialist Howell into the Intelligence bunker just before sundown after their return from the village of Cu Chi, where they met with the staff of the local orphanage and showed them the picture of the woman Billy and Kim-Ly identified as Tran Thi Cai. While his team gathered around the small conference table, Christen poured himself a cup of coffee and scratched the red fuzz on his head as he seated himself.

"Let's go over what we've got."

Howell shuffled his notes. "One, we confirmed that a certain Tran Thi Cai was in the Catholic 'Child of the Night' orphanage up until some six years ago, as Kim-Ly reported."

"Did they confirm that this Cai girl is actually Tiger Woman from our photograph?" Master Sergeant Pierce asked.

Howell shook his head. "The Nuns presently at the orphanage weren't there during the time she was, but their records, though incomplete due to a fire years ago, verified a girl by that name was there from the age of thirteen until she turned eighteen. However, they did give us a lead on an older Nun called Mother Sara who was there during that period and is currently running an orphanage in Saigon."

"She Tiger Woman," Billy insisted. "I confirm picture of Cai. Kim-Ly confirm picture of Cai. She Tiger Woman. I earn reward now."

Pierce scowled. "We require *three* unrelated verifications, Billy. You and Kim-Ly are only two."

"I think it's fair to assume she is Tiger Woman at this point," Christen soothed. "Now let's focus on how to find her. The surviving orphanage records indicate this Cai girl's uncle, a certain Tran Duc Thinh, arranged for her to marry a man named Nguyen Dien Pin upon her departure from the orphanage. She is thought to have given birth to a child and moved away from this area shortly afterwards."

"Were there any indications as to where they moved to?" Pierce asked.

Howell shrugged. "Not really, and it seems logical to assume her husband and child will be as difficult to locate as she is. But if we *can* find them, it stands to reason we'll find *her*. In any case, they all seem to have disappeared some five years ago and no one has seen or heard from them since. Another possible lead is the uncle who arranged the marriage. The Nuns couldn't give us much to go on where he's concerned, other than his being listed as her only known surviving family member."

"Lay on a chopper to fly us to Saigon tomorrow morning to interview this Mother Sara," Christen directed. "Maybe she can help us locate Cai's uncle or has some knowledge of where Cai and Pin moved to. What have you two turned up?"

Pierce shrugged. "Billy and I flew to three more ARVN outposts, distributed her picture around, and had the camp commandants question their troops. Not a single lead materialized from any of them. We plan to visit more outposts tomorrow."

"Good. Add the name of her husband and uncle to your list."

"Right." Pierce wrote the names Nguyen Dinh Pin and Tran Duc Thinh on his pad.

"What else can we do?" Christen asked.

"Go to Vietcong prisoner of war camp," Billy suggested. "Offer reward for information."

Christen nodded. "That might be worth a try."

"Is everything about money with you?" Pierce demanded.

Billy shrugged. "It capitalistic way. You Americans taught us this."

Pierce turned to Christen. "Pardon me, Cap'n, but what the fuck does it matter what her name is, or where she was born, or who she is married to, or anything else along those lines? The real question is where the fuck is she *now*? We're wasting our time on all this irrelevant bullshit. We should be concentrating on where to *find* her."

"We've got ten thousand troops out there in the bush, Sergeant Pierce," Christen answered. "Their tactical mission is to find her and destroy her. I assure you they're pursuing every avenue. Our mission is to compile a profile on her in hopes it will help them accomplish that mission, or at the very least, to help capture her so we can put her on trial as a war criminal."

Howell grimaced. "Capture her, my ass, Captain; that's going to be one dead chick if I get her in my sights."

"I think you no capture her," Billy asserted. "She never surrender."

"Tell us more about her, Billy," Howell insisted. "You spent three weeks with her training to be one of her bloody butchers."

"Not more to tell," Billy answered. "I tell you she train us hard. She no talk much. She very demanding. Drill over and over on every detail. What more to tell?"

"Tell us more about the psychological warfare part," Pierce insisted.

"I not know more. She just say fear weakens enemy mind. Make them not think clear. She say we must instill fear. She not say how."

"Well, she sure as hell's doing that," Pierce swore. "She's got every soldier in this division scared shitless when the sun goes down. It's as if an evil blood-sucking vampire was lurking around out there somewhere in the dark. But where?"

"She very close."

"So how do we find her, damn it?"

"That very difficult. I think it more likely she find you when she ready."

"You're no help at all," Pierce complained.

"I tell you what I know. I tell you what I think. You do with this what you want."

"Why did she initially select you for her band?" Howell asked.

"I not know why she pick me. I with my wife and child one day when she come. I have no say in matter. I just do what she say."

"You have a family? Where are they now?"

"American gunship kill them during battle near our village when I away training with her," Billy replied.

"I'm... sorry to hear that," Christen said in the uneasy silence.

"It very sad accident," Billy replied softly. "The Communists fight Americans near our village. They put my family in harm's way. I turn myself in to ARVNs afterwards. I grow tired of war. I help you drive them from our land now."

Christen cleared his throat. "Let's go back over what we've got one more time."

Chapter 27

Bubba chuckled as they lay on their cots in the hospital room. "I tell you, Bo, I just about lost it in there during the interrogation. I mean it. I just about fell over laughin'."

Allen scowled. "You *said* to make stuff up."

"But, Bo, you're *supposed* to make it believable; a *cook* trying to get *promoted* by a commander that requires his men to go on at least one *combat* patrol? Come on! Give me a break."

"They didn't beat me this time," Allen argued.

"True. But what the shit are you gonna tell 'em the next time when they ask you for the recipe for 'shit on the shingles,' Bo?" Bubba demanded, referring to toast covered with gravy and chunks of beef that the army served at breakfast on a regular basis. "Or even better, what if they want you to whip up a batter of fried chicken for 'em? And what about the *Sanitation Company* you're supposedly assigned to? I just 'bout exploded when you told 'em your unit went around burnin' barrels of shit from the base camp latrines all day. I mean it, Bo. I 'bout died right there on the spot!"

"They didn't beat me," Allen repeated.

"I gotta speed up our escape plans, Bo. I won't last through another interrogation session with you. They'll be beating my ass 'cause I'm rollin' on the floor laughin' like a fuckin' hyena!"

"It wasn't that funny, Bubba."

Bubba wiped at his tears. "I'm sorry, Bo. I can't help myself."

Allen scowled. "Man, I'm so hungry I'd eat about a dozen eggs right now and a whole pan of biscuits. It must be morning, Bubba. Breakfast was always my favorite meal."

"Bo, you can't tell me 'bout no biscuits. My Momma's the best biscuit maker in the whole world. She makes 'em from scratch, Bo, all hot, and fluffy, and dripping with butter. I'd eat a dozen right now. When we get outta here, you come on down to Georgia and I'll get her to make us all the biscuits we can eat. That's a promise, Bo."

Allen's mouth watered as hunger pangs flitted through his stomach. "Man, Bubba, that's one damned promise I'd like to hold you to!"

CHAPTER 28

"Gentlemen, you know Captain Christen," the general introduced. "Chris, what have you got for us today?"

Christen nodded at the assembled staff as he settled in behind the podium and arranged his notes. "Good morning, Sir. It's been a busy few days since I last briefed you, but I think we've assimilated an impressive profile on Tiger Woman.

"First, the woman in the photograph has been positively identified as Tran Thi Cai. As you may recall, the Kit Carson scout made the initial identification. A woman named Kim-Ly, who was childhood friends with this woman and grew up in the same village with her, also confirmed her identify two days ago."

"Do you consider this woman reliable, Captain?" the G-2 asked.

"Yes, Sir, I do. Kim-Ly has since married and has two children. Her husband is a decorated soldier with an ARVN Ranger Battalion located in Trang Bang, ten clicks west of us. From all indications, she is a loyal citizen to the Republic of South Vietnam. She also gave us some additional leads, which we have since followed up on and believe to be conclusive verification."

"What are these other leads you mention, Captain?" the G-1 asked.

"According to Kim-Ly, Cai was born in the village of Ly Van Manh, which we have code named 'Nightmare Village' in past operations. Nightmare Village, as you know, is nine clicks southwest of Cu Chi." He used a pointer to indicate the village on the map approximately five miles to the southwest of their base camp. "Today, the village is mostly a cluster of burned-out hooches with few inhabitants due to our previous engagements and the saturation patrolling we have employed in that area. Years ago, during the French era, it was a thriving village infested by the Viet Minh, the predecessors to our current Vietcong forces. I think it's safe to assume Cai's father was a member of the Viet Minh movement.

"According to Kim-Ly, the French attacked the village and killed both of Cai's parents in the engagement. She further stated that Cai herself was kidnapped during the siege by five rogue French soldiers and released several days later when their forces withdrew. Her uncle, Tran Duc Thinh, placed her in the orphanage here in Cu Chi afterwards. Records at the orphanage verified that a female by the name of Tran Thi Cai was with them for five years until she turned eighteen, but could not identify her from the photograph. However, they did refer us to a Mother Sara in Saigon who ran the orphanage during that era, and who positively confirmed that our photograph was indeed of Cai, leaving no doubt that she is the woman in the picture we call Tiger Woman."

"You say she was a captive of the Frenchmen who attacked her village and killed her parents, Captain?" the G-2 asked. "She would seem to have been too young at the time to have been a member of the local resistance along with her parents."

126

"The reason she was initially held and then later released is unknown for sure, Sir, but Mother Sara informed us that Cai was a tiny child for her age and required a long period of hospitalization after her uncle placed her in the orphanage, but would not disclose the exact nature of her injuries or treatment received. However, Mother Sara did state that during the five years Cai spent in the orphanage, she was withdrawn and made no friends. Specifically, she would not talk to the other children, or play with them, and performed poorly in her schooling. Her uncle, Thinh, arranged her marriage to a Nguyen Dinh Pin, shortly after her eighteenth birthday. Mother Sara never saw Cai after she left the orphanage, but she believes that a child was born to her and Pin five years ago, just before Cai and Pin disappeared."

"So where do we go from here?" the G-3 asked.

"Our next task is to find the uncle, Tran Duc Thinh, who most likely is a member of the local Vietcong network, and the husband, Nguyen Dinh Pin, who almost certainly is. We are also trying to obtain information on the child who may have been born to Cai and Pin. Additionally, we plan to visit several different South Vietnamese prisoner of war camps in search of information on Cai, Thinh, and Pin. That concludes my briefing, Gentlemen. What are your questions?" Christen collected his notes and looked expectantly at the assembled staff members.

The general nodded. "Chris, you've done a marvelous job of assembling this data in such a short time."

"Thank you, Sir. I realize none of this information helps you tactically, but hopefully as we continue our investigation, we'll find something useful to help end her reign of terror."

"Such as, Captain?" the G-3 questioned.

"It's a long shot, but if we can find her family members or her child, we could possibly lay a trap for her."

"Captain, you mentioned before that she was thought to be the mistress of Nguyen Van Chien, the VC district commander. Has there been any verification of that?" the G-2 asked.

"Not at the present time, Sir. All we have to go on is the Kit Carson scout's report, which he admits is based largely on rumor and speculation. But I will add, Sir, that everything he has told us up to now has been verified as true, which would tend to give credibility to that as well."

"It would seem so, Captain," the G-2 agreed. "But if that be the case, and she is in fact Chien's mistress, would it not also indicate that she is no longer married to this Pin fellow?"

Christen nodded thoughtfully. "Yes, Sir, I see your point. I think that would be a strong indication that Pin is probably dead or incapacitated in some way."

"Why not divorced?" the G-1 asked.

"That's possible, Sir, but not likely," Christen advised. "Divorce is almost unheard of in this society, especially in arranged marriages. The female is a virtual slave to her male counterpart and almost considered as property in such circumstances."

"Based on what I've heard here today, Captain, the theory that she may indeed be a psychopath has grown in merit," the G-1 observed. "It's only natural to assume that whatever ordeal she suffered at the hands of the Frenchmen, which required such extensive rehabilitation, may have been festering in her sick mind all these years."

Christen nodded. "That may very well be the case, Sir." He turned his attention back to the General. "There are two other pieces of information before I go, Sir, but I'm not sure what they mean yet. During the last attack, only the wounded were tortured. It's also noteworthy that they took all four of the MIAs that were rescued by the Wolfhound Company Platoon into captivity unharmed. That's a significant change from her previous tactics. Also, for whatever reasons, she did not leave her photo behind this time."

"Do you have a theory as to why, Captain?" the G-3 asked.

"No, Sir, but I do have some theories that may help you tactically that I have developed from viewing the actual ambush sites after her attacks."

"What are those observations, Captain?"

"They are unsubstantiated, but the pattern seems reliable. One, I think she has scouts follow the platoons and watch them set up. Two, she is familiar with our troop dispositions in our employment of night ambushes. She always strikes at the rear of the ambush perimeter, where the concentration of men and firepower are the weakest. Three, she uses stealth to surprise and overrun the perimeter after they've been there several hours and are at their most fatigued and least vigilant posture. Once her force has breached the line, it's impossible to bring our fire-superiority to bear on her because all command and control is lost after the defensive position is compromised.

"What happened during the last attack is significant as well. In talking to the surviving soldiers, we learned that their platoon leader, who unfortunately did not survive the attack, instructed his men that if hit, they were to run out of the ambush site and fight independently. It proved to be unorthodox, but sound tactics. As you know, most escaped, and it would seem that they inflicted a number of casualties upon her force as well. Another key point is that the platoon leader put starlight scopes orientated in all four directions instead of primarily to the front. I believe this may have helped them spot her force moving into position behind them. In my opinion, that Lieutenant did a superb job of neutralizing the tactical advantage she employs against us. That concludes my briefing, Sir."

"Thank you, Chris. We appreciate your observations. We will certainly take your points under consideration." The general turned to the G-3. "Tell me about this second engagement that occurred, the platoon from the 1-27 Infantry that apparently attacked her force as they were withdrawing and rescued the four prisoners."

"That was a strange one, Sir," the G-3 answered. "The Platoon Sergeant, uh, actually the *Acting* Platoon Leader, a Staff Sergeant Adkins, moved his unit at double time for over a mile to set up a hasty ambush. Her force walked into his trap and suffered nine confirmed kills and numerous blood trails indicating at least another eight or ten wounded. Unfortunately, two of the four prisoners rescued received wounds during the attack as well before they were able to identify themselves, but thankfully none of them seriously. It was quite a remarkable operation, given the circumstances."

"Who directed them to move?" the general asked.

"No one did, Sir. Sergeant Adkins took it upon himself to do so. His after-action report says he looked at the tactical situation and thought that was the most probable route of withdrawal when he heard the attack start and he moved to block it. I would say he came real close to killing that bitch, if you'll pardon my choice of words, General."

"A Staff Sergeant?"

"Yes, Sir. Actually, he's an *acting* Staff Sergeant. His Battalion Commander speaks highly of him. He currently holds the highest body count of any platoon in the Division, Sir."

"That's amazing," the G-1 observed. "Half the troops out there are scared to death of even meeting up with this lunatic, and this youngster picks up and runs off through the night to ambush her while she's still conducting a full-scale attack. Truly remarkable."

"It was indeed an admirable response," the general concurred. "And one filled with valor under the circumstances. Insure he gets proper recognition for it."

The G-1 nodded. "Yes, Sir; it is done."

"Chris, you may be excused from the rest of the briefing. I see you squirming around over there," the general said with a supporting laugh from his staff.

"Sorry, Sir, but I've got some urgent matters waiting for me. I appreciate your understanding." He collected his notes and left the conference room. When he entered his small office Pierce, Howell, and Billy followed him in.

"You look better than the last briefing, Cap'n," Pierce appraised.

"The General was pleased with the progress we've made. Let's keep the momentum going."

"I'm all for that, Captain. What have you got in mind?" Howell asked.

"I want you and Billy to go to the prisoner of war camp and run down any information you can find on Cai, Thinh, and Pin. Sergeant Pierce and I will go out to Trang Bang in the morning to check in with Kim-Ly and her husband to see if they can help us locate any of Cai's family."

"I'll lay on the chopper, Cap'n," Pierce acknowledged.

CHAPTER 29

First Sergeant Vickers glared at Sergeant Adkins as he sauntered into the orderly room and filled his cup with coffee before flopping down in the chair beside his desk.

"You wanted to see me, Top?" Adkins sipped and grimaced as he stared suspiciously into his cup analyzing the mystifying ingredients.

Vickers fought the budding annoyance from Adkins' insufferably benign manner, which had a tendency to piss him off before he could contain it. "*Good morning*, Sergeant," he replied with heavy sarcasm.

"Why, thank you, Top," Adkins replied warmly, looking him in the eye as he sipped at his coffee. "Not many people give a damn what kind of morning I'm having."

Vickers sat back in his chair and puffed on his cigar furiously. "Mind telling me what that stupid stunt was all about?"

Adkins frowned. "Which one, Top? I get my stupid stunts all mixed up sometimes. You see, they run together in my head and ..."

"*Quit* fucking around!" Vickers shouted. "I asked you a fucking question, now give me a fucking answer, goddamn it!"

Adkins sighed. "Okay, so I took a long shot. It almost panned out. We busted their ass big time and nearly got the bitch. Next time we will. And we rescued four of our guys, even if we did almost kill them in the process. Can I be excused now, pretty please?"

Vickers fought his exasperation. "You are one *pigheaded, conceited, dumb son-of-a-bitch*, Sergeant! How did you get from your appointed ambush site to that unauthorized position in the first fucking place?"

Adkins grinned. "We ran."

Vickers grimaced. "You took *fifty* men, at *night*, in *hostile* territory, while a fucking *firefight* was raging right in front of you, and ran *blindly* for over a mile, without *security*, into an area that you had *no idea* of what godforsaken *danger* might be lurking there, and you call it a *long shot*? Not to mention that *no one* in this whole fucking *Division* had any idea of where you were because you *neglected* to clear your movement with Battalion or *anyone* else—and knowing *full well* that we had gunships buzzing around like hornets looking for anything that *moved* that could take you under fire at *any* fucking given moment? Are you fucking *crazy*? Or just fucking *stupid*?"

Adkins shrugged. "I figured by the time I called Battalion and got the mission cleared by those dunderheads, it would have been daylight and the opportunity lost."

"I thought I told you not to take this thing personal, Sergeant."

"You did."

"Then why the *fuck* are you *ignoring* me?"

"Uh, how long is this ass chewing going to take, Top? I've got to see to my men and get them ready for..."

Vickers snatched the cigar from his mouth and jabbed it at him. "*Your* fucking time is *my* fucking time, Sergeant, and you don't have a fucking *thing* to do unless I *tell* you to do it, and right fucking now I'm *telling* you to sit your ass back down in that fucking *chair*. *I* put those fucking stripes on your fucking arm, and by god *I* can take them the fuck back *off.*"

Adkins glowered. "You want these fucking stripes, Top, you can have them." He ripped the stripes off his left sleeve and tossed them on his desk.

"Don't even *think* about fucking with me," Vickers warned softly. "I'll put your ass so far down in the bottom of a dark pit you'll have to stick your head up your own asshole to see sunshine."

Adkins stood. "Do what you gotta do, Top. I've got a job to do until you tell me it's not my responsibility anymore." He turned for the door.

"One last thing, *Sergeant*," Vickers called. "The fucking General says to decorate your simple-minded ass for your stupid antics. Any particular fucking award you want to receive for exposing your whole fucking unit to total fucking annihilation?"

Adkins turned back to him. "Sure, Top. I'd like a decent cup of coffee when I come in here for one of your little pep talks. That would be more fucking reward than I could ever *imagine*." He strolled out, stretching the screen door to its maximum tolerance before allowing it to slam closed behind him with a resounding *whap!*

Vickers sat back and grinned as he puffed on his stogie. Adkins was going to be a hell of an NCO someday—if he didn't get killed or court-martialed first.

135

CHAPTER 30

Kim-Ly was not pleased to see the Americans again when they drove up to her hooch in three ARVN gun jeeps with her husband the day before, creating a great deal of curiosity among her fellow villagers. The tall one with red hair and many freckles talked to her husband as the short, thick one with no hair stared at her and bounced her baby on his knee. She did not like her children held by strangers. At her husband's direction, she made them tea, which they hardly touched. Her husband proudly showed them the new ox cart he purchased with the money they gave him at their prior meeting and seemed eager for them to talk to her again in hopes of receiving another reward, though she could not imagine what information they found so worthy concerning a schoolgirl she had known years earlier. They questioned her through an interpreter for over an hour as a silent group of her neighbors gathered to watch from a distance while the children of the village cavorted about trying to attract the American's attention.

She grew weary discussing the details of Cai's life as a child, which she could sense they found of no value. When pressed, she admitted she had seen Cai's uncle, Tran Duc Thinh, at market the previous week. They seemed disappointed she had not spoken to him, but showed keen interest when she confirmed he still lived on the outskirts of the village of Ly Van Manh, where she and Cai were born. Her husband grew irritable when she was unable to identify the specific location of Thinh's hooch on the confusing map they showed her.

After the Americans finally departed with their ARVN escort, her husband chastised her for not being of more help to them, and seemed especially disappointed when they did not give him more money, seeming to find fault with her for this as well.

He further insisted she accompany them to Thinh's village on this the following day with his ARVN Ranger Company to show them Thinh's residence and identify him. This displeased her greatly. She did not like to be around soldiers and their guns, or to be away from her children. She wished she had never divulged that she knew Cai. She would not have done so if she had known it would cause so much turmoil within her serene life. She was also concerned that they thought Thinh might be part of the liberation movement, which often sought reprisals against those who cooperated with the American and South Vietnamese governments. When she expressed her fears on these matters, her husband grew gruff with her and reminded her that Cai was now their enemy and no longer her childhood friend. Try as she might, she could not imagine the shy, withdrawn little Cai drawing so much attention from the Americans. She certainly could not imagine Cai as her enemy, or that she was such an important person in the liberation movement. Surely, this was all a mistake on the American's part. She wanted all of this to end so her life could return to its former tranquil bliss.

Earlier that morning she and her husband flew with the two Americans from his outpost to the village of Ly Van Manh in another American helicopter. From the air, the scores of

ARVN soldiers in long lines surrounding the village fascinated her. As she stood to the side, the soldiers herded all of the villagers together and watched over them with poised rifles. Her husband then required her to walk before them and look each in the face. It was a most unpleasant experience for her, especially when one of the village men stared back at her in open contempt, sending her pulse racing. She stood traumatized as her husband knocked the man to the ground and kicked him, offended by his insolence towards her. The tall American with many freckles appeared disappointed when she did not identify Tran Duc Thinh among the villagers. Afterwards, she reluctantly led them to Thinh's empty hooch with its mud walls and thatched roof, and stood with downcast eyes as they searched its interior.

Abruptly, a series of buzzing sounds startled her, followed by the popping of rifle fire. The soldiers dove for cover in a clamor of harsh gunfire as she cupped her palms over her ears in terror. Her husband shoved her down as bullets kicked up dirt in front of them in the deafening roar as she clutched at his arm screaming. He shook her off as he yelled orders and disappeared into the green growth with his men. The American with red hair rushed in after them with his pistol drawn. When the chaos ceased, she raised her head off the ground, shaking and crying, consumed with fear for her husband's safety.

The American captain came out of the jungle with his pistol holstered and hurried over to help her up from the ground as he uttered soothing sounds. When she found her legs too weak for her to stand, he slipped his arm around her waist to support her. Other soldiers came out of the thick shrubbery, with two of them dragging a man by his arms behind them. She wailed in relief when she saw her husband and ran to him as two other men stumbled out carrying another man between them with blood on his chest. She collapsed onto her knees before her husband, sickened by the sight of the injured men, trembling and crying.

Her husband took her by the elbow, guided her into the darkened interior of Thinh's hooch, and returned to his men outside. She tried to calm herself and attempted to drink a cup of water, but spilt the liquid down her chin because she could not control her shaking. She lay down on a straw pallet on the floor, closed her eyes, and drew air deep into her chest in measured gulps until her husband returned for her, led her back outside, and forced her to look at the enemy soldier they had killed. The red haired American seemed relieved that it was not Thinh. She followed her husband back to the helicopter, which flew them back to their village. When the helicopter landed in front of her hooch, she ran crying to her children as her husband got back onto the helicopter with the Americans and flew away. Afterwards she hugged her children to her breast, vowing she would have no more to do with the Americans, no matter how much it displeased her husband.

Exhausted from her ordeal, she allowed her mother-in-law to settle her onto her mat with a cup of hot tea and soon succumbed to the deep exhaustion weighing her down.

CHAPTER 31

Cai sat at the end of the long table with Chien in the middle. Four other of his commanders sat at the table with them. Chien had not visited with her in her quarters nor spoken to her for three days now. Though he was stoic, she knew he was still furious with her. It had been a grave insult to turn her back on him, and an even worse offense to take a lowly member of his staff to her bed. Chien had the man shipped out to another underground complex the following day. She had made a very bad mistake in both of those actions. Now she awaited her own punishment puzzled by his seemingly indifference to her and the fact that he had not made any demands on her body throughout this period.

As a member of his tactical staff, she listened to the reports from outlying posts to help assess the enemy movements and select their countermeasures. Later, she hoped to interview replacements for her depleted force. The three days had been intolerably long for her to wait for this event. She was most anxious to get her force rejuvenated and to seek out the Americans again, but she dared not approach Chien in his present state to hasten the process.

As her mind wandered, she was startled to see her uncle, Tran Duc Thinh, standing before them as the previous courier departed. She had not seen Thinh since he arranged her marriage to Pin. She was not fond of Thinh. He had shown her little interest as her sole surviving relative. She knew of him only vaguely as a sergeant in the local guerrilla forces in the Ly Van Manh District, whose strength both the French and the Americans had depleted over the years, but were still a viable threat. Thinh made a bow to Chien and stood at attention before them.

"Sit, Sergeant," Chien directed.

"Yes, my Colonel." Thinh sat in the single chair facing them.

"Report," Chien directed.

"The Americans came in force to Ly Van Manh yesterday, Colonel. A Company of ARVN Rangers supported them. We suffered two of our men wounded and one killed. The ARVNs recovered his body, I regret to inform you." Thinh squirmed as Colonel Chien stared impassively at him—losing the body of a fallen comrade was serious.

"Why are you rendering this report and not your Captain?"

"I am sorry to inform you that my Captain was one of the men wounded, Colonel. He directed that I render the report to you in person because of the special circumstance of the American and ARVN joint operation."

"Tell me of this special circumstance," Chien directed.

"They were looking for me, Colonel."

"How do you know this to be true?"

"They questioned the villagers about me and they brought along a woman who could identify me, Colonel."

"Was this woman herself identified?"

"Yes, Colonel. She is Cao Thi Kim-Ly. She is formerly from Ly Van Manh. She is now married to a Sergeant in the ARVN Ranger Company in Trang Bang who assisted the

Americans. Kim-Ly was the childhood friend of my niece, Cai, and knew me well."

Cai's pulse quickened as Chien absorbed this information. She had not seen Kim-Ly in over ten years.

"What is the American interest in you, Sergeant?"

"This I do not know, Colonel. I regret to say that I have not distinguished myself in any commendable way, nor have I done anything that would draw their attention to me."

"What does your Captain recommend?"

"He instructs me to seek your permission to turn myself in to the Americans at Cu Chi, Colonel. He suggests this for two reasons. First, he does not desire to attract attention to me as a member of the Liberation Forces. He believes my willingness to be interrogated by the Americans will remove suspicion. Secondly, he wishes to discover why such a large force would search for a lowly soldier such as me. He feels that the Americans will return if I do not submit to their interrogation. He does not desire me to leave the District at this time to go into hiding."

"Your Captain is a clever man, Sergeant. What is your opinion of submitting yourself to the Americans for interrogation?"

"I have no fear of the Americans, Colonel. I have been in their custody before. I find them naïve and stupid. I have no doubts that I can fool them again. If it gives my Captain the information he needs, I am honored to be of service to him in our glorious cause."

"I am impressed with your courage, Sergeant. You have my permission to do as your Captain requests. I require that you report to me upon your release. I too am curious as to why the Americans want to question you so badly."

"Yes, Colonel. I will obey."

"You are dismissed, Sergeant."

143

Chien turned to Cai. "Captain, I instruct you to travel to Trang Bang to visit your friend, Kim-Ly, and inquire as to her knowledge in this issue. You must be discreet."

"But, Colonel, I have not seen Kim-Ly in many years," Cai protested. "Would my time not be better served in bringing my unit back to strength as quickly as possible?" She immediately regretted her decision to speak out when she saw the color change in Chien's face, realizing she had spoken rashly and inadvertently questioned his judgment in front of his staff.

"If I thought such, Captain, I would have so directed it. You will depart immediately. Bring in the next courier," Chien ordered without looking at her as he spoke.

She rose from the table and hurried out to prepare for her trip, mollified by her actions and by the fact that additional time would be lost while she sought out Kim-Ly for no apparent useful purpose.

"I trust you are well, Niece?" Thinh greeted when she entered the outer room, where he was preparing to depart.

"I am well, Uncle," she replied as she moved to pass him in the narrow tunnel.

"You have brought great esteem to our family. I am honored by your status."

She turned to him. "I am merely a soldier, such as you, doing my duty, Uncle."

"Your actions have paralyzed the American dogs with fear."

"The Americans are pigs. They are deserving of worse than I have served upon them."

"You have changed in the years, my little Cai." His eyes narrowed. "With the influence you have now attained, I hope you do not forget those who are of your own lineage."

Her demeanor chilled. "Do you seek something specific of my position, Uncle?"

144

"Perhaps a promotion?" he suggested slyly. "Or possibly even a place on Colonel Chien's staff, if it pleases him?"

"Promotions are awarded for courage shown on the battlefield in pursuit of our glorious cause, Uncle, and I do not choose the members of Colonel Chien's staff. I recommend you approach him on this issue."

Thinh stepped closer to her and lowered his voice as he smirked. "It has been said that the woman who warms the emperor's bed wields greater influence than the generals who expand his empire."

"Then perhaps you should curry favor with the emperor's bed warmer, Uncle, in order to advance without having earned the progression through merit."

Thinh stiffened angrily as she turned and hurried to her room.

After she dressed in her black pajama peasant disguise with sandals and conical straw hat, she summoned four of her most loyal female soldiers as her escort and informed them they would travel in an ox cart disguised as women going to market. She then selected an older male soldier to drive the cart. She had them stash their weapons within easy reach, hidden under the straw on the bed of the cart, a ploy that had served them well in the past.

She had no desire to see Kim-Ly again, suffering only bad memories of that period of her life. Kim-Ly's shyness had held her back when the French imperialists coached her closer and had ultimately spared her the brutal fate Cai herself faced. Kim-Ly only brought back the bad memories and shame of that experience. She was pleased when Kim-Ly stopped coming to visit her afterwards in the orphanage.

Now, after all these years, she was required to confront her and the degrading experience once again.

CHAPTER 32

"Cap'n?" Pierce paused at Christen's door. "You're not going to believe this. There's a gook at the front gate that says he's Tran Duc Thinh and that we were looking for him out in Nightmare Village a couple of days ago."

"You're kidding me?"

"The MPs at the gate called G-3 for verification and they referred them to us. It's the damndest thing I've ever heard of. I sent Howell and Billy up there to fetch him."

When Howell and Billy returned they escorted a short, lithe man in his mid-fifties, with scars on his left forearm and the left side of his forehead that appeared to be shrapnel wounds, into Christen's office and sat him in a chair. The man's dark eyes darted about fretfully as he clasped his hands in his lap.

"Do you speak English?" Christen asked.

Thinh shifted as he averted his eyes. "Some English. Not good."

"I am Captain Christen. These are my assistants. Thank you for coming to talk to us."

"I away from my village. They say many soldiers come look for me. I not do anything wrong. I am farmer. I not want to make trouble with Americans. I grateful you help my country."

"We appreciate your help as well," Christen assured him. "We're looking for a woman named Tran Thi Cai. Do you know of her?"

Thinh's eyes widen. "I not see her for many years now. She my niece. She marry and go north with her husband and child, five, maybe six years ago."

"We have reason to believe she is back. Can you identify this picture?" Christen held out the photo of Tiger Woman.

Thinh took the photo and stared at it as he frowned. "Yes, this Cai." He handed the photo back.

"Have you seen her recently?"

"Not since she go north."

"If she came back to the south, where do you think she would go?"

"I think she come to me. I her only relative. Her husband from my village."

"Is her husband a member of the Vietcong forces?"

"It dangerous to ask that question. I not ask. I farmer, not soldier."

"How did you get those scars on your face and arm?"

"American artillery. They fight many times around my village."

"Can you identify any of the men or women in this picture?" Christen handed him the original photo with the men and women in the background behind Tiger Woman with their AK-47 rifles raised triumphantly.

Thinh looked at the photo and handed it back. "I not know them."

"But you do agree that is your niece, Cai, in the foreground?"

"Yes, it Cai."

"But you haven't seen her in five or six years and you don't know any of the communist soldiers with her?"

"I not know them. I not see her."

Sergeant Pierce leaned forward. "What if we told you there was a sizable reward being offered for information leading to the capture of Cai?"

"I not understand what you say."

"Let me try," Howell offered. He held a lengthy conversation with Thinh in Vietnamese and turned back to them. "That got his attention, Captain. He wants to know how much of a reward."

"Tell him 50,000 piaster," Pierce offered with a smug smile.

Howell spoke to Thinh, whose eyes widened in wonder. Thinh spoke to Howell.

Howell turned to them. "He wants to know what he would have to do to earn that money and who would know if he helped us."

Pierce banged his fist on the table triumphantly. "I *knew* the son of a bitch was lying the whole time!"

CHAPTER 33

Allen listened closely as Bubba sat next to him on his cot in the infirmary, acting casual as he talked in a low, intense voice to shield his words from their guard ten feet away conversing with one of the wounded Vietcong in the ward.

"We've gotta pay attention to the different tunnel channels, Bo. Commit them to memory each time they move us around. We've gotta map this place out in our brain so when the time comes we'll have some idea of where to go."

Allen shook his head in despair. "How are we going to know which tunnel leads to the exit, Bubba? This whole place is a maze."

"Pay attention to where they *don't* carry us, Bo. They're not gonna let us get near an exit. Watch where they steer us away from, that'll be a clue."

"We can't just run off in a direction we *think* we should be going in, Bubba," Allen argued. "We've got to know for sure."

"Nothin' in life is for sure. We're gonna just have to eliminate as many possibilities as we can and then roll the dice."

"Snake-eyes will get us killed, Bubba."

"If that's the case, let's take as many of these slopes with us as we can."

"With what, Bubba? Our fists?"

"No, with their own fuckin' AKs, Bo." Bubba inclined his head towards their guard who had his weapon slung casually over his shoulder. "We'll use his to get others. We're gonna have to fight our way outta here. There ain't no other way."

"What about the other prisoners, Bubba?" Allen asked. "Are we going to try to take them with us?"

"If we can, but I haven't seen 'em in a long time. They may have already been moved outta here."

"Moved where?"

"Probably up the Ho Chi Minh Trail to North Vietnam. I expect that's where we're headed too, when we heal up. That doesn't leave us much time. We gotta make our move soon."

"When we get out of here, where do we go then?" Allen asked.

"We go south. We got hit on the north side of the base camp. It was dark and I was sorta lost, but I'm sure we moved further north, about two hour's travel, maybe a little more, to this fuckin' hole in the ground. If we go south, we've gotta hit our base camp sooner or later."

Allen grunted. "Yeah, with them chasing us every step of the way."

"What's the alternative? Do you wanna rot down here in this fuckin' hole in the ground, or spend the rest of your life in a POW camp up in Hanoi gettin' your ass beat every day with a bamboo switch? We're *soldiers*, Bo! We gotta *act* like soldiers. We're here to fight, so by god, let's *fight*!"

"I'll do my best, Bubba. When the time comes, I'll try not to let you down. But I'm not as strong as you are, or as smart. If I slow you down, don't hesitate to leave me behind. I mean it. Leave me if you have to. Don't let me get you killed or recaptured."

"Ditto, Bo. When we go, the main thing is for at least one of us to make it. We've gotta expose this place and destroy it. If either one of us is not able to go on for any reason, we leave him behind. Deal? No questions asked?"

"Deal, Bubba. But if you make it and I don't, would you visit my mother for me? Don't tell her everything that happened to me, just tell her I loved her and died honorably. Will you promise me that, Bubba?"

"Consider it done. Will you do the same for me, Bo?"

"I promise," Allen swore. "I'm scared to death, Bubba. I'm ashamed to admit that, but I'm just not as brave as you are."

"It ain't about bravery, Bo, it's about justice. I'm so pissed I can't wait to get at these fuckers! I'm gonna give some bullshit back to these fuckin' slopes before it's all over with. It's not natural what they've done to us. Neither of us deserves the treatment we've received from these cowardly little piss-ants! I'm gonna teach 'em a little respect before I'm through. I been walkin' around grinnin', stoopin', and bowin' every since I've been here. When the time comes, I'm gonna show 'em what a real fuckin' wild man is like. I mean it, Bo. They think I'm just a harmless little pussy. I can't wait to show 'em what a Georgia boy's like when you get him riled. And, Bo, just you let me come across that little cunt that leads this group. You don't *even* want to be around if that happens!"

"I might want a piece of that action myself," Allen allowed with a deadly hiss.

"That's my man! Get mad as hell. When the time comes, don't hesitate, and don't show no mercy, Bo! I can double-damn guarantee you they're not gonna show us none!"

CHAPTER 34

Kim-Ly followed the woman in front of her as she led her into the thick vegetation outside her village, her heart filled with joy at the prospect of seeing Cai again, even under such puzzling circumstances. When they came to a clearing she rushed forward eagerly to greet Cai, who waited with several other women and a man spaced about in watchful positions armed with rifles.

"No one followed you or noticed you leave?" Cai demanded of her guide, ignoring Kim-Ly.

"No, Captain. I stayed with her the whole time as you instructed. She talked to no one but her mother-in-law to instruct her to watch her children."

"Leave us now."

The guide and the others moved away from them quickly.

"*Cai*," Kim-Ly whispered endearingly as she stepped forward to embrace her friend, pleased that she had blossomed into such a radiant woman over the years, and then paused abruptly when Cai's unique eyes fixed on her glinting with anger.

"Why did you go to Ly Van Manh with the Americans to attempt to identify my uncle, Tran Duc Thinh?" Cai demanded.

Kim-Ly paused, baffled. "I... I was instructed to do so by my husband. I have missed you so, Cai! I am so pleased to see you again. Are you well?"

"That is of no concern to you, Kim-Ly. I do not have much time. You will tell me everything about this search for Thinh."

"M-My husband brought home a picture of you," Kim-Ly stammered. "I told him I knew you from our childhood."

A chill passed swiftly down Cai's spine. *A picture*? "Tell me of this," she demanded.

"I-It was of you in a strange army uniform holding a gun."

The shiver worked its way back up Cai's spine. She had never considered the Americans might be shrewd enough to use the photograph she had pinned to a stake in the first two massacre sites to identify her. She had committed a strategic blunder in taunting the Americans in such a manner after her devastating victory over them. *Were they even now pursuing other leads to identify her through her soldiers around her? If she had not anticipated this, what else might she be missing?*

"Were you asked to identify others in the photograph as well?"

"No, Cai. The picture was only of you. I hardly recognized you."

Why had the Americans altered the photograph? "Tell me more of your talk with the Americans!"

"The Americans flew us to Cu Chi in one of their helicopters. T-They were very excited that I knew you. They asked many questions about you."

"How does this photograph relate to your attempt to identify Thinh for them?"

"Later the same Americans came to my village and asked me about Thinh. I told them what I knew, which was little. My husband insisted that I come to Ly Van Manh to help identify Thinh for them. He was not there. There was much shooting. It was terrifying. Several men were hurt."

Somehow, the Americans had identified her uncle and mounted a pursuit for him in hopes of locating her! "What exactly have you told them about me, Kim-Ly?"

"I could give them very little information about you, but still they gave my husband money with which to buy an ox cart. They... seemed to know much about you already... I can not imagine knowledge I had of you from years ago to be of such importance to them now ..."

The simmering anger boiling within Cai for her thought-less naivety in leaving the photograph behind to mock the Americans fused into sudden, blinding rage, propelling the back of her hand across Kim-Ly's cheek to send her stumbling backward to the ground with a cry of surprised pain.

"You were very foolish to collaborate with the Americans and give them information about me, Kim-Ly! You were even more foolish to try to help them identify Thinh! *You may no longer consider yourself my friend!"*

"What does all this mean?" Kim-Ly sobbed as she lay on the ground at Cai's feet. "Why do they have such interest in you that they would pay for useless information about a schoolgirl I knew from many years ago? Why are they interested in Thinh? I don't understand. I mean you no harm, Cai! I hold you deep in my heart and will always treasure you as my friend forever!"

"You are a foolish and weak woman, Kim-Ly. Go back to your family and enjoy the little time you have left with them!"

"Cai! Please, Cai, don't be angry with me!" Kim-Ly begged as Cai turned and stalked away. *"I meant you no harm!"*

Kim-Ly stood on quaking legs and saw that all of the other women and the man had disappeared into the foliage with Cai. She hurried back to her hooch crying softly for her friend and the unknowing displeasure she had invoked within her. Everything that had happened since her husband brought home the picture of Cai had been frightening and caused her great distress.

A great emptiness grew inside her. Filled with anguish, she ran weeping to her children.

CHAPTER 35

Cai interrupted her troubling analysis of her meeting with Kim-Ly and lurched up quickly from her seated position in the back of the cart as they thumped along behind the water buffalo. Her eyes narrowed, surveying the thin dirt road they were plodding along on in the middle of the large paddy area spanning four hundred meters in all directions.

To their immediate front, ten Americans stripped to the waist worked on a culvert crossing under the road. She tensed as their cart bumped over the rutted detour the men had provided until they could get the cement culvert in place. Four men with rifles were spaced fifty yards out from them facing into the paddies providing security for the workers. There were no other people as far as she could see. Keen anticipation flashed through her as the Americans paid no attention to the five women in the cart with the old man driving the ox. She noted their weapons stacked carelessly nearby while they worked, safely out of their reach as they toiled under the hot sun. The four guards with their backs to them appeared bored as they gazed outward for signs of danger in the far tree line.

These Americans boys had surprised and embarrassed her. She was sure to face Colonel Chien's wrath due to their extraordinary attempts to locate her using her own humiliating lapse in judgment concerning the photograph. Perhaps there was a way to displace Chien's looming displeasure... and punish these imprudent youngsters for attempting to make her look foolish.

"Prepare!" she hissed to her surprised companions. "We will attack the imperialists. Each of you will take one of the guards," she directed to the four women in the back of the cart with her. "Bao and I will take the workers."

Bao turned from where he sat driving the cart. "Is this wise, Captain?"

"We must strike them before they have a chance to reach their weapons," she instructed. "We will take as many prisoners as possible from the workers. We will kill the guards quickly before they can turn on us. We will strike when we regain the main road."

Bao frowned. "Colonel Chien will not be pleased."

"You will obey," she ordered curtly.

As the cart jostled through the detour and climbed back up onto the main road, the women reached under the straw to pull their weapons out and shifted to clear their fields of fire as Cai passed Bao his rifle through the slats in the side of the cart. When the cart regained the road, Bao brought it to a halt.

"Attack!" Cai ordered.

They brought their weapons up and opened fire in an abrupt, jarring roar, dropping the four guards almost instantly. Most of the men working on the culvert dove for the nearest available cover, but three rushed for their weapons. She and Bao dropped them in a crescendo of automatic fire and then trained their weapons on the remaining seven men cowering on the ground in shock. It was over in less than ten seconds.

"Quickly, take their belts from the loops of their trousers and tie their hands! Put them in a line on their knees before me!" Cai instructed, eyes glazed, stomach boiling in avid hunger. She laid her rifle aside and jumped down from the back of the cart as her soldiers rushed to herd the men together with poised rifles.

"Captain, we have no time!" Bao cautioned. "It is too dangerous! We must hurry from here. Others will be coming who have heard the shooting!"

Cai pulled her knife as she walked up to the first American soldier in line, leaned down, and sliced his stomach open as he grunted in pain, his lips pulled back in a tight grimace.

The American next to him shuddered. "Fuck! It's that crazy bitch we've been hearing about! She's gonna kill us all!"

Cai moved to him and sliced one of his ears off as he jerked and cried out. She sliced his stomach open and then cut his tongue off as he screamed. She turned and sliced the throat of the man beside him as he bellowed in terror. She paused in front of the next one as he sobbed, savoring the moment before she poked him in the eye with the tip of her knife and then sliced his stomach as he gasped. She moved on to the next weeping man.

"Please, Ma'am, I've got a wife and little girl," he pleaded. "Please don't kill me, please! I'm an engineer. I'm here to help build *awwww!*"

Cai sliced his stomach from side to side, ending his pleas. She reached in and pulled his guts out, gasping, trembled with pleasure as the warm, sticky mass covered her hands. She moved to the sixth man and sliced both of his ears off as he howled and tried to dodge her flashing blade. She then disemboweled him in a slow curve across his belly as he panted in anguish. She moved to the last man in line and quickly poked him in both eyes with the point of her knife as he attempted to jerk away from her. She sliced his tongue off as he screamed, and turned from him in rapture, her lust fulfilled. She looked down the line of squirming men on the ground, savoring their pain and the gore of their bowels as they thrashed their life away.

"Captain. Please! We must go!" Bao called as the other women hurried to climb aboard the cart.

Cai backed towards the cart, entranced by the quivering, bloody bodies before her, chest heaving with satisfaction, and then climbed aboard as Bao lashed out at the oxen to get it going, keeping her eyes on the dying men as the other women hid their weapons under the straw. One of them took the bloody knife from her hand and slipped it under the straw as the cart rumbled down the road. When they reached the safety of the trees bordering the paddies, Bao slowed the cart to a steady pace as the oxen stumbled along wheezing from the effort. None of her comrades spoke or looked her in the eye. She looked down at her bloody hands, which still shook, and tried to gather her senses. When they crossed a small stream, she ordered Bao to stop the cart. She climbed down and dipped her hands in the muddy water, finally able to control the shaking as the blood washed away. She climbed back into the cart and they continued their journey.

CHAPTER 36

Sergeant Adkins surveyed his platoon strung out around a small cluster of hooches after calling a break in the early afternoon heat. He sat off by himself, brooding, watching as his tired men opened their cans of C-rations and ate. A few of them held kids brave enough to venture near in their lap and shared bars of chocolate with them as their worried parents squatted at a distance watching apprehensively.

He considered their search and destroy mission outside the Cu Chi base camp, ostensibly to find and destroy the crazy woman in the picture, a relative waste of effort. He figured the vixen to be far more intelligent than to jump his or any of the other innumerable platoon-sized elements saturating the area in broad daylight. She would anticipate their reaction forces back at the division airstrip waiting to launch upon her, or any other hapless VC who took a potshot at them, in an immediate counterattack by land and air. His particular cynicism came from the knowledge that though they now romped bravely through the paddies and hedge-rows in their daylight quest for her, confident they possessed the strength to overcome any opposition, dusk brought on an entirely different perspective.

Half of their day patrols would remain in the field to set up night ambushes as the other half returned to the sanctuary of their base camp. The platoons left out changed attitude with the coming darkness as each element hunkered down fearfully for a long phase of terror on 100 percent alert. Though they owned the day, she owned the night. The pendulum of power swung to and fro with the setting and rising sun. The aggressive avengers of the day became the meek prey of the night as they shivered through the darkness waiting for one of her sudden, devastating attacks to materialize from out of the gloom and swarm over them in a menacing tide of surging death.

His platoon, slated to stay out on this night, was no exception. He sensed the tension in his men as the day wore on, even though they had boldly bloodied her force just days before. He was not overly concerned himself. With all the patrols in the area, he surmised she would keep a low profile for a time, possibly ten days to two weeks. Tonight's ambush would be as fruitless as today's search. In this, he was disappointed. He would much prefer that she be active. The only way to catch her was when she struck. They would never flush her out with useless daylight search and destroy missions. Based on this belief, he pushed his platoon at an easy gait to keep them fresh in the mind-warping heat, certain the she-vampire would eventually return to mutilate the corpses of their dead and bathe in the warm blood of the unfortunate survivors. A brief, raging firefight erupted in the distance, drawing his attention from his gloomy review.

He sat his can of peaches aside, listening intently. "Bryant! Bring my radio!"

Bryant set the little girl on his lap aside, handed her the rest of his chocolate bar, grabbed the PRC 25 radio, and hurried over. "What's up, Sarge?"

Adkins cocked his head, listening. "Damned if I know. All I hear is AK's out there. Unless the fucking VC have started fighting each other now, it doesn't make a lick of sense!"

CHAPTER 37

Cai sat with her back against the rail of the ox cart, her thoughts growing darker as those around her refused to meet her eyes. It had been an overpowering impulse on her part when she saw the careless Americans. A whim born of hatred. Bao was right; Chien would be displeased about the attack on the gullible engineers, even though they killed fourteen of the hated imperialists. This was of heavy concern to her, even in her current state of sated tranquility after satisfying her peculiar cravings with the prisoners. She would have enjoyed more time with them, but Bao was also right in that others would be rushing to investigate the shooting. Even now, several helicopters overhead hurried towards the site. Chien would view it as a foolish act on her part, but the Americans, whose arrogance saw no danger in five women and one man in an ox cart, never anticipated such an attack in broad daylight. The whole affair had taken less than five minutes. It was more troubling that the Americans were using her photograph to help track her down. The American dogs could be very clever at times.

A helicopter flew low overhead in a crescendo of whipping wind and thumping noise, diverting her attention from Chien's pending displeasure with her impulsive actions and the irksome photograph she had foolishly left behind in the other ambush sites. She squinted up at the aircraft as it circled back around to take a closer look at them, and then braced herself as the ox shied in panic from the clamor when the craft hovered over them. One of the soldiers in the big side door near the middle trained his machine gun on them as he looked them over while Bao attempted to control the bucking oxen. She clutched at her conical hat irritably as the whirling hurricane from the thumping blades whipped it about violently. Finally, the aircraft turned and flew off at tree top level as the crew apparently decided they were harmless. Bao got the ox under control and they continued their plodding journey.

When they arrived at their secure hooch a short time later, where they would wait until darkness before moving on to the tunnel complex, Bao took the cart and continued alone, leaving her and the other women there. She lay on a straw pallet pretending to sleep as her four companions lay silently near her, her thoughts on Colonel Chien and his reaction to her attack on the Americans. Undoubtedly, he would punish her body greatly for her initiative... and even more so if he discovered they had unwittingly uncovered a means with which to help identify her. As in the orphanage after the horrifying experience with the French imperialists, she withdrew deep within herself to a private place she shared with no one.

Her thoughts wandered to her uncle, Thinh, who the Americans had somehow traced to her. Even now he was talking to them, unknowing that he was but a pawn in their efforts to find her. This was of great concern to her. His sole past interest in her had been in selecting a husband for her on her eighteenth birthday in order to obtain a small dowry. At the time, he had made it clear to her that she was impure and lucky for any man to want her after her childhood ordeal.

166

Now he was meeting with the Americans, who were offering a substantial reward for her.

Her thoughts drifted fleetingly to the husband Thinh chose for her, and of how filled with mounting terror she had been on their marital mat after the brief ceremony. Thankfully, he had simply pulled down her bottoms impatiently without bothering to engage her in conversation or give consideration to her own satisfaction as he sated his hunger for her body. The experience was not as brutal as before with the Frenchmen, and she was actually relieved he required no response on her part other than to lie placidly beneath him.

Afterwards, though the terror of receiving him subsided, it was never a pleasurable experience for her, only an annoyance she withstood in a stoic mode. In time, she came to accept that he viewed her merely as a possession; a warm vassal with spread thighs within which he could satisfy his desires. Much to his delight, she quickly became with child.

Shortly afterwards, he joined the transport corps through the local Vietcong network and pressed her into service with him, intent on placing their child in the safety of his parent's home in the North until the imperialist American forces were repulsed. They journeyed there together along the Ho Chi Ming trail, where the infant was born on a dark, stormy night amid great personal pain to her. When they reached his parent's home, he placed their newborn son with them and they began their trek back to the South laden with war supplies. American bombers killed him on the return trip and she herself received a concussion during the event.

She had not loved her husband, even though she had been an obedient, dutiful wife to him, therefore she did not grieve at his death. Upon her release from the infirmary, she eagerly sought out the courier service in lieu of returning to live with her husband's parents in order to nurse her husband's son.

Immediately pressed back into duty, she had not seen his child in the four years since.

Once widowed, many of the single males expected to share her bed mat in the transport service, but she coldly rebuffed all attempts to woo her. Due to her attractiveness, it was a constant source of irritation to her in the beginning, but over time, her snubs garnered the seclusion she sought. She deliberately made no friends with the other females in the transport corps, preferring solitude to companionship. She became a reticent transporter who walked with her burden on her back day in and day out as required. She gave no thought to the future and cared little for the present, her thoughts never shared with others. Her needs were simple and her pleasures nonexistent. She was not happy, nor was she sad. She moved in a world that had little effect on her other than to avoid death from the bombs the hated Americans showered down on them along the Ho Chi Minh Trail day and night. She saw many of her comrades killed, and escaped death herself on several occasions, but suffered no further personal injury.

Her two years in the transport corps were difficult. Females were preferred as transporters because they could march twelve hours a day as compared to a male's ten-hour marches. A female could also bear one and a half times the back weight that a male could handle. She and the other women carried three mortar rounds strapped to a backboard as compared to two mortar rounds for a man. The females departed the night's rest area one hour before the men, and at the end of each day's grueling march, were required to prepare the evening meal for their contingent and pack the following day's lunch of boiled rice before the male transporters arrived. The advantage to her being in such a thankless, tedious assignment was that she did not have to share herself with anyone.

Chien changed all that. He first selected her when he was traveling south with her column to assume command of the Cu Chi district where she was born and raised. He initially sought information she could provide on the Cu Chi area and sent for her each night to probe her mind. He also, as a matter of course, made advances to her, which she received with indifference in spite of his high rank, as she did all others. After several weeks, he grew impatient and forcefully fulfilled his physical needs, as she lay impassive beneath him. However, he went far beyond the basic act of relieving his desires in a quick and impersonal manner as her husband had done. He seemed to enjoy her unresponsiveness during the times he joined with her body, which became frequent. When their long journey ended, he pulled her from the transport corps and attached her to his headquarters staff in order to keep her close, which she accepted with aloof indifference.

At first, she served as a simple courier for his far-flung forces, but in an abrupt, impromptu firefight between the Americans and her escorts, she distinguished herself when she took up an AK-47 from a fallen comrade and supported their floundering attack. Her first memorable thrill was with an American soldier wounded in that encounter. The experience forever changed her. It served to thrust her back into the present, to snap her out of the shadowy shell where she witlessly subsided and launched her on her present glorious path as a warrior.

Their chance engagement had evolved into a running battle. She stumbled upon the American during the confusing skirmish. She knelt next to him as he lay panting for breath with his blood bubbling from his chest. He clutched at her, his hands covered with his blood, begging her to help him. An astonishing thrill ran through her as his warm blood contacted her skin, a sensation similar to what Chien and her husband experienced when they mounted her in the night and trembled after fulfilling their needs with her. The encounter confused her and energized her beyond comprehension. She smeared her hands in his blood as he lay dying, the act filling her with inexplicable delight.

She campaigned afterwards for Chien to allow her to transfer to the Liberation Forces, which he eventually conceded to do only with great reluctance. She quickly mastered the hit and run tactics they employed against the American and ARVN forces, and grew bolder with each encounter. The next opportunity to explore the amazing phenomenon occurred with yet a second injured American soldier.

With him wounded in the leg, she volunteered to guard him while the others continued to pursue the American force. She dipped her fingers in the man's blood from his wound and became flushed with heat. When he tried to snatch her weapon, she slashed his arm with her knife. The blood spurted from the cut onto her hand, its warmth filling her with animalistic joy. Initially perplexed by the experience, she soon embraced the raw desire building within her and gave in to the uncontrollable impulse surging through her, slashing at him randomly. As he weakened and begged for his life, she grew intoxicated with her power and lustfully fulfilled her insatiable cravings by bathing her arms in the heated blood pouring from his wounds.

With her distinguishing combat career on the rise, the cadre abruptly selected her to attend the advanced tactics warfare school in the North. Though initially disappointed in having to leave the Liberation Forces she had grown to cherish, she nevertheless learned much from this training and swiftly moved to capitalize on it when she returned. Now she was reaping the fruit of those long months of schooling, and in a position to satisfy the desperate urge within to fulfill the bizarre longings that haunted her. She had waited for months to experience that emotion again. Following her unit's first attack on the American ambush position, she succumbed to the encompassing temptation with the pleading, helpless American prisoners before her. Now Chien seemed intent on extinguishing the only true pleasure she had ever known.

This could never be.

CHAPTER 38

Christen ducked under the whirling blades and led his small team in a crouch to the disheveled soldier waiting to greet them.

"Captain Christen, special investigating officer for the Commanding General."

The chopper lifted off from the dirt road to their rear, forcing them to grab their helmets and turn away from the blowing sand.

"Sergeant Adkins, Captain," the man replied when the whirlwind dissipated.

Christen took in the man's soiled, tattered uniform with the chevrons hanging off one sleeve and the dangling threads where the other set of stripes should have been, thinking him the sorriest looking NCO he had ever seen. Smoke grenades, hand grenades, pouches of ammo, and three canteens clung to his shabby web gear. Festering scratches covered his deeply tanned, dirt-encrusted arms. Rips and tears adorned his threadbare jungle fatigues above a bright new set of canvas jungle boots encasing his feet. The faded camouflage covering on his helmet depicted a crude drawing of a fearsome wolf's head with a hapless Vietnamese wearing a conical hat in his dripping jaws.

"What happened here, Sergeant?"

"We were on patrol about two clicks from here when we heard the gunfire and hurried over to check it out," Sergeant Adkins replied. "I secured the area and called it in to headquarters. They instructed me to wait for you." They walked together to the massacre site with Pierce, Howell, and Billy flanking them.

"Get this mess documented," Christen directed to his staff grimly. "When did this happen?"

"About an hour ago, Captain," Adkins replied. "We reached the area about twenty minutes after the shit hit the fan. I thought it odd at the time because we heard only AK-47 fire and no M-16 counter fire. It looks like they took them by surprise. None of the guards around them got off a single shot. It appears these three here made a rush for their weapons stacked over there, but didn't made it. They obviously took the other men over there prisoner."

Christen looked around uneasily in the deathly quiet. "Where did the attack come from? This area is wide open for five hundred meters around us. They *had* to have seen *something*."

"They were in a vehicle of some sort, Captain. Look here." Adkins led him over to the spot where the detour rejoined the road. "There are spent brass AK rounds in this area. It looks like they drove right up to them and opened fire."

"How did they do that without arousing suspicion from the guards?"

"This is the work of that crazy woman," Sergeant Adkins observed. "She moves in mysterious ways. This is some sick shit, but the CG is wasting your time investigating it."

Christen turned to him. "And why is that, Sergeant?"

Adkins looked him in the eye, sending chills racing down his spine. "Because I intend to kill the bitch before he gets the chance to prosecute her for any silly-assed war crimes."

Christen studied him closely. "Adkins... I remember that name. Are you by chance the one that counter-ambushed her force the other night?"

Adkins nodded. "That would be us, Captain. Damned near got the bitch too."

"I sat in on the briefing with the CG. That was quite a maneuver, Sergeant. The general was quite impressed."

Adkins grinned. "I understand he passed his admiration for my brilliant tactical maneuver on down to my First Sergeant, Captain. I appreciate that, since Top took a mighty dim view of the overall operation himself."

Christen turned grimly to the line of bound, dead men. "In any case, Sergeant, this does seem to have her signature in the murder of her prisoners, but she has never attacked in broad daylight before, especially in such an exposed area. This is at odds with how she's operated in the past. We had patrols all over the area and aircraft in the air within minutes of the attack. All they spotted was one Lambretta filled with straw baskets, and an ox cart driven by one old man with five women in the back. She seems to just disappear into thin air after she strikes."

Adkins turned to him. "An ox cart with five women?"

"Yes, it was observed about two clicks from here."

"Which way was it traveling?"

"Away from ..."

"Son of a bitch!" Adkins moaned as he hurried to his RTO. "She rolled right through us in a fucking ox cart! *That's* why they didn't raise any suspicion! I'll get on the radio and get some aircraft looking for that cart and the women!"

"It looks like we let her slip through our hands," Christen advised Howell, Pierce, and Billy when they finished taking their pictures and rejoined him. "That sergeant thinks that ox cart with one man and five women in it observed by one of our aircraft a couple of clicks from here was her. He thinks she rolled right up in the middle of them without raising an alarm."

Pierce shook his head. "She's one gutsy bitch."

Howell frowned. "She keeps changing her tactics. We need to revise our profile of how she operates. This is getting crazy, Captain."

"Crazy, but effective," Christen agreed bitterly.

"She take time to torture prisoners," Billy added. "But she no leave picture again."

"I think we've got two psychopaths on the loose, Cap'n," Pierce observed. "The last two attacks don't fit the pattern of Tiger Woman."

"It's Tiger Woman," Howell argued. "The mutilation is her signature."

"Nevertheless, whoever did this jumped them in broad daylight this time, and like Billy said, there has been no picture left the last two times," Pierce argued. "And the corpses aren't hacked up like the other times. This time they only hacked up the prisoners; the time before they didn't hack up the prisoners, but they did hack up the corpses and the wounded. I'm telling you, we've got at least two copycat psychos running around out here."

"Captain," Sergeant Adkins called from his position near his radio. "They've found the ox cart!"

Christen hurried over as the others hugged his heels.

"About five clicks from here the ARVNs had a check point set up," Adkins continued. "The driver attempted to avoid them, which aroused their suspicions. They popped him when he jumped off the cart and tried to run. They searched the cart afterwards and found six AKs and a lot of spent brass in the straw. They also found a bloody knife."

"What about the women?"

"No sign of them, Captain," Adkins reported. "He must have dropped them off before they capped him."

"Damn! Call our chopper down, Sergeant! I want to see that cart!"

CHAPTER 39

Chien sat impassively at the table with his staff as Cai and her four soldiers stood arrayed before them, his mood coldly reserved.

"It was a glorious victory for our cause, my Colonel," Cai finished her report.

Chien nodded. "It would seem so, Captain. The killing of fourteen imperialists is indeed a glorious victory, though our own loss of Bao is unfortunate. Were prisoners not taken?"

"Yes, my Colonel... but regrettably... we could not risk bringing them with us..."

Chien sensed the four women beside her shift uncomfortably. "In what fashion were they disposed of, Captain?" he asked in a neutral tone.

Cai's eyes flashed defiance. "Quickly and quietly, my Colonel, since we could not risk drawing additional attention to ourselves."

"And what of your mission, Captain?" he asked softly. "I speak of your visit with your friend Kim-Ly, for which you were dispatched."

Cai paused, choosing her words carefully. "Kim-Ly admits selling information about me to the Americans, though I am certain it is of no significance since we were but children then and it has been many years since we have had contact. She also admits she accompanied the Americans to Thinh's village in order to identify him, and even led the imperialist dogs to his hooch."

"Did Kim-Ly give you insight as to why the Americans have an interest in you and your Uncle Thinh?"

"Kim-Ly... seemed uncertain as to why the Americans were interested in me and my uncle, my Colonel."

Chien stiffened. "I am informed Kim-Ly identified you from a photograph the Americans sent out to the ARVNs, Captain. I am surprised you friend did not share this information with you."

"Kim-Ly... did inform me of this, my Colonel," Cai replied tersely. "But I... do not think it of any importance."

Chien picked up a photograph on the table and studied it. "I am informed you left a copy of this on two instances after you attacked the Americans, Captain." He held up the photograph of Cai and her men. "Is this not so?"

Cai nodded. "Yes, my Colonel ..."

"Captain, have you not been taught that we must blend in with the peasants and not draw attention to ourselves?"

"Of course, my Colonel..."

"And in spite of this teaching, you provided the Americans with a photograph of you and a number of your soldiers to use in their search for you?"

"I considered the photograph of no consequence, my Colonel, merely as a tool to antagonize the Americans, who are apparently chasing their tails like the rabid dogs they are in their attempts to find me."

"But by this action, you also seem to have compromised another member of our organization, your uncle, Tran Duc Thinh. Do you not consider this a grave breach of our security, Captain?"

"I... meant only to instill fear into the American dogs, my Colonel. In the North I was taught …"

"*Surely* you were not taught to make our enemy's job in locating and destroying us *easy*, Captain?"

"Of course not, my Colonel, but…"

"But in fact you have done so, Captain, have you not?"

"I... did not anticipate our enemy would use the photograph to…"

"Then you underestimate our enemy, Captain. In your misguided attempt to instill fear in them, you seem to have filled them instead with vengeance due to your unorthodox methods in dealing with their slain and your prisoners. The Americans have a very high sense of morality when it comes to war, Captain. They may be stupid, but never underestimate their resourcefulness or their high principles. The Germans and the Japanese discovered this to be so in the Great War. I fear you have gravely compromised your ability to operate against our enemy in a veiled manner. They have distributed hundreds of these pictures containing your image across the country and are offering large rewards for information concerning you, as your friend Kim-Ly seems to have used to her advantage. Through their vendetta against you, they seem to have identified your uncle, Thinh, as well. I fear you have started a process that could compromise our whole liberation movement in this district due to your personal arrogance, Captain. This course could ultimately destroy us all. The bizarre warfare you pursue in spite of my disapproval has turned our enemy into an unrelenting machine of resolve with but one purpose in mind: *to find you and destroy you!*"

She stiffened angrily as her heart hammered. "Then I welcome their efforts, my Colonel! My life is of no significance if it advances our most worthy cause!"

"*You do not advance our cause by diminishing our ability to prevail!*" Chien countered coldly. "Our cause is not merely to inflict pain on our enemy, Captain. Our cause is to defeat our enemy in order to reunite our country."

"Of course, my Colonel." She lowered her lashes as she shook with fury. "I regret I have met with your disapproval in this matter. I unfortunately do not possess your vast wisdom or dauntless experience."

"You are dismissed, Captain," Chien replied abruptly.

Cai departed under a tight veil of exasperation, chaffing under Colonel Chien's harsh criticism of her in front of his staff. She must learn not to challenge him openly. She attempted to force her mind to more pleasant thoughts as she bathed, imagining the kneeling Americans as they groveled for their miserable, undeserving lives, but her simmering frustration drifted back to Chien's chastisement of her. Her force had accounted for more enemy casualties in the last few weeks than his entire command combined. The American dogs were terrified of their own shadows. For this, she must suffer the reprimands of a weak, shortsighted commander who viewed her merely a vassal for his own lustful pleasure.

She stiffened when the cloth covering rustled behind her and turned with her eyes downcast as Chien stood just inside the opening. She blanked her mind of the repulsion she felt and numbed herself for the ordeal to come. Chien stared at her nude body for a long minute and then turned and walked out of her cavern. She lifted her head to stare at the swaying cloth in surprise, Chien's silent departure troubling to her, over-riding the faint relief for not having to submit to him. Perhaps he was finally tiring of her and would now seek his pleasures elsewhere.

The cloth pushed aside abruptly and Chien drew up in front of her. She quickly lowered her lashes, but not before catching the glint of anger in his eyes. He drew his hand back and slapped her to her knees with a swift blow. Kneeling before him, she raised her hand to her cheek, tasting the blood from her lips, her heart hammering as she fought the impulse to lunge for her knife.

Chien began undressing.

Reluctantly she rose and turned to her cot instead. Now was not the time.

But soon. Very soon!

CHAPTER 40

"General," Christen addressed the commander and his staff. "Since I last reported to you, we visited several POW camps, distributed Tiger Woman's picture to additional ARVN outposts, and posted a reward for information regarding her. As of yet we've had no takers, but we have located Tran Duc Thinh, her uncle. He has agreed to cooperate with us in laying a trap for her in return for a sizable reward."

The G-3 sat forward. "Is this man Thinh trustworthy, Captain?"

"It's hard to say at this point, Sir. He did turn himself in to us and appeared cooperative. However, since he is a suspected member of the Vietcong infrastructure, betrayal is not out of the question. I think he can be trusted to the point of the reward, but that is only my opinion. I will admit that my staff does not necessarily share my views."

"How will this trap be sprung, Captain?"

"I don't have the answer to that yet, Sir. Thinh claims he doesn't know the current whereabouts of Tiger Woman, but will attempt to make contact with her. He'll advise us when this happens. We'll form a plan of action from there.

"But I do have some tactical information that may help in your search." Christen walked to the map on the wall as the staff shifted to follow him. "The attack on the Combat

Engineers yesterday afternoon occurred here, as you know." He used a pointer to indicate the spot on the map. "We now know that an ox cart was used to breach their security and launch their attack upon the unsuspecting men. The cart was found here, approximately five clicks due west of the attack area." He pointed at the spot and moved back to the podium.

"An aircraft sent to search the area spotted this cart initially two clicks from the attack site and reported that it was occupied by five women and one man. When the ARVNs stopped the cart later for a routine search, it contained only the man. Somewhere along the route between the two click and the five click locations, the women left the cart. I recommend that a large part of your search efforts be concentrated within a circle in the middle of that three-click area. I believe the women were dropped off at their base."

"How certain are you that the cart and the women were involved in the attack to begin with?" the G-2 asked.

"Certain, Sir. Upon inspecting the site, it was apparent that the attack occurred from a central location. We found scattered shell casings in one spot only. The cart would not have aroused the suspicions of the engineers or the guards because hundreds of them dot the countryside and they are relatively passive. When the ARVNs searched the cart later at the checkpoint, they found six AK-47 automatic rifles, spent shell casings, and a bloody knife. The knife was presumably used to execute and torture the seven prisoners."

"Was the man captured?"

"No, Sir, unfortunately he was killed attempting to flee from the ARVNs. I'm certain that it was the same cart used in the attack and that Tiger Woman and the other four females were dropped off somewhere along this three click route."

"It appears there are a considerable number of women in her band," the G-3 observed. "Should we give any significance to that?"

"Not a lot," the G-2 answered. "We've known for years that females make up a large part of the VC infrastructure. Most are simply couriers and transporters, but it's not unusual to face them on the battlefield either. Our troops in the field report they are tenacious fighters. Why specifically do you think it was her, Captain?"

"Honestly, Sir, this has caused us some concern," Christen admitted. "Some members of my staff are convinced it was not Tiger Woman who made this attack, but a copycat. I don't agree with this reasoning. However, there were differences. The attack occurred in the daylight with a small band in a wide-open area, instead of at night with a concentrated force. The prisoners taken were butchered, but the corpses weren't disfigured, as she has always done before. She took no prisoners this time, which is also unusual. Nevertheless, I remain convinced that it was her because of the wounds inflicted upon the prisoners. I've seen enough of her handiwork to know no one else could exactly duplicate it."

"This area you are recommending we search has been saturated with troops many times, Captain," the G-3 pointed out. "We've found nothing. In fact, it's fairly well pacified and we encounter little or no resistance there."

"Yes, Sir. I pulled the after-action reports and studied them. We've rarely encountered the enemy in that area. But the fact remains that she and her group disappeared there. That has to carry some weight."

"But what would we be looking for that would be any different from the hundred times we've looked before, Captain?" the G-3 asked.

"Anything out of the ordinary, Sir, of course, but this time I would also look hard at anything that is *too* ordinary," Christen recommended. "I suggest we distribute her picture to our ground forces and have them scrutinize each female they encounter. I'm convinced her base of operations is somewhere in that area."

The G-3 nodded thoughtfully. "With the General's permission, I'll plant a battalion dead in the center of that area on an extended operation and saturate the whole sector with day patrols and night ambushes. If she is in that area, she won't be able to take a crap without us smelling her passing gas."

The general nodded. "I agree with the recommendation. Chris, your team is better equipped to detect subtle inconsistencies than our combat troops. I'd like to see you spend some time on the ground during this operation to make your own observations."

"We'd be glad to participate, Sir, though we have little tactical field training."

The G-3 nodded. "Captain, I'll assign one of my best combat platoons to you for your personal use outside of the operational control of the battalion. You'll be free to pursue your own search in whatever manner you choose."

"Thank you, Sir. We'll do our best. Oh, uh, in that regard, Sir, is there any way we could get Sergeant Adkins' platoon assigned to us for this operation?"

The G-3 frowned. "Sergeant Adkins?"

"Yes, Sir. He's the one from the 1/27th Infantry that countered-ambushed her force a week ago. He also was the one securing the engineer site when we got there. Quit an interesting man, Sir. He seems dedicated to finding Tiger Woman and destroying her. In fact... he assures me the General is wasting my time in investigating her because he plans to kill her before she can, and I quote, 'be prosecuted for any silly-assed war crimes.'"

The general smiled as the staff guffawed. "A right interesting young man."

The G-3 nodded. "I like how he thinks and operates. I'll see what I can do to get him assigned to you, Captain."

CHAPTER 41

Chien left Cai's cavern physically sated after satisfying his every whim upon her tiny, exotic body. Her stoic acceptance of him made her the perfect sexual partner: beautiful, pliable, and accommodating, without need for personal arousal or emotional satisfaction an essential prerequisite for his own pleasure. However, her new mindset disturbed him. She was becoming a disciplinary problem within his command, openly displaying hostility and acting independently of his instructions. She was losing sight of their objectives, giving consideration only to her own perverse personal whims. The emerging sadistic side of her left him unnerved.

After he dismissed her from the briefing room, he questioned her four soldiers, who gave a graphic, sickening narrative of what occurred after the capture of the men from the engineer detachment. He agreed it would have been too dangerous to attempt to bring the captives in under the circumstances, and that their execution was preferable to leaving them behind, but a simple bullet in the back of their head would have sufficed instead of the intolerable methods she employed. The abnormal fetish to torture her prisoners served only to inflame the hearts of their enemy, and to distress her own soldiers as well.

Afterwards, all four of her soldiers requested reassignment to other Liberation Force units. He did not grant their request of course, but he did understand their wish to serve under another, more conventional commander. He must find a way to restrain her before his superiors took the matter out of his hands. The thought of this was unbearable. Trying to reason with her only brought flashing resentment to her captivating eyes. Issuing directives to discontinue the practice of mutilating her captives only produced defiant hostility.

He was losing her. This knowledge only served to strengthen his craving for her. In the beginning, she had been an accommodating mistress, but now that she had experienced combat, she became bolder with each mission—and he grew less capable of dealing with her. Other commanders under him were watching this battle of wills, which only served to weaken his influence with them. Now he had even resorted to striking her, desperate to bring back the docile Cai he once knew. Even though she had submitted afterwards and withstood his drawn out exploitation of her body, he could sense the coldness she exuded towards him versus the previous indifference with his use of her.

Tran Duc Thinh also troubled him. Thinh had returned from his interrogation with the Americans and reported they were obsessed with finding Cai, whom they referred to as Tiger Woman. Thinh reported the Americans had offered him 10,000 piaster for information about her. He claimed he had told them he had not seen her in five years. His mannerisms indicated he was being less than truthful. He assumed Thinh gave the Americans more information than he had admitted to.

Thinh also brought back the American photograph of Cai, and from Le Loi he obtained a copy of the original.

He was stunned that Cai would provide such documentation to their enemy under any circumstance. This proved she was not rational in her behavior. Stealth and deception was the key to their survival as a guerrilla force. It was unthinkable to give their enemy photographs with which to trace her and her soldiers. The growing revulsion of Cai's own soldiers to her gruesome acts, and the huge reward offered by the Americans, set the stage for potential betrayal. This combination of temptations would only grow stronger with each atrocity she committed. Cai's hatred for all foreigners blinded her, and she failed to see their strengths. She focused only on their weaknesses. It was a given that she exploited them better than any of his commanders, but to ignore their strong points could be dangerous to them all. He must find a way to bring her back to reality; otherwise, he would lose her forever. This could never be.

CHAPTER 42

"Cap'n, I've laid on a chopper," Master Sergeant Pierce reported from the door to his office as Christen raised his first cup of coffee to his lips the next morning. "We need to get out to Trang Bang as fast as possible."

"What's up?"

"The ARVN outpost just called in. Kim-Ly and her children were murdered by the VC last night."

Christen's stomach clutched as heat rose to his face. "*What?*"

"Sorry, Sir."

"Let's go!" Christen grabbed his hat and rushed out the door as Pierce, Howell, and Billy followed. Fifteen minutes later the chopper dropped them off in front of Kim-Ly's hooch, where a captain from the ARVN ranger battalion surrounding the village waited to greet them.

"Sir, he says it is regrettable to greet you under such unpleasant circumstances," Howell interpreted over the noise of the chopper.

"Thank you, *Die Wee*, I too am sorry to meet you under these circumstances." Christen replied as he shook hands with the ARVN captain while Howell translated. They turned and accompanied the ARVN captain to the entrance of Kim-Ly's hooch, where they drew up abruptly at the sight of Kim-Ly's severed head and those of her two children mounted on stakes.

Christen abruptly turned away from the grisly scene, his empty stomach heaving in spasms at the sight of the shards of skin dangling below the bloody faces with the eyes rolled back until only the whites showed. "Oh my god," he gasped.

Howell listened closely to the Vietnamese captain. "Sir, he says a small group of Vietcong came to the hooch around midnight. They severed the heads of the children first as Kim-Ly pleaded with them to kill only her. Several of them raped Kim-Ly before beheading her as well. They pinned a message to the stake warning the other villagers against collaborating with the Americans," he reported between pauses as he listen to the captain.

"Oh my god," Christen moaned. "I'm responsible for this!"

"Cap'n, you can't accept responsibility for this crime," Pierce argued. "They did this to control the other villagers. There was no way we could have anticipated something like this happening!"

The Vietnamese captain talked as Howell listened. "Sir, he says Kim-Ly's husband is grief stricken and unable to meet with us right now. He says her husband told him Cai visited Kim-Ly the day before yesterday and was very angry with her for talking to us." He listened again. "He says that Cai wanted to know why we were searching for Tran Duc Thinh and seemed unaware that we were searching for her by name until Kim-Ly told her about the photograph. He says Cai knocked Kim-Ly to the ground and told her they were no longer friends."

"Tiger Woman was here the day before yesterday?" Pierce demanded. "That puts her on the road directly between here, the scene of the Combat Engineer massacre, and the location of the cart where the ARVN's found it. I guess it *was* her and not some other loony tunes trying to imitate her."

"I knew it was her all along," Howell swore. "Nobody else could do what she does the way she does it."

Christen drew a deep breath to calm himself. "This woman is truly a psychopath!" he whispered, averting his eyes from the heads on the stakes before them.

"I know what was wrong with the whole engineer setup now, Cap'n," Pierce mused. "She didn't plan it. She found herself in the middle of them, saw a target of opportunity, and took it. It wasn't planned at all."

"I think you're right," Howell agreed. "She was rolling along in the cart and took advantage of the opportunity when it presented itself. Nothing else makes sense."

Billy nodded. "That why she not take time to butcher the dead or take prisoners. She in big hurry!"

"Document this crime," Christen ordered weakly. "Thank the Captain for calling us. Ask him to please tell his sergeant that we are deeply grieved by this unjust tragedy." Howell translated as Pierce took pictures of the three heads on the stakes from different angles. The Vietnamese captain stepped forward and shook Christen's hand.

"He says he is sure his sergeant will be grateful for your compassion, Captain," Howell translated. "He says nothing can ever right the full injustice of what has occurred here, but that the death of the woman who caused this will go a long way in bringing Kim-Ly's husband the justice his soul cries for."

"Tell him he has my solemn pledge that we will seek justice on his behalf," Christen replied. "Now let's get out of here before I embarrass myself further." He turned to the chopper as Howell translated.

CHAPTER 43

When the jeep deposited them back at their bunker from visiting Kim-Ly's murder scene, a gaggle of fifty fully combat-clad infantrymen lay in disarray on the ground, most sleeping. As they dismounted, Sergeant Adkins strolled over to them with his rifle held loosely in his left hand. The men on the ground ignored them as he tossed a careless salute in Christen's direction.

"Sergeant Adkins reporting as ordered, Captain."

Christen returned the salute even though Adkins dropped his hand and mopped his face with a green towel draped around his neck, noticing he wore new jungle fatigues now with bare sleeves versus the tattered set with staff sergeant stripes clinging to his right sleeve and only threads dangling from the left. "Good to see you again, Sergeant."

"My Company Commander said we were to be your personal bodyguard for the next week or ten days, so here we are. Don't know who's fucking with you, Captain, but you're in safe hands now."

"Where is your Platoon Leader?" Sergeant Pierce asked.

"I don't have a Lieutenant of my own, Sarge. Butter Bars don't last long in the bush anyway." He glanced back at Christen. "Does our mission include watching over these other REMFs here and the slope too?"

Christen blinked. "REMFs?"

"Uh, don't go there, Cap'n," Pierce injected quickly. "Sergeant Adkins, we didn't get the chance to formally introduce ourselves the other day. I'm Sergeant Pierce, the NCOIC of this group. This is Billy, our Kit Carson scout, and Specialist Howell. Come on in the office and we'll fill you in on your mission."

"You shits stay loose," Adkins called to his sprawled men as he passed, who seemed to take no notice of him.

Pierce poured a cup of coffee and handed it to Adkins. "Sergeant, I assume you've heard of Tiger Woman?"

Adkins shrugged as he sipped at the coffee. "If she's the bitch we've been chasing after for the last month or so, I've seen her leavings twice now and bloodied her once."

"We're a special intelligence team working for the CG," Pierce continued. "Our sole mission is to gather information on her in order to help eliminate her."

Adkins looked around the office with seeming disinterest. "Uh huh."

Pierce flushed. "We're going on an extended operation to find her."

Adkins leveled his brown eyes on him. "Okay."

"How long have you been in Vietnam?" Christen asked in the ensuing silence.

Adkins glanced at his watch. "Two hundred and forty-three days, seven hours and fifty-two minutes, Captain. Why?"

Christen cleared his throat. "Well, uh, you just seem awful young to be running a platoon without an officer."

"Huh," Adkins grunted and sipped at his coffee as he turned back to Pierce. "When do we pull out?"

"Pull out?" Pierce asked.

"We ain't going to find that bitch standing around here in base camp scratching our ass. I assume you have a plan of some sort?"

"Oh, yeah, well, we depart tomorrow morning on an extended operation into an area that we believe she is based out of," Pierce replied. "A firebase will be set up in our target area. We'll be inserted by helicopter first thing in the morning to begin the hunt."

"Uh huh," Adkins replied and turned to Christen. "Captain, my men have been out off and on for nine straight days now, so if you don't object, I'll herd them on down to the company area and get them fed, shit, showered, shaved, and drunk. I'll have them back here at dawn."

Christen nodded. "That sounds fine, Sergeant."

"Thanks for the sludge." Adkins sat his cup down and ambled out the door. "You sorry shits get on up off your tired asses," he called to his men as he passed through them.

Christen and his staff moved to the door to watch the men rise and fall into two lines as they trailed after their curious sergeant, seemingly uncaring of where he led them.

"What the hell was that?" Howell asked. "I thought the G-3 was giving us one of his *best* field units?"

Christen laughed. "Don't let their looks deceive you. They might not seem like much in garrison, but they've proven they know their way around out there in Indian land."

"What did he mean by him 'blooding her once'?"

"This is the platoon that jumped her force the last time she struck one of our night ambushes."

"Do tell," Howell mused as he watched them straggle away. "So what's a REMF?"

Pierce chuckled. "That, Specialist, is what we are, and Grunts don't too much care for us. It means 'Rear Echelon

Mother Fucker.' With these men you earn their respect, it's not a given."

Howell scowled. "I think I noticed that somewhere in his demeanor. He's definitely a man of few words—and I don't think he's especially enamored with our mission either."

"Did you notice his eyes?" Pierce replied. "He was constantly analyzing everything around him. I have a feeling he doesn't miss much."

Christen turned away from the door. "I think we're in good hands, even if he doesn't think much of us or our mission. Let's study the area we're going into tomorrow and see what we can figure out. Billy, you used to be the enemy. Tell us where you'd hide if you were still out there."

"I stand next to you and pretend to help you find me," Billy replied.

Howell laughed and turned to refill his cup. "Want some more *sludge*, Captain?"

Christen grinned. "Hell yeah, and throw in a little gunpowder for sweetener."

"Consider it done, Super REMF," Howell replied, laughing.

When Christen arrived at his office the next morning shortly after daylight, he found the platoon of infantry again lying around in a haphazard cluster, with most of them sleeping. He threaded his way through the strewn bodies and entered, where he found Sergeant Adkins sipping on a cup of coffee in the deserted office.

"Morning, Captain," Adkins greeted. "You guys start a mite late around here."

"The others should be here by 0700 hours." Christen poured himself a cup of coffee, annoyed that he sounded like he was apologizing. He grimaced with his first sip of coffee and stared into his cup. "Damn, that's strong."

"I didn't have any bourbon to cut it with," Adkins advised.

Christen seated himself at Pierce's desk across from Adkins. "So tell me a little about yourself, Sergeant."

"There ain't much to tell, Captain. I'm from Texas. I've been in the Army about a year and over here about eight months."

"I'm from New Jersey," Christen offered.

Adkins nodded. "I pegged you for a damned Yankee from the start."

Christen swept his annoyance aside. "How did you make sergeant so fast?"

"There wasn't anybody else left to hang stripes on."

"Why haven't they assigned you a platoon leader?"

"I reckon we do just fine without one."

"It must be difficult to run a platoon by yourself."

"It's a damn sight easier than training a boy-wonder," Adkins replied, referring to new second lieutenants right out of officer candidate school. "Those jackasses can get you killed."

Master Sergeant Pierce came through the door. "Good morning, Sir; morning, Sergeant Adkins. I see you guys are ready to roll." Pierce poured himself a cup of coffee and took a sip. "*Damn!* What's this shit?"

"I didn't have any bourbon to cut it with," Adkins advised.

"Morning," Howell greeted as he entered and turned to the coffee pot. "You guys are up early."

"Watch out, it's poison," Pierce warned as Howell took a tentative sip and grimaced.

Christen winked at Howell. "Sergeant Adkins didn't have any bourbon to cut it with."

"So what's the deal with the gook?" Adkins asked.

"Billy? He was training to be one of Tiger Woman's guerrillas before he became a Kit Carson scout," Pierce replied.

"Good. We've got a walking body count if we have a slow day," Adkins observed as he took a sip of his coffee.

"Damn, this stuff will eat the fur off your tongue," Howell complained. "I'll dump it out and start a fresh pot."

"What do you mean by a 'walking body count if we have a slow day'?" Christen asked.

Adkins shrugged. "We can always shoot him if we don't find anything else to entertain ourselves with."

"He's just kidding, Sir," Pierce reassured Christen with a chuckle, and then frowned when Adkins stared at him with unblinking eyes.

"Billy is a member of my staff... and as such, under my personal protection," Christen advised hesitantly.

Adkins sighed. "That's a shame. I better let my men know that upfront, I reckon."

Christen nodded. "I... would appreciate that."

"Good morning, *Die Wee*," Billy greeted as he entered.

Adkins turned to him. "Out late last night, Charliesan?"

"What you mean?" Billy asked.

Adkins walked over to him. "I saw a slope pacing around about 0530 hours this morning writing on a piece of paper." He reached out, unbuttoned the left flap on Billy's shirt pocket, slipped two fingers into the cavity, and extracted a piece of paper, never losing eye contact with him. He opened the paper, peered at the Vietnamese writing, and handed the sheet to Christen. "You might want to check this out, Captain."

Billy flushed. "It not important."

Adkins stared at him evenly. "Maybe, maybe not: but it could be the distances to key buildings and bunkers around here. That would bring some quick cash from the local bad guys who lob mortar rounds in here on occasion."

"Let me see that, Captain," Howell requested and took the sheet of paper from Christen's hand to study it. "It doesn't make sense."

Billy drew himself up. "It just poetry I write!"

Howell laughed. "That's it! It's poetry!"

Billy blustered. "I do nothing wrong. I work for Americans now, not VC."

Adkins leaned in to him, his stare ice. "Sure you do, Charlie-san, and for anybody else that will pay you, I suspect. Now listen to me real close. If I get one of my men hurt out there and even *think* you *might* have had something to do with it, your own Momma-san ain't gonna recognize you when I get through with you. You *bic*?"

"*Die Wee*, you tell him," Billy pleaded, backing away a pace. "I make deal. I work for you now. I not work for VC now."

"Uh, Sergeant, uh... I don't think, uh ..."

"I get your drift, Captain. I just hope your pet slope here gets mine." Adkins turned to the pot and poured a cup of the freshly brewed coffee, sipped, and frowned. "Now that's a tad weak. Can I pour you a cup, Charlie-san?"

Billy sulked. "I get my own."

Adkins shrugged. "Help yourself then, Billy-Bob, but make it quick, we need to get this show on down the road. Time's wasting."

CHAPTER 44

Cai climbed out of the stream she was bathing in and shielded her eyes against the early morning sun to observe the American helicopters filling the sky and landing in waves to the north of her. She quickly donned her peasant garb and rushed to the tunnel complex as big helicopters with two blades carrying artillery pieces slung under their belly flew overhead, knowing the Americans only brought their artillery when they built small base camps and stayed for extended periods.

The Americans were landing virtually on top of them. They only built their bases in the most heavily contested areas. Chien always kept the fighting to a minimum in this sector so as not to jeopardize their vast tunnel system. Their entire command structure was now in grave danger. Chien would direct all operations to cease until the Americans departed in order to fool them into thinking they were wasting their efforts. There had to be a breach of security for them to be here. Now that they were, they would saturate the area with their patrols day and night. This would disrupt her recruiting plans and hamper her training of new soldiers. Nothing could be worse than this for her, and would set her back a considerable amount of time.

Where could a breach of their security have occurred? There had been no recent capture or interrogation of their soldiers. Except for Thinh! He was in a position to bring attention to this area when he voluntarily submitted to the American interrogation, although even he did not know the exact location to the tunnel complex. He, as most others, met at the secure hooch and waited for a guide to blindfold and lead him to the entrance on each occasion. They left again blindfolded to return to the secure hooch. She tried to quell her anger as she slipped into the hole in the ground and re-placed the cover to the camouflaged entrance. She rushed to the operation's room, where she found a courier briefing Chien. All eyes turned to her abrupt entrance.

"Colonel! The Americans are landing in force to the north of us! There are many helicopters and they are bring-ing their artillery with them!"

Chien glared at her as if she were at fault. "Seal the en-trances! Have them checked for proper concealment! No one will enter or depart without my direct permission. Send the old women decoys to gather information. Do these things now!" Those around him hurried off to carry out his orders. "You might have interest in the rest of this report," Chien directed to her coldly. "It concerns your friend Kim-Ly."

Cai moved to her place at the table with a heavy heart, her apprehension far removed from Kim-Ly as in the back-ground workers hurried to fill in the entrances with dirt to hide the tunnel openings. When completed, the Americans would find only spider holes such as their snipers used on occasion and would not discover the adjoining caverns. With this action, they also sealed themselves underground until Chien directed otherwise.

Filled with dismay, she scarcely listened to the courier's report of the execution of Kim-Ly and her children.

CHAPTER 45

Christen watched the paddies flash by below his feet as the nose of the aircraft lifted and their forward speed slowed. One lone man hurrying down the dirt road away from their landing zone drew his attention. The man seemed familiar as they passed him by, but he was unsure of what piqued his interest. When the chopper settled down with a thump, he leaped out behind Sergeant Adkins with Pierce, Howell, and Billy following and ran in a stoop away from the side of the chopper as the wind whipped around their heads in near hurricane force. The troops from Adkins' platoon poured out of the line of choppers behind them with lowered heads against the whirling debris.

A guide from the battalion headquarters staff hurried over to them, his head turned away from the blowing sand and grass. "Captain Christen, Sir?"

"Yes, I'm Captain Christen."

"You and your men follow me, Sir. I'll show you your area."

"Lead the way," Christen instructed. They followed him to the center of the firebase, where the guide indicated an area marked by four stakes with white engineer tape on the tops.

"This is your sector, Sir. You can draw sandbags from the S-4. The Headquarters bunker is going up over there."

"Thanks," Christen replied as the guide hurried off to meet the next lift of aircraft settling down on the LZ.

"All right, you slackers," Adkins shouted. "I want First Squad here, Second there, Third over there, and Fourth back here, tied back into the First Squad. Set your positions, drop your gear, and build me an eight by eight by six-foot bunker right here in the middle. When you're finished, dig your individual fighting positions and get your personal gear squared away. I don't want to see no ass dragging either. Move it!"

Christen watched the troops scatter to their assigned sectors and peel off the layers of equipment as the squad leaders made final adjustments in the circle of two-man fighting positions. Within minutes, the squad leaders had men transporting sandbags and metal engineer stakes from the supply point as others stripped to the waist and dug a hole for the command bunker, depositing the dirt into the sandbags to build the walls.

The efficiency of the men and the speed with which the command bunker rose up around the deepening hole in the ground amazed him. He watched as Adkins assigned Howell the task of stringing the commo wire to connect them to the headquarters bunker, and Pierce to supervise the raising of the radio antenna. When he moved to help some troops struggling under a heavy load of sandbags, Adkins intercepted him.

"Begging the Captain's pardon, but you need to go find some officer stuff to do," he advised sternly. "My men get nervous when the brass is around, and right now they don't need the distraction."

"Officer stuff?"

"We have this situation under control, Captain. You're in our way."

"Uh, okay, Sergeant," Christen replied as he meekly moved off to find some officer stuff to do, although he had no clue as to what that should be. He paused on the fringe of their designated area and surveyed the twelve hundred men of the accompanying battalion working around him seemingly without direction, quickly shaping the firebase into a large circle of fighting positions manned by four infantry companies strung around the outer perimeter. Small company command bunkers rose out of the ground centered on each unit. Within the circle of infantry, other sandbag walls grew around a battery of 105-millimeter howitzers. A larger battalion headquarters bunker steadily sprouted out of the ground in the center of the evolving firebase near Christen's own bunker. Sweating men around the outer perimeter strung circles of concertina wire thirty yards in front of the infantry and placed out trip flares and claymore mines. Others dug two-man fighting positions lined with sandbags behind the concertina wire and erected waterproof poncho shelters behind them to sleep under when not on guard. A long, grassy strip in the middle of the firebase provided a secure LZ for the helicopters.

When he saw Adkins' men laying metal engineer stakes across the tops of the walls to his bunker and placing sandbags on them to form a roof as others carried olive drab tables and cots inside, he deemed it safe to return. As the men dispersed to prepare their own positions, he entered his bunker and found a table with metal folding chairs around it, a large operation's map on the wall, and a communications center hooked up and operating. Each side of the bunker held two canvas cots situated on the four feet deep earthen floor below the four foot high sandbagged walls, giving plenty of headroom. Two battery-operated lamps with a red lens to preserve night vision hung on the steel beams supporting the roof.

Now what? he wondered absently.

CHAPTER 46

Thinh anxiously watched the American helicopters flashing overhead in long lines with hundreds of soldiers in them, knowing this was more than a typical air assault. The Americans were setting up one of their temporary bases practically on top of the tunnel complex. Now Chien would seal the entrances to the underground network against the threat and he would not be able to render his weekly report. Though his captain had sufficiently recovered from his wounds to make the trip, Chien had directed him to come in his place. This disturbed him. Chien had a vast intelligence-gathering network and was no fool. It would be a mistake to consider him so. The Americans were notoriously loose with their tongues. Had they compromised his agreement to help them find Cai, which prompted Chien to send for him personally after rendering his initial report upon meeting with the Americans?

As he hurried away, he glanced up at the helicopters flying low over his head and was startled to see the red headed captain he had met on his visit to Cu Chi staring back at him from the wide door of the aircraft. This gave him further unease. What was the captain doing here with these soldiers? He had given no indication to the Americans that Cai might be in this specific area. The Americans had distributed hundreds of fliers offering enticing rewards for information leading to Cai. He had personally reported this to Colonel Chien. Had they somehow discovered her base of operations through some other source? Would Chien blame him for someone else's indiscretion or disloyalty? Surely he was not Chien's only suspect.

He quickened his pace with growing unease, relieved he would not have to face Colonel Chien on this day. He was not adept at deception, and Chien made him nervous. The fact that it could take several weeks before the Americans departed and he would have to face Chien again gave him comfort. This would give him time to calm his nerves and perfect his story... as well as devise a plan to lure Cai out to the Americans before someone else beat him to the reward.

He dreamed of the riches soon to come his way. Cai would regret rebuffing his request for assistance in advancing his status within their organization, a most serious error in judgment. Her chastisement of him for seeking her support was humiliating, her unwillingness to use her influence to help the only remaining member of her family intolerable. After all, it was he who found her a husband, though that had not been difficult as attractive as she was, and he in fact had profited from the moderate sum paid by Pin for such a prize, even though she was not pure.

Still, he would not forgive her this transgression.

CHAPTER 47

Pierce glanced up and grinned as Christen entered the bunker. "This is one hell of a platoon, Cap'n."

"They're no slackers," Howell agreed. "When they move, they don't mess around, and they definitely seemed to know what they're doing."

Adkins entered the bunker carrying a small portable gas stove with a coffee pot. "Since you gents don't care for my brewing talents, who wants to do the honors?"

"I believe that'd be me," Howell volunteered. He drew water from a five-gallon can as Adkins set up the stove and got it going.

"Everything meet with your approval, Captain?" Adkins asked.

Christen nodded. "I'm impressed, Sergeant."

"Good. Now that we've got the housekeeping chores out of the way, let's get on with the mission. What do you have in mind for us?"

Christen hesitated. "Find Tiger Woman."

Adkins nodded. "Right: if you'll point her out, I'll go shoot the bitch and we can pack up and go on back home."

Christen flushed. "I... guess the plan is for the Infantry to saturate the area day and night with patrols."

Adkins nodded. "That's original. What do *we* do?"

"Uh, we'll look for things they might not see."

Adkins arched his eyebrows. "And what might *we* see that they don't?"

Christen frowned. "Something that seems normal, but in fact isn't, I guess."

Adkins nodded, bemused. "Well, *okey-dokey* then …"

"What I mean is—we're looking for the hidden-but-obvious sort of thing."

"Can you be any more specific than that, Captain?"

"Look, Sergeant, to be honest, I don't have a specific plan, but I feel very strongly she's out there somewhere," Christen insisted.

Adkins grinned. "So you've got a whole damned battalion out here on a *hunch,* Captain?"

"I'd... like to think it's stronger than just a hunch, Sergeant."

Adkins shrugged. "Hell, I don't guess it really matters none since she hasn't been any other damned place we've looked. With dinks, a hunch is as good as an educated guess most of the time anyway."

"I admit I may be off base here," Christen conceded. "The G-3 thinks this area is pretty well pacified. I looked up the after action reports and there has been very little contact in this area that would indicate we're on the right track. But I do have a strong hunch, as you say, that she's somewhere in this vicinity."

Adkins filled his cup and sat at the table. "Why is that, Captain? Why are we *here* instead of somewhere else?"

"The fact is, we don't have a clear plan of action, but here's our thinking," Pierce interjected to save Christen further discomfiture. "After the engineer disaster, the women in the cart disappeared somewhere between the point where the aircraft spotted them and the ARVN checkpoint where they killed the man driving the cart. Based on that, we think her base of operations is somewhere in this area."

Adkins nodded thoughtfully. "That's logical: it elevates this production to an educated guess instead of a wild-assed hunch." Adkins turned to Howell. "Specialist, can you plot all the coordinates on the map where there has been previous contact in this AO?"

Howell grabbed a folder and a grease pencil. "Sure."

"What have you got in mind?" Pierce asked.

"If your theory is correct, it would only make sense that the limited contact they've had here in the past would be in the areas where they're protecting something," Adkins advised.

"That's a good point," Pierce agreed.

"If that's so, that's where we need to be looking. These are wily little bastards. You never know exactly what they're thinking, but it may be that they deliberately limit their contact in this area to throw us off. Sort of a variation of 'don't shit in your own nest,' so to speak. By not drawing our attention to the area, they can better protect whatever they're afraid of us finding. What do you say, Billy-Bob? You're a Chuck."

"I not know what *Chuck* mean."

"Chuck, Charles, Sir Charles, VC, Viet Cong, Cong, they all mean the same, Billy-Bob: a walking, talking, fucking target. You *bic*?"

"I bic. But I not Chuck now."

"The jury's still out on that issue, but we're talking about what you *think*, not what you *are*."

"I think it not make sense to fight for no reason. I think they protect something."

Howell turned from the map. "I should have plotted these coordinates before. There's definitely a pattern here.

217

Look, there are four distinct groupings, or clusters of points of contact, one each in the north, the south, the east, and the west of us."

"You're right, and they're almost exactly spaced," Pierce agreed. "Now that *is* strange."

Christen stared at the four clusters on the map. "But what does it mean?"

"I can guarantee you it means something," Adkins allowed as he inspected the four clusters. "Hell, let's pick one and go have a look. The one here in the south is the closest."

"You mean right now?" Christen asked.

"We've got five hours of daylight left, Captain. We can get there and back easy in that time. We sure as hell ain't accomplishing anything sitting around here on our ass drinking coffee."

Christen cleared his throat. "Uh, I've never been on a combat mission before."

"No kidding?" Adkins chided dryly. "Get your rifle and all the canteens of water you can carry. Leave the rest to us. Just move when I tell you to move, walk where I tell you to walk, and don't get curious about anything. Curiosity will get you killed if you poke at the wrong thing."

"Billy-Bob," he continued, turning to Billy. "I expect you know what you're doing out there, since you've probably laid half of the mines and booby traps in this cesspool you call a country. You stay close to me so I can keep my eye on you, understand? Specialist, you and Sergeant Pierce stay back here and monitor us on the radios in case we overload our ass. Breaking in one newbie at a time is about all I care to handle. Plot this area here to the south on a map and run it on over to the Headquarters bunker and tell them we're going to make a platoon-sized sweep through that area so they can plot artillery and such. We move out in half an hour." Adkins drained his cup, set it on the table, and left the bunker. "All right you shits, get saddled up now!" he called. "It's time to earn your keep. Uncle Sam ain't paying you to sit around fiddling with your dongs all day. Let's move!"

Pierce grinned. "He's pretty damn decisive, ain't he?"

"Definitely a man of action," Howell agreed. "Captain, are you sure you want to go along on this mission?"

Christen sighed. "No, I'm not sure of anything, except that we seem to have just gone from no plan to a damn good plan, and I haven't a clue as to how it happened."

"This Sergeant not like me very much I think, and I not understand much of what he say," Billy mused. "But if he not kill me too quick, I think we someday be friends."

They laughed as they turned to their assigned tasks in preparation for the mission.

CHAPTER 48

"Somethin's goin' down, Bo," Bubba whispered as he eased over and sat next to Allen on his bunk.

"I know," Allen whispered back. "Everybody's rushing around everywhere and they've doubled our guard."

Bubba nodded grimly. "They're runnin' aroun' with shovels and baskets and shit. If I didn't know better, I'd say we're bein' buried alive."

"That must mean they're afraid of something near us," Allen speculated. "I did pick out one tunnel they were rushing into. If you're right and they are filling in the entrances, that's one of the channels we need to watch."

"It also affects our timing, Bo. It's for sure we ain't goin' nowhere with all the exits covered up. Whatever's got 'em spooked is not necessarily a good thing for us."

"What do you think is scaring them, Bubba?"

"It's gotta be our guys, Bo, and I'm thinkin' they're real close."

"Should we make our move now? Before they seal the exits?"

"Not with two guards. They'd bust us in a skinny minute. We've got to be patient and wait for the right opportunity. But when it presents itself, Bo, you better be ready. I don't know when it'll happen, but when I move, you move with me."

"Try to give me a little warning, Bubba."

"I'll do the best I can, but when the time comes, I think you'll know it as well as I do. Just don't hesitate and don't show no mercy."

"You no talk. You no talk!" one of their VC guards ordered.

"Yea, yea, you little pig fucker," Bubba grumbled. "I bet your momma-san sucks water buffalo ding-dongs for sport."

The guard lifted his cane in the air. "You no talk! You go to own bed. You crawl. You move!"

Bubba slid off the cot and crawled to his own bed a few feet away. "See you, Bo. Stay alert now!"

CHAPTER 49

Cai stood in the operation's room until the reports were rendered to Chien confirming the tunnel entrances were now sealed, which their soldiers accomplished by filling the horizontal cavity with dirt to a length of five feet and tamping it solid. Workers from the ground level poured dirt into the vertical shaft for a depth of five feet above the entrance to the horizontal opening, tamped it, and then poured water into the vertical shaft, further disguising any loose soil. The ground workers then checked the camouflage covering over the hole and departed the area, entombing them below the surface.

Their primary source of oxygen would be the air pumped down to them through the inadequate system of vents made of hollow bamboo poles with the tops ten feet above the ground. Their only link to the outside world was four telephone lines. The handsets were battery operated with the connecting wires buried under the topsoil, over which they would receive operational reports from the observers above ground. These old men and women who reported to them aroused little suspicion from the Americans as they moved about tilling their paddies. This enabled them to track all enemy movements, which Chien's staff posted on the large map located in the operation's room. They would prepare their meals only at night over small, smokeless oil fires. Movement and noise would be restricted to a bare minimum. No one would enter or leave the complex without the authority of Chien.

When Cai was satisfied that all was going according to plan, she returned to her room in dismay.

Now the interminable wait for the Americans to leave would begin.

CHAPTER 50

Christen followed Billy, where Adkins positioned him near the middle of the fifty-man platoon, as they wound their way single file through the turns in the concertina wire and out of the firebase. As instructed by Adkins, Billy dogged the heels of the radioman, which followed Adkins. The platoon medic brought up the rear of their headquarters group. First and second squads strung out in front of them, with third and fourth squads trailing along behind.

They swiftly crossed the paddy area and entered the tree line heading south. Adkins raised his hand above his head with two fingers aloft and the platoon split efficiently into two columns fifty yards apart, with Adkins, his RTO, Billy, Christen himself, and Doc in line in the center.

In spite of the heat and their heavy loads, the men moved quietly through the light vegetation, pausing on occasion for the point man to check out danger zones. Christen stayed close behind Billy, and was careful not to stray off the invisible path that Billy walked so as not to fall victim to booby traps, mines, or punji pits as he placed one foot in front of the other praying only moist earth would received it. When the brush thickened, the two columns edged closer to maintain contact.

Christen marveled at the proficiency of the platoon. There was no talking and very little noise in their movement through the underbrush. The absence of directives belied the fact that the men were well versed in their individual roles. Adkins simply made eye contact and nodded his head, sending a member of the platoon to perform an unspoken task quickly and competently, verifying he was in the capable hands of professionals as the stress of his first combat patrol dissipated somewhat. However, the soaring heat and stifling humidity as millions of insects swirled around them in humming clouds clinging to their sweat drenched faces was worse than he ever imagined. His fatigue shirt was soon soaked white with sweat even though he carried less than half of the equipment the other men carried.

As he swiveled his head in all directions looking for signs of danger, he was temporarily stunned to find himself all alone, the men around him having vanished without warning. A surge of relief washed through him when Adkins leaned out from behind a bush and held his palm horizontal to the ground, motioning him down. He squatted behind a bush and waited, his lips slightly ajar in order to better hear in the stifling quiet as he swiped at the sweat trickling down his face and tried to decipher what was evolving around him. His heartbeat increased tempo when he picked up the sing-song chatter of Vietnamese voices close by. He froze, resisting the urge to swat at a mosquito drawing blood from his cheek. Brush rattling off to his left and the soft thud of footsteps in the strained hush drew his attention through the tangled shrubbery to two black pajama clad figures with straw conical hats, oblivious to the fifty heavily armed men crouching within feet of them. When they disappeared to their rear, the silent men around him reappeared and moved surreptitiously forward again. After an hour of steady movement, the platoon again halted without apparent command. The squad leaders appeared and arrayed themselves around Adkins as he squatted on his heels to study his map.

"About two hundred meters now," Adkins whispered. "First and Second Squads, on-line; Third and Fourth Squads, in flank column: let's go see what these fuckers are so afraid of us finding out here." The squad leaders faded back into the jungle without a word. "Stay close to me, Captain," Adkins advised as he moved forward with his RTO following. Billy dogged the RTO's heels. Christen fell in behind Billy, and the medic brought up the rear.

They moved at a cautious pace, slipping around bushes and placing their feet to ensure they did not step on fallen limbs and twigs. Fifteen minutes passed without incident before the sudden barking of rifle fire from their left front sent him dodging as spent bullets whizzed overhead. He flung himself to the ground in panic as a volley of M-16 fire answered the enemy rifles. He saw Adkins slip forward in a crouch with his RTO and Billy shadowing him, and disappear into the brush.

Doc rushed by him. "We've got to keep up, Captain!"

Christen pulled himself up on rubbery legs and stumbled after the medic as more rounds whined overhead against the ragged clamor of M-16 counter fire.

"*Fire and Maneuver!*" Adkins shouted from somewhere to his front.

The firing picked up as unseen bodies crashed though the undergrowth. Christen lost sight of the medic as he ran forward in a crouch, trying to stay low and behind trees as the firefight hammered around him. Again, he found himself alone, which filled him with even greater anxiety than the barrage of gunfire to his front.

He hurried forward, guiding on the jagged roar ahead of him. When he judged the surging fight was moving rapidly away from him, he threw prudence to the wind, his fear overcoming his teetering caution as he twisted and turned frantically through the thick vegetation trying to catch up, becoming more disorientated and confused by the clamoring battle. Abruptly the firing stopped. He thrashed through the jungle, finding the eerie silence more terrifying than the shooting, and stumbled into Adkins' kneeling headquarters section. He collapsed beside them gasping for breath.

"I warned you to stay with me, Captain," Adkins admonished with a wry grin as he stood and moved forward again.

Christen fell in on their heels feeling foolish, but staying so close to the medic this time that he actually stepped on the poor man's heels twice. They drew abreast of the men of the platoon strung out in a line. The squad leaders converged on them and Adkins asked for a headcount. Each squad leader reported all accounted for, no casualties taken.

"Looks like we got their attention," Adkins observed. "But their hit and run tactics don't smell right. They gave up too quick. Let's move back through the area to look for what we may have missed."

The squad leaders slipped silently away.

CHAPTER 51

"*That was M-16 fire, Bo!*" Bubba whispered.

"It was so far away I couldn't tell," Allen whispered back.

"Sounded like a platoon throwin' down on a couple of snipers," Bubba insisted. "It's gotta be our guys up there. Maybe they've got a lead on us down here."

"They'll never find us buried down here like this, Bubba."

"Then we've gotta help 'em find us."

"How?"

"Hell, I don't know, Bo. *Think*! There's gotta be some way we can signal to 'em. We can't just sit around down here on our ass doing diddly-squat with them right on top of us lookin' for us, now can we?"

Allen lifted his head, his eyes alert. "How are we breathing, Bubba?"

Bubba frowned. "What kind of dumb ass question is that?"

"Look, Bubba, if we're buried, where is the air we're breathing coming from? Don't you see?"

"No, Bo, I don't see. What tha' hell are you talkin' 'bout?"

"I mean they've got to have some sort of a ventilation system. Fresh air has to come in to us and the carbon monoxide has to get out. If we can find out how they circulate the air, we can send up some kind of a signal through the exhaust system. Don't you see?"

"Yea, I think I see what you mean. Like a smoke signal or somethin', right?"

"Yeah, that's what I mean."

"But what if it's dark, Bo? We don't know night from day down here."

"I'm beginning to notice a pattern, Bubba. I've been watching the activity around us. When the others sleep and when they get up, that sort of thing."

"That might not mean much, Bo. The VC are as active at night as in the daytime—maybe even more active at night. That's when we both got our asses kicked, remember? How do you tell the nightshift from the dayshift, Bo?"

"Hell, I don't know, Bubba. It was just an idea. You said to *think*. Maybe we could send up a signal during both periods to make sure."

"We're only gonna get one chance to get it right, Bo, and how are we gonna create enough smoke to signal even if we know when to send it?"

Allen scowled. "I thought up the idea, Bubba. You figure out a way to do it!"

"Okay. So how do we find this circulation system?"

"Look for a change in temperature, Bubba. That will tell us when we're close to it. It's real cool down here. When they bring in the outside air, it should be warmer. Pay attention to that."

"You're smart, Bo. I'd never of thought of that: and another thing, if we create enough smoke, it don't matter where the exhaust system is. The smoke's gotta get outta here somewhere. If we fill the tunnel with smoke it'll find the exhaust port on its own."

"You're right, Bubba. That narrows it down to only two things: how do we create a lot of smoke and when do we know when it's daylight to do it?"

"Yeah. That 'bout puts us right back to where we started."

"Let's *think*, Bubba. *Think*!"

"I'm doin' the best I can, Bo!"

Chapter 52

Cai hurried to the operation's room when muffled gun-fire erupted near their south entrance, knowing Chien deployed snipers in the vicinity of each entrance to lure patrols away from the area as an added precaution against them discovering the tunnel complex even with the entrances backfilled. Chien stood before the map on the wall studying it as his aides updated information called down to them by the observers above ground. She moved beside him to study the large circle covering over a thousand meters depicting the main American base and the single dotted line that led to their south entrance.

"With what force do the Americans search, Colonel?" she asked, masking her eagerness.

"A small reconnaissance force," Chien replied, preoccupied with his analysis of the map before him. "It is thought to be only a platoon."

"My band could bloody them at this distance from their base before reinforcements could reach them," she suggested.

"Engaging them serves no purpose except to draw further attention to the area, Captain," Chien reprimanded her as the faint drumming of gunfire from the engagement tapered off.

Cai choked back her annoyance as Chien turned to an aide at his elbow.

"Colonel, the snipers drew the Americans off, but now they have turned back towards the entrance again."

Chien frowned. "Have them strike a second time."

"Yes, Colonel." The aide hurried back to his landline to issue instructions.

"This is most unusual," Chien observed.

"Perhaps they are simply returning to their base," Cai offered.

"Or perhaps they are looking for something specific …" he retorted, turning to her, his eyes accusing.

Cai bit her tongue and steadied the angry tremor coursing through her body. *Surely he was not implying that she was responsible for the Americans being here?* A strong flash of remorse flashed through her as she envisioned the mocking photograph she had left to taunt the Americans, which led to Kim-Ly's identification of her and the subsequent search for Thinh.

If a culprit existed who had led the imperialist's to this area, it was unquestionably Thinh!

CHAPTER 53

Christen crept along behind the platoon as they reversed their direction and swept back through the area they had just covered. Within fifty meters rifle fire sprouted from their rear, one round zipping so close to his head he again flung himself to the ground convinced the sniper was taking him personally under fire. Adkins quickly ordered the platoon to reversed course and they again attacked through the jungle towards the unseen enemy blasting away at them.

Christen kept up this time as Adkins strode upright at a steady pace through the thick growth. The men on the left side of Adkins fell prone and fired as the line on the right side of him lifted up and surged forward. After thirty yards, they fell to the ground providing covering fire as the line on the left rose up and raced thirty yards beyond them.

As Christen watched them execute the perfectly coordinated fire and maneuver tactic, he now understood how they were able to move so swiftly, though he was still disorientated and unsure of exactly what was occurring around him. He marveled at Adkins' cold reserve as he strode boldly ahead with the alternating lines of men rushing forward on each side of him in the roaring firefight. The man seemed to know no fear as he led his men by example, giving them courage with his own unflinching exposure to danger. He darted after Adkins, self-conscious of his own cowering progress, ducking and dodging through the thick vegetation as the rounds whistled overhead, envious of Adkins' daunting leadership.

He had often tried to imagine himself under fire. Now faced with the situation, he was less than pleased with himself. He had not anticipated the very personal essence of someone trying to harm him, or the helplessness of not knowing what was going on in the intimidating noise and confusion of battle.

Christen almost sagged in relief when the firing abruptly ended. He stumbled along at the rear as Adkins continued the sweep for another two hundred meters. When they received no additional enemy fire, Adkins reformed the platoon, turned them around, and swept back through the area again, this time without drawing fire.

Adkins then placed them in two columns and set a course for the firebase.

CHAPTER 54

"There it is again, Bo!" Bubba shouted with both fists raised in the air. "Tell me that's not M-16s firin' and a carbine or two. *Give 'em hell, guys!*"

The nearest guard rushed over and whacked Bubba across the head with his cane. "You no talk! You no talk!"

"*Fuck you, Gook-san*! That's our guys up there and they're gonna come on down here and kick your slope-eyed little ass! You hear me, fuck-face? They're gonna ..."

Both guards rushed to beat at Bubba as he rolled off his cot and under it in an attempt to ward off their blows, covering his face and head with his arms in the onslaught.

"You no talk! You no talk!" the guards yelled as they clubbed at him.

"Aw shit, Bubba!" Allen cried in disgust as he spread his arms and dived onto the attacking guards, bowling them over the top of Bubba's cot as he cowered under it.

The other Vietnamese in the room began yelling as Allen and the two guards rolled around grappling on the floor. Bubba rolled out from under his cot and jumped onto the pile of squirming bodies, yanked one of the guards cane from his hands and commenced to beat him with it as other guards ran into the room. Several of them pinned Bubba to the floor as he gnashed his teeth and tried to bite them.

Allen grappled with the other guard and grasped the man by the throat as the newcomers swarmed around him trying to pry his hands loose. Another man whacked him across his back with a cane, causing him to release his grip on the guard's throat. He rolled up into a fetal position as the others beat and kicked him until he blanked out.

When he came to, he was dizzily aware of two men dragging his limp body along a corridor. From somewhere in the distance he heard Bubba yelling above the resounding whacks of canes impacting on flesh.

His vision dimmed and all pain subsided.

CHAPTER 55

"The Americans are such fools," Cai observed as their snipers again engaged the Americans, who responded with spirited enthusiasm.

"You give our enemy little credit," Chien replied gruffly. "I fear that will be your downfall one day."

"The American dogs waste their bullets," she spat in disgust. "They exercise no moderation!"

"They have the finest supply system in the world," Chien replied. "They have no need to conserve as our own forces do. You would be wise to put aside your contempt for our enemy and study them. They have much to offer in the art of waging war."

"They are an Army of young pampered boys," Cai retorted. "They have little discipline and no culture. Their cause is unworthy and their low morale reflects such. They are not equal to our forces on the battlefield. Only their superior firepower makes them worthy adversaries."

"Your views reflect the rhetoric of a political officer from the North instead of a combat veteran who has engaged them in our glorious cause here in the South. It is ill advised to regard their youth as a disadvantage, when it is actually their strength. The Americans have proven themselves remarkably adaptable to our method of warfare and the resolve of their soldiers we face is strong. Their political system is their weakness. This is where we shall prevail. We will not win this war here on the battlefield. It will be won in their homeland by their inability to unite behind their soldiers to support the principles under which they were deployed against our people."

"I do not wish to challenge your wisdom, my Colonel," Cai replied stiffly as the muffled firing overhead ended abruptly. "I am but a simple soldier trained to drive our hated enemy from our land through battle. I do not know of their political system or their homeland weaknesses."

She turned and withdrew, furious with his rebukes.

CHAPTER 56

Christen straggled back through the concertina wire as the men dispersed into their interior fighting positions.

"What happened, Cap'n?" Pierce asked as he stumbled into the command bunker in near exhaustion.

"Damn if I know," Christen replied as he shed his web gear and hung his rifle off the back of a chair by its strap. "We got jumped two different times. Everything happened so fast and was so confusing, I stayed lost and scared shitless most of the time. I know one thing; these men know their business. I mean, they're pros. They were as calm as hell through it all. The G-3 wasn't kidding when he said he was giving us one of his best combat platoons."

"He gave you his *best* combat platoon, Captain," Adkins corrected as he entered the bunker. "I hope you REMFs didn't drink all the damn coffee."

"I just put on a fresh pot, Sarge," Howell replied. "Can I go out with you next time?"

"I reckon we'll take on another newbie since your Captain here earned his combat stripes today, and did a pretty decent job of it for his first time out."

"Sergeant, I swear, I've never been so confused," Christen allowed, the adrenalin still pumping in his veins. "I have no clue as to what was going on out there other than somebody was trying their best to kill me."

Adkins motioned as his squad leaders hesitated at the entrance to the bunker. "Come on in, damn it, and quit lurking around in the doorway like a bunch of stray kittens. Coffee's brewing, but these REMFs drink it pretty weak. Sit down over there at the table and mind your manners since we've got an officer present. Let's have a recap of the mission for the Captain here and see what we've learned."

Christen sat at the table with the squad leaders as Pierce and Howell took up positions on the cot to their rear to listen to the after action report. Adkins moved to the map on the wall and drew on it with a grease pencil.

"We moved in a U formation to this point here. We took fire from two carbines from this point here, which we maneuvered against to this point here, where they gave up the fight. We turned and swept back to here, at which time we again took fire from the same two jackasses from this point behind us right here. We turned and assaulted to this point here, where they again faded away. We then turned and swept back through the area, reformed, and moved back to the base camp on this route here." Adkins turned from his drawings and poured a cup of coffee. "So what did we learn?"

"We learned that the VC are still defending that position in the south," Howell offered.

"I wouldn't call it *defending* exactly," Sergeant Handler scoffed. "They didn't put up much of a fight. But they sure seemed irritated that we were there."

Christen looked at him in astonishment. "*That* wasn't much of a *fight*?"

"Heck no, Captain," Sergeant Fielding offered. "All they had was a couple of rusty old carbines and a pocketful of shells. Wait 'till you meet up with a group of real bad asses carrying AK-47s. They'll make you eat dirt and like it."

"They gave up ground too fast," Sergeant Gonzales observed.

"And then jumped us a second time after we turned back to sweep through the area again," Sergeant Brooks added. "They weren't *defending* anything with us going *away* from them. Mighty peculiar."

"All good points," Adkins praised. "We've got a weak attack; giving up ground too quickly; and attacking from the rear instead of defending from the front. What does it mean?" When no one answered, he grinned.

"As usual, I can see I'm the only real genius in the group."

CHAPTER 57

Captain Christen briefed the battalion commander and the S-3 operations officer on the afternoon's encounter with the enemy as Howell marked the four areas of concentrated contacts on the map. Christen stepped over to the map and continued.

"What we propose is an experiment, Sir. We would like you to send out one platoon to each of these four locations to the north, south, east, and west to see what happens. In addition, we would like to see another four platoons sent out at a forty-five degree angle in the middle of these four points to see if they draw fire."

The battalion commander pursed his lips speculatively. "I believe we can accommodate you on this, Captain, but what are we looking for specifically?"

"First, to see if you draw fire in these four areas, as we expect you will. Additionally, to see if you do not draw fire in the other four areas between them, as we expect you will not. This should confirm or dismiss our theory that these are protected areas of some sort. I have another request as well, Sir. My Platoon Sergeant has another theory he would like you to try out if you do draw fire. He wants your platoons to engage the enemy as usual. When the enemy slips away, he wants two of the platoons to then turn around and sweep back through the area they just covered to see if they draw fire a second time. He would like the other two platoons to continue the pursuit of the enemy as they normally would do."

The S-3 shook his head dubiously. "Why would he want them to cover ground they've already cleared, Captain? That doesn't make sense. Our mission is to engage the enemy and destroy him. I've never heard of abandoning the pursuit. What kind of crazy theory does your Platoon Sergeant have that would justify such an unconventional action?"

"He is convinced that the snipers employed there are what he calls 'Prairie Chickens.'"

The S-3 blinked. "And what is a Prairie Chicken, exactly?"

"According to Sergeant Adkins, it's a bird of some sort that lives in nests on the ground back in his native Texas. When a coyote comes near a Prairie Chicken's nest and threatens her young, the hen will run out in front of the coyote and act like its wing is broken. The coyote will chase after the hen, but each time he gets close enough to catch her, the hen flies off a short distance and fakes injury again. She does this in leaps and bounds staying just out of the coyote's grasp until she has lured him far enough away from her nest that she can then pick up and safely fly back, leaving the coyote far away."

The S-3 scowled. "Sounds a bit far fetched to me."

"Perhaps," the battalion commander mused. "But it is an interesting theory, nonetheless. Let me get this straight: your Sergeant's theory is that there is something in these four areas the VC feels the need to protect, and they do this by luring our patrols out of these areas in pursuit."

"That is his theory, Sir," Christen agreed.

"What happens if his theory is proven?" the S-3 asked.

"I would suggest we then concentrate on each of these areas to try to find what they are protecting."

The battalion commander nodded. "I like the plan, Captain."

"Thank you for your support, Sir, and so we don't get caught up in a friendly fire situation, Sergeant Adkins plans to trail along about an hour behind one of your platoons that will continue the pursuit on the same course as they took," Christen continued. "He wants to see if the Prairie Chicken returns to her nest after luring the coyote away."

The battalion commander chuckled. "I like this Sergeant of yours, Captain. I think he's officer material."

Christen grinned. "I'm not sure he would stoop to that level, Sir—he seems to hold a rather dim view of officers in general."

"I can't say as how I blame him with the crappy leadership we're dumping on our field troops over here. We're turning out boy scouts to lead men and rotating them out of the field as soon as they learn how to do their job, if they survive that long. It's the dumbest thing I've ever seen."

"I'll draw up the plans," the S-3 acknowledged. "We'll have the east and west sectors pursue, and the north and south turn back."

"Then I guess my platoon will take the eastern route one hour behind the initial platoon's sweep," Christen replied.

"Good hunting, gentlemen," the battalion commander replied. "Captain, I'd like you and your staff to dine with me tomorrow after this operation. We should have a lot to talk about one way or another."

"Thank you, Sir. It would be our pleasure."

CHAPTER 58

Chien sat alone at his table in the operation's room studying the large map on the wall as his staff updated the enemy movements. Cai and his other commanders sat at a larger table to his right. Small enemy units on the move saturated the map. The Americans appeared to be in complete disarray as they scattered in all directions without reason. It appeared they had no specific plan in mind other than to strike out blindly in search of targets of opportunity. Within an hour, the north sniper screen engaged the enemy to pull them out of the area to that entrance. Then the eastern sniper screen engaged the enemy, followed rapidly by the southern and western screens. Deep in their cavern, the muted sounds of rifle fire drummed all around them as staff members tracked their movements on the map.

Chien watched with pride as his forces deftly lured the Americans away. Trained by his best commander, they were operating with efficiency now as the clumsy American platoons lumbered after them like water buffalo chasing antelope. He yearned to be young again. He once jabbed and feinted at the French in such a fashion, loving the chase and the intoxicating high of combat. He ardently recalled his youthful days in the Viet Minh when he had proven his courage on the field of battle, his soul longing for the comradery of his men as they faced death together and made sacrifices for their cause. The higher in rank he climbed, the further he seemed to get from the fellowship of his warriors. It indeed was a lonely place at the top. One did not have the faithful friends or the bonds of trust forged only on the field of battle through shared hardship and mutual danger. At this level, he could trust no one and must suspect all who sought his favor. That was his greatest attraction to Cai in the beginning. She sought nothing of him, not even his companionship. She alone among his commanders attained her rank strictly on merit and not for her political favoritism or alliances with others in power. In the beginning, she alone served him without expectations of anything in return.

He was vaguely aware of the firing above them tapering off, first in one direction and then another until silence surrounded them. He watched absently as his staff updated the American positions on the map, nodding in satisfaction as he saw the eastern and western lines extending as they chased his invisible screen. He waited for the extensions of the northern and southern lines, frowning impatiently as the lines remained stationary. The ragged pitch of renewed fighting to the south puzzled him further. The American patrol of the day before had curiously reversed its course. Could they be doing so again? If so, why? It made no sense to him. Then the firing to the north started again. Both locations showed no movement by the enemy force as the eastern and western lines continued to extend. He walked to his map willing the lines to the north and south to extend.

He turned to the men operating the field phones in consternation. "What are the reported enemy movements?"

"Colonel, the force in the south has turned as they did yesterday. Our comrades are again engaging them."

"This is so to the north as well, Colonel," the second man reported as he held the receiver to his ear. "The Americans have turned back and our forces are reengaging."

"Our comrades to the east has broken contact and are returning to their positions, Colonel," the third man reported. "The Americans are continuing to pursue thin air."

"The west has broken contact and is returning to their position, Colonel," the fourth man reported. "The Americans are continuing in their pursuit as expected."

Chien stared at the map as his aides continued to draw the lines to the east and west away from the entrances and the north and south remained inactive. The firing to the north and south continued unabated. He watched uneasily as a second line of enemy march began dotting its way to the east along the same route as the earlier enemy force. What did this mean? They were obviously not reinforcements. Why was a second enemy detachment marching along the same route? This made no sense to him at all. He stared at the map in puzzlement as another line sprang up and moved westward much the same as the line going eastward, along the same route as the previous platoon's movement to the west. He checked the north and south. There were no secondary marches occurring there. He backed away from the map in astonishment to take in the big picture the map was telling him. It appeared like a starburst, with lines moving outward in all directions except the north and south. The secondary lines to the east and west were advancing rapidly behind the other lines in front of them. The lines to the northeast, northwest, southeast and southwest were streaking along as well. Above and in the distance the muted sound of the east engaging the secondary line advancing on them filtered down to them. The enemy lines farther out to the southeast began to curl back towards the east and collapse inward in an arc much like a flare returning to earth. He could see that his western screening force drawing the first American advance outward was now fading back into a trap as the first enemy advance now turned to sweep back at them. The west engaged the secondary advance and he had fighting on all four sides again. What did this mean? What were the Americans doing? He watched the western first wave turn and close in on the second wave, trapping his forces between them as the eastern waves had done to his forces there. Suddenly the southern and northern line began extending outward, following his sniper screen, but he realized in dismay that his screen was now backing into a wall of blocking forces provided by the Americans who had deployed in the quarterly directions to the northwest and southeast before turning to double back. Abruptly he saw the brilliance of the American plan and the cunning trap they had sprung.

He turned to his operation's officer in panic. "Break contact! Withdraw! It is a trap!"

The operation's officer stared at him. "But Colonel, our observers are isolated from our heavily engaged sniper screens! They can not give them your command!"

Chien turned back to the map and stared in horror as the lines converged on the front and rear of his entrapped forces, crushing them between their massive jaws of lethal steel. The eastern front firing died out. Two minutes later the northern front, then the southern front, and then at last the western front faded away like embers in the night as his brave soldiers were crushed between the two advancing lines.

He turned to his table and slumped at his desk staring at the map in disbelief as the American routes converged back towards their base after eliminating his sniper screens to the last man in the most tragic event he had ever witnessed.

He dropped his face into his cupped hands as the extent of the catastrophic event sank in. What he had just witnessed was impossible. It was as if the enemy had anticipated his every move. How could they have known? He lifted his head from his hands to stare at those around him, searching for signs of accosting demeanor. Only Cai dared meet his eyes as the others looked away in shame for witnessing his humiliation.

He rose abruptly and left the room for his quarters.

CHAPTER 59

"Sir, the final results of the mission are twenty-seven guerrillas killed, with eleven wounded and captured. Five additional suspects were taken who we believe disposed of their weapons prior to their capture," the S-3 completed his briefing in the packed command bunker.

The battalion commander turned to Christen and his crew. "Sergeant Adkins, I believe you've just given one Vietcong Commander his worst nightmare. You called it down to the last detail."

"Thank you, Sir, but I only had a theory. You devised the rollback plan that actually destroyed their snipers deployed against us."

"But it was a plan that could not have succeeded, Sergeant, unless your theory was correct. Any commander can defeat his enemy if he knows their battle plan. It was as if you were in his head. Now, gentlemen, I have some good French wine and some steaks grilling that are five inches thick. If you'll accompany me, I'd love to hear what you think our next plan of action concerning the protected areas should be."

Sergeant Adkins stood. "Begging your pardon, Sir, but I need to see to my men."

The commander grinned. "I figured you'd try to slip out of this, Sergeant, and I'll tell you why—because you're an honest to god *soldier*, son! Rest easy; right now, your men are savoring their own steaks and a ration of beer I had prepared especially for them. You come along with us and let them enjoy their meal and spirits. I believe they can survive a couple of hours on their own without you hovering over them."

Adkins nodded. "Thank you, Sir. I appreciate you looking after them. There's no way I could've choked down a steak while they were eating C-rations out of a can."

"And I respect you the more for that, Sergeant. Come along now and let's plan our next coup. Now that we've proven your theory that they're trying to protect something in those areas, we need to figure out a way to find it!"

CHAPTER 60

Cai watched Chien depart without remorse. With the defeat of his snipers, he no longer had a fighting force above ground with which he could oppose the American imperialists. He must now open at least one of the tunnels to deploy more of their forces from within the cavern. She meant for that force to be hers.

She hastened to Chien's chambers, where she swept aside the cloth covering to the candle lit room to find him lying on his cot with his hands folded on his chest as he stared up at the earthen ceiling.

"Why do you come to me?" he demanded.

"I come to volunteer my force to be dispatched to the surface to oppose the Americans, my Colonel."

"Why do you assume I will deploy additional forces against the Americans? Would it not be wise to allow them to tire and go to another area to plunder?"

"We must have forces on the surface to ensure they do not discover our entrances. This is a risk we cannot take."

"I have not sought your advice in this matter."

She softened her tone, her heart hammering with anticipation. "Nor do I seek to displease you by giving my counsel, my Colonel. But I do ask that my force be deployed if this is the course you choose. I... could depart in the early morning hours if you desire …" She waited breathlessly with the invitation hanging in the air.

"I will take your request under consideration," he replied after a pause. "You may go now."

"Yes, my Colonel." She turned to leave.

"I will visit you later," he said softly to her back.

"Yes," she answered, and swept through the door experiencing a delectable thrill. Chien was weak. She would conquer him with his perverse needs—and then dispose of him by leaving him sealed in this hated dark vault while she languished in the sun and slay their enemies at will. At last, she would be free of his strangling control and nauseating moderation.

Once her force was running free in the open air they would wreak havoc on the imperialist dogs. Yes, and they would take many prisoners in the process, she vowed as delicious swirls of anticipation swept through her. She would have no one to answer to in the matter of the prisoners and no one to control her movements or temper her tactics. Nothing could stop her now. She would slay them with vengeance by day and night until she had driven them from this sector in terror.

The Americans called her Tiger Woman. The name suited her, she decided. She would claw them and bleed them until her boundless lust for their blood was sated. Her bosom heaved at the prospect as she projected their cries of terror and imagined them pleading for their unworthy lives as she disemboweled them and soaked their blood into her skin. The foreign dogs would curse the day they used her so badly.

She bitterly recalled the French imperialists coming to her village. Five of them in an armored car enticed her close as her friend Kim-Ly held back shyly. When they grabbed her, Kim-Ly fled in terror, leaving her to her brutal fate at their hands. She suffered great pain and degradation afterwards as they used her horribly, often with two of them on her at the same time plundering her body until she could no longer physically comply with their demands. They then beat and used her in even more horrible ways.

Now they would feel the same pain in their bellies she had felt in hers as she pulled their intestines out with her bare hands. They would suffer the same shame she suffered as she exposed and castrated them. Ultimately, their souls would die in their bodies as her spirit had virtually died in hers when they smothered her helplessly under their overbearing weight while they satisfied their depraved lust within her. Nothing could stop her now from fulfilling the vengeance her inner psyche cried for.

Moreover, with this justice served, she would at last be safe from the clutching darkness that incessantly beckoned her since the day the imperialist pigs tossed her battered body into a ditch filled with slimy water. She shuddered as she recalled landing on one of the many bloated corpses left lying about, this one with its lips pulled back in a sardonic grin. As she disentangled herself from the rotting stench, she was mortified to find it was the carcass of her father, killed some four days previously and left to decay in the sun. She screamed incessantly as the darkness snatched her down into its bottomless pit, until somehow, she had managed to fight her way back up to the light. Now she was ever vigilant of the deep murkiness waiting for her.

Upon her release from this hated place, she could howl with the injustice of what they had done to her and her family in their once loving, tranquil life. She and her soldiers would come out of the ground like a swarm of wasps to cover the Americans in a cloud of stinging pain and confusion.

She savored the moment as she prepared for Chien's impending visit.

CHAPTER 61

A llen drifted into consciousness, growing aware that he was in a different ward now. It was still an infirmary, but not one with which he was familiar. He rolled his head to the right and saw a guard watching him. He propped up, swung his legs off the cot, and sat on the edge, steadying himself as waves of nausea engulfed him.

"You not move. You cause enough trouble for yourself for one day," the guard warned in remarkably good English.

"Where is Bubba?"

"He get shit beat out of him too. You not very smart, G.I."

"Is he hurt very bad?"

"He worse than you."

"You speak good English."

"I once work for you Americans. My American name is Joe."

"Why did you switch sides?"

"How you know I switch sides?"

"So you were a VC when you worked for us?"

The man stared at him passively.

Allen's hopes soared. "Are you a South Vietnamese soldier spying on the VC?" The man again gave no answer. "Can you get us out of here, Joe?"

A group of men entered the room and Joe stood. The man in the lead spoke and Joe turned to him. "You come! You crawl on hands and knees, American dog! You move!" Joe cuffed him on the side of his head and shoved him down onto his hands and knees as the group led the way. Joe nudged him to follow them. "Move, dog! You hurry! *Be humble, G.I.*" Joe whispered tersely as Allen crawled along, and then cursed at him and poked him with his cane until they entered the interrogation room where the colonel and his staff sat at a table, minus the evil woman who normally sat in her customary position on the end. Allen squatted before the table and waited.

"You break rule. You cause disharmony. Why you do this?" the colonel asked.

"They were beating my friend for no reason, Sir," Allen replied. "I was trying to get them to stop."

"You foolish man."

"Yes, Sir. I apologize for causing a disturbance."

The colonel nodded his head. Joe stepped forward, whacked him across the back with the cane, and stepped back. "You not be so foolish again."

"No, Sir. I won't. I'm sorry."

The colonel nodded again. Joe stepped forward, whacked Allen three blows across the back, and then stepped back as he cowered.

"You move. Move here." Joe poked him with the cane and guided him to the side of the room, where he again squatted. Bubba crawl into the room on his hands and knees as another guard prodded him along.

The colonel stared at Bubba as he squatted in front of the table. "You break rule. You cause disharmony. Why you do this?"

"I got carried away when I heard our men kickin' your gook asses," Bubba replied sullenly, his left eye swollen shut, tilting his head to see out of the right eye, also swollen and purple. "It seemed like the thing to do at the time."

The colonel nodded and the guard behind Bubba stepped forward and brought the cane down across his back as he cringed.

The colonel stared at him impassively. "You foolish man."

"Not as foolish as you're gonna be when I get my hands on you, fuck-face," Bubba snarled. The guard struck Bubba briskly as he cowered on the ground.

"Stop being stupid, Bubba, for god's sake," Allen called.

Joe stepped forward and whacked Allen across the back. "You no talk! You no talk!"

"Okay, okay, I'm sorry," Allen whined as Joe threatened him with the raised cane. "I was just trying to help."

"Be cool, Bo. I got this under control," Bubba called back as he regained his knees. His guard whacked him across the back again and yelled for him not to talk.

"You not show respect. You not obey rule. You must to show proper obedience." The colonel nodded and the guard stepped forward and methodically beat Bubba as he curled into a ball on the floor whimpering in pain.

Allen turned his head away, grimacing as the blows struck. When the beating stopped, Bubba lay unconscious. Two guards grabbed him by the arms and drug him from the room.

Joe poked Allen with the cane. "You come, dog. Move quickly."

Allen crawled in the indicated direction with Joe prodding him along cursing at him. Back at his cot, he lifted himself up and sat back. Joe settled down a few feet from him and looked over his shoulder to ensure no one was paying attention.

"You not dumb as I think. Your buddy stupid."

"If you're not really VC, can you help us escape?"

"Be patient. Be humble," Joe advised softly.

CHAPTER 62

After discussing the operation long into the night over their steaks and wine, Christen ruefully admitted he still did not have a clue as to what they were looking for.

The battalion commander turned to Adkins. "So where do you suggest we go from here, Sergeant?"

Adkins shrugged. "I admit I'm as stumped as everyone else, Colonel. For lack of a better direction, I guess we can search the sectors again. Captain Christen and Billy can accompany my platoon to the northern sector. I'd like a platoon from the company remaining behind to protect the firebase to reinforce us. Pierce and Howell can tag along with other platoons to the east and west sectors. Our basic plan if engaged should be for one platoon to pursue the snipers while the other stays in the sector to conduct an in-depth search for whatever these jokers are trying to hide. It's not much of a plan, but it's the best I can come up with under the circumstances."

"We've got nothing to lose," the battalion commander allowed. "Let's do it."

The following morning Christen followed Billy in his designated spot within the headquarters group of Adkins' platoon as the reinforcing platoon led the way, which would be the pursuit platoon if engaged, leaving them to search the area. As they neared the sector, firing erupted to their east. Adkins called a halt and squatted down as his squad leaders and the platoon leader from their reinforcing platoon converged around them.

"The bastards have upped the ante," Adkins observed.

"It's definitely more than a sniper screen," the lieutenant from the support platoon agreed.

Christen listened intently to the firing in the distance. "What do you mean?"

"They're better armed and they're standing and fighting, Captain," Adkins replied. "They've got AK's instead of carbines, which means a fighting force instead of a screening force, and the group on the right is a bunch of women. They don't usually make good snipers."

"How do you know they're women?" Christen asked.

"Listen to that group on the left, Captain," Adkins offered. "Hear the rhythm of their fire; short and fading back? Now focus on the group on the right. Hear the longer bursts? And they're pulling back slower than the group on the left."

Christen listened to the two different groups for a long minute. "I do hear a difference. I hope you aren't making fun of me. The one on the right is women? You can tell that by the way they're fighting? Why do they fight differently?"

Adkins allowed a wry grin. "Hell, Captain—I reckon because women are just more bitchy and stubborn by nature. Even you should know that."

Christen grinned. "You *are* pulling my leg, aren't you, Sergeant?"

"He's not joking, Sir," the lieutenant advised. "The group on the right is definitely women."

"We'll make an Infantryman out of you yet, Captain," Adkins encouraged. "Billy, why *do* your women fight differently?"

266

"Women not smart like man. They not like to give up what they have."

"See, Captain, even the VC agrees with me," Adkins teased.

"I not VC now," Billy insisted.

Adkins chuckled. "Yeah, right, and my grandmother don't dip snuff neither."

As the others laughed, Christen cocked his head to listen to the raging firefight. "Should we go help them?"

Adkins shook his head. "Naw, I figure the platoon leader's getting pissed off along about now. He'll be sprinkling some 105 rounds amongst them pretty soon. That'll put them on the run. Nasty shit when the artillery gets involved." Even as he spoke, a cannon boomed from the firebase, first one round, and then a half-minute later, a second round. After a short pause, the whole battery opened up in a reverberating barrage as they found the range. The firing to their east quickly dissipated and died out as the VC withdrew.

"I guess it's our turn now," Adkins warned. "Let's move out. Lieutenant, I expect you'll take fire in the next few hundred meters. If they get stubborn like that bunch to the east of us, drop some arty on them to chase them off. If they circle around you back to us, trap their ass between us like we did yesterday."

The lieutenant nodded. "You've got it, Sergeant. Let's rock and roll!" They dispersed back to their positions.

"Captain, stay up tight with me," Adkins ordered. "Billy, stay in my sight. You bic? If I have to come looking for you, I'm going to be pissed."

Billy nodded. "I be your shadow. I not lose sight of you."

Adkins stood. "Let's move."

Within fifteen minutes, the support platoon engaged in a huge firefight to their front. Christen hugged the ground grimly, now understanding AKs versus carbines as the rounds passed furiously overhead and zinged all around him, cutting leaves and chipping bark in a buzzing storm. Adkins had his platoon hold their own fire and let the support platoon in front of them handle the situation. Soon a single artillery round hummed overhead and impacted to their front. A short period later, a second round whistled over them and exploded. After another pause, a third round streaked overhead.

"That Lieutenant can't adjust artillery for shit," Adkins growled as a fourth round roared overhead, followed a few seconds later by the full battery firing. "About goddamned time he found the range," he griped as the ground under them trembled and billowing smoke filled the air ahead of them. "The rabbit's on the run and the hounds are giving chase. Let's slip in and see what we can find while they're jerking each other around."

For the next hour, they searched the whole grid foot by foot, finding nothing but a couple of abandoned spider holes and one wrecked hooch. As they probed, the western and southern forces engaged the enemy and sent their pursuit forces out while they searched their own areas.

Christen followed after Sergeant Adkins as he turned the platoon around and searched the area again, looking for anything that would merit their attention. They found nothing. Their support platoon returned in early afternoon and they split the sector and searched it a third time. Discouraged, they formed up and returned to the firebase as the other units drifted in as well.

In the debriefing, they discovered that none of them found anything of importance. The eastern platoon scored two enemy kills in their battle. The rest of them came up empty handed. Adkins settled his men in for the night and then entered the bunker. Pierce brewed coffee as they sat in silence at the table staring at the map.

Adkins sighed. "You know, we could be all wrong about this. It could be that the areas they engage us in are not the protected areas at all. The areas in between may hold the real secret and they let us walk through unopposed in order not to draw attention to them."

Pierce scowled. "If there's anything out there in the eastern sector, I sure as hell couldn't find it. We went over it with a fine-toothed comb. A few spider holes and that was it."

"Same here," Howell reported. "I personally looked under every rock and leaf out there. If something's there, I'm blind and stupid."

"It just doesn't make sense," Adkins mused. "They had a sizable force in each of those sectors today and they were not of the sniper class either. They were much better trained and armed, and they didn't fall for our enveloping tactics like the other group of amateurs did yesterday. Now why would they jump us in the exact same sector each time if they aren't protecting something? I think it's right under our nose and we're too dumb to see it."

"What should we do next?" Christen asked. "The battalion commander is depending on us to give him some direction."

"Damned if I know, Captain," Adkins replied. "I guess we search the areas in-between as a process of elimination, but I'm still convinced we're looking in the right area now. We just aren't seeing what's there."

CHAPTER 63

"Listen to me, Bubba," Allen insisted. "I'm telling you, Joe can be trusted. He showed me where to get out of here."

"Bo, you're full of shit. I'm tellin' you, you can't trust these fuckers. It's a trap."

"He says every few days the exit is opened for a few hours at night to let couriers in and out. He doesn't know in advance when they'll do it, so we have to be ready to go at any time. He says he'll give us a signal."

"And why would this gook son of a bitch help us escape?" Bubba demanded.

"Hell, I don't know, Bubba! I think he's some sort of a spy for our side or something. It's not like we can debate these things freely. He gives me information in bits and pieces."

"If he's a spy, why ain't half the Wolfhound Battalion diggin' their way down here to rescue us right now?"

"I don't think they let him out of here, Bubba. Their security is very tight. He wants us to get out so we can lead them back here, I guess."

"You guess, Bo? *You guess*? You're talkin' about gettin' our ass killed if you guess *wrong*."

"Have you got a better idea?"

"Yeah, that's why I got my ass beat half to death. I'm gonna fake injury 'til they relax their security and then I'm gonna make a run for it on my own."

"That's a hell of a plan, Bubba! You can't even walk right now, much less run, you dumb ass. I think you need a change of plans."

"I'm not as crippled as I'm pretending to be, Bo. When the time comes, I can hobble faster than you can run."

"I'm going to do this thing, Bubba," Allen insisted. "Are you in or out?"

Bubba hesitated and then sighed. "I guess I'm in, damn it. You're too dumb to make it without me."

"Okay, here's the plan. When Joe gives us the signal, we make a run for it. Joe says there are only a couple of guards at the entrance. We'll jump them and take them out."

"How much time is all this gonna take?"

"I figure not more than two minutes flat, Bubba. We've got to move fast before they have time to get organized and stop us."

"How many guards are up above us, Bo? What're we gonna find up there when we crawl out of this stinkin' hole?"

"Joe doesn't know for sure, but he thinks we'll mostly find a couple of workers up there to refill the hole."

"He *thinks* and *mostly*? There you go again, Bo. You fuckin' well *better* know what we'll find up there, or we're gonna get out ass busted for sure."

"You said there's nothing in life for certain, Bubba. You said sometimes you just roll the dice. It'll be night and that'll help us some."

"I wish you'd quit repeatin' every bullshit thing I ever said, Bo. It sounds dumb."

Allen smirked. "I wonder why that is, Bubba?"

Bubba grinned as they interlocked palms and thumbs. "If you get me killed, Bo, my Momma's gonna be real pissed at you."

"No way, buddy. I want some of those biscuits you promised. By the way, what was the name of that girl of yours again, Bubba? If you *don't* make it, I'll look her up on my way through Georgia too."

"Fuck you, Bo. You couldn't handle her. Our little Georgia peaches are too sweet and ripe for you corn-fed clods from Ohio."

"You no talk!" their guard ordered from his position near them.

CHAPTER 64

At 0230 hours that morning, Christen bolted upright and listened for a brief, grim minute to the carnage occurring to the west of them before rushing to the door of the bunker, his senses filled with dread.

"You shit's saddle up!" Adkins yelled as he rushed by. "The bitch is on the prowl again and those boys sound like they need help!"

Christen scrambled after Sergeant Adkins. "Where are you going?"

"To coordinate with the reaction force," Adkins yelled. "I'm going with them!"

"You're doing *what*!"

"Ain't that what we're here for, Captain?" Adkins answered as he darted in the door of the battalion command bunker.

"I figure you need some company, Lieutenant," Adkins advised the Reaction Force Platoon Leader, who was clustered before the map with the S-3. "We'll trail along behind you and provide rear security."

The lieutenant nodded. "Glad to have you along, Sergeant. We'll be pulling out in about two minutes. Be prepared to travel fast."

Christen dogged Adkins' heels as he hurried out. "Are you sure we want to do this, Sergeant?"

"You better sit this one out, Captain," Adkins replied. "It's subject to get real hairy out there."

"I'm going with you," Christen insisted, his heart pounding as the artillery boomed in support of the hapless men in the dark distance.

"Suit yourself," Adkins growled. "All right, you shit's! Form on me! We'll be tail-end-Charlie to the Reaction Force. Keep your head out of your ass and your eyes peeled unless you want to wear a body bag home. Let's move it!"

Christen darted into his bunker to grab his gear, his heart pounding.

In the distance the firing began to slacken, indicating the attack was virtually over before they could even clear the firebase.

CHAPTER 65

Cai stood in the middle of the ambush site glowing with satisfaction as the four prisoners knelt before her with their hands tied behind their back. One, wounded in the arm, appeared to be in shock, but two others whimpered fearfully as they eyed the knife glinting in her hand. She savored their extreme anxiety as they watched her soldiers administer to the eighteen bodies strewn around them. Over half of the American pigs had escaped in the initial stages of the assault, a disappointing, but tolerable ratio due to her depleted force. Pockets of scattered resistance broke out around her as her soldiers pursued the fleeing survivors. They would account for more; perhaps even take additional prisoners. She shuddered with anticipation.

After leading her band to the surface the previous morning, they spent an exhilarating day skirmishing with the Americans. At dusk, she positioned her scouts around the perimeter of their base to follow their ambush patrols. She selected this group as the most vulnerable. She studied the young men at her feet, enjoying their desperation. They were just boys, really. They knew nothing of war. Chien made them out to be worthy warriors serving a decadent political system that flaunted its vast powers but was ultimately incapable of uniting behind its unprincipled causes. She knew them to be merely puppets of their pathetic leaders, following mindlessly where led, fighting without passion, groveling and begging for mercy when conquered.

She considered them naïve representatives of a spoiled, pampered nation of soft, ignorant people who had never known hunger, or seen their families destroyed, or suffered the depravities of an unjust, corrupt political regime. They cared for nothing but their own comforts and pleasures. They were coarse, vulgar, and arrogant. They deserved to die like the dogs they were.

She lifted the knife from her side and moved to the first kneeling man as he shrank back. She trembled eagerly as she grabbed a handful of his hair and twisted his head up, forcing him to look into her eyes as he wept. She smiled as she drew the blade across his stomach, gasping as his warm blood washed across her hand. She took her time carving him, relishing the feel of the blade slicing cleanly through his skin as he moaned. She released him and watched him twitch as he clung to the life draining away from him. She turned to the second man in line as he cowered back from the blade in her hand and worked on him methodically as the one next in line groveled. The third man attempted to bite her hand as she grasped his hair and slit the crotch of his pants open to expose his genitals. She laughed when he attempted to spit in her face as tears of anguish washed down his cheeks while she castrated him, but the effort fell short and the spittle hung off his chin. She disemboweled him with one slow sweep of the blade and ended with two quick punctures to his eyeballs, leaving him wheezing as she moved to the last man in line.

"I'll be waiting for you in hell, you fucking bitch," the man, much older than the others, with chevrons on his sleeves, gritted. "Because that's where you're going. I'll be waiting for you there, you little bitch. Go on, kill me, you fucking slut. One day we'll meet again. The fucking devil himself can't save you from me. I promise you that, you sick, depraved little cunt. Kill me, bitch. Take your time and enjoy it. Then multiply everything you do to me a million times and that's what I'm going to do to you for eternity while we burn in hell together."

She paused as she held the blade against his stomach. She had never experienced such lack of fear in a person before. She tilted her head, confused, searching for the terror in him, but finding nothing but hate directed back at her from his black eyes glinting with the yellow light of the American flares floating overhead. The effect sent a chill trickling through her. She stepped back from him filled with uncertainty as a distant, dreadful memory darted out at her from the indistinct, forbidden recesses of her mind.

"Don't you dare leave me alive, you cunt! *Kill me*! Do you hear me? *Kill me*. You bic? I want another day with you! *Kill me and send me to hell to wait for you*!" he raged at her.

She stepped back from the man with the yellow glint in his eyes as horrifying recall surged to the forefront. She flung the knife aside and turned to Le Loi, shuddering. "Assemble! We go now!"

Le Loi raised his rifle. "I will shoot him."

She stared in fascination at the man who had no fear. "No! Leave him!"

Le Loi hesitated. "But Captain, we can not take the prisoner with us. We have no place to hide him. He will only slow us down."

"You will obey! Leave him!"

"Is this wise, Captain?"

"Let us go now!" She backed away from the man as he cursed and raved at her, begging her to kill him, and then turned and fled as his shrill voice taunted her, chasing her into the night.

She stumbled along filled with anxiety. The man with the glittering eyes filled with hate confused and frightened her. No one faced with certain death failed to show their fear, but he had no fear, of this, she was certain. He begged her to die. He *wanted* to slide into the eternal darkness. *He promised to wait there for her*!

Unnerved, she hurried past those near the end of her rapidly withdrawing force, wanting to surround herself with her comrades to ward off the man and his flickering yellow eyes seeking the eternal darkness. She had never sought death, though death welcomed her when the pain and humiliation of her ordeal with the Frenchmen drove her into the darkness. On one occasion, when several of them were tearing at her body at once, she withdrew so deep into the darkness she had trouble finding her way back. Afterwards, she kept the darkness behind her and backed into it with her face towards the light. She never sought the total darkness as this man was so want to do. This demon man begged to go there. He promised to meet her there. She had spent the years since the ordeal avoiding that cold, empty place. She could not allow him to pull her back down into there!

She panted with fear as they slipped through the night, turning her eyes to the flares overhead, seeking light and warmth to chase away the cold tremors sweeping through her. The man's taunting voice echoed in her mind as she imagined his flickering eyes of death staring into her own. She knew those eyes from before, involuntarily crying out at the memory of the first Frenchman carrying her into the dark interior of the armored car, forcing her onto her back, tearing at her clothes as she fought. His eyes glinted and flashed from the small yellow light inside the armored car as he laughed and his heavy form crushed her, filling her with pain as he pinned her to the floor and thrust into her, staring into her eyes with the wicked yellow glint reflecting from his own.

Tears streamed down her cheeks as she pushed faster into the night, fleeing from those evil eyes. A hand grabbed her arm and jerk at her. She cried out and lunged away, clawing at the man grappling with her.

"*Captain*! *Captain, it is me, Le Loi!*" her lieutenant soothed as she lashed out at his grasping hands. She sagged against him, gasping in gratitude, burrowing into the safety of his encircling arms.

As the panic subsided, she grew conscious of her soldiers turning their heads, shocked by her collapse into Le Loi's arms, confused by her display of weakness. They had never known her to cling to a man. They had never known her to show compassion, as she had to the prisoner she left behind. They had never known her to show fear or emotion, as she was doing now, trembling and sobbing as Le Loi held her in bewildered confusion.

She jerked free of his soothing embrace, shamed by her weakness, and stalked off as they straggled after her in a disorderly cluster.

Behind her, she could still hear the devil man shouting at her from the darkness and shivered as she hurried forward.

CHAPTER 66

A fter forty-five minutes of hard, harried marching, what they found left no doubt in Christen's mind that Tiger Woman had struck for the fifth time. Surprisingly, they discovered one lone survivor amongst the grisly dead, tied up and raving like a lunatic. Unable to make sense of his ranting, the reaction force lieutenant called for a dust-off to extract him.

Afterwards, the lieutenant and Adkins placed their platoons in defensive positions around the perimeter of the ambush site to wait for morning amid the occasional bursts of fire erupting around them as elements of Tiger Woman's force happened upon fleeing survivors from the American platoon. The rising sun brought Pierce, Howell, Billy, and the Battalion Commander out to the site to document Tiger Woman's latest atrocity. Adkins' platoon again drew the grisly task of loading the dead into body bags and placing them onto the choppers. With the job complete, the two platoons quickly regrouped and divided into chalk orders for the extraction back to the firebase. The reaction force flew out first, as Adkins' platoon waited for the next lift.

"Thank god we're flying," Christen said wearily as he stood with Adkins at the far right of the six lines of men spaced down the LZ. "I'm too pooped to walk."

"It's been a long night, Captain," Adkins agreed. "My men are mighty touchy right now after cleaning up that crazy bitch's leavings again."

"I'm not a coward, Sergeant, but seeing what she does to our men unnerves me."

"Mustang Alpha One-Six, Rough-Rider Six, over."

Adkins reached for his handset from his radioman and keyed the mike. "Rough-Rider, Mustang Alpha One-Six, over."

"Roger, Alpha One-Six, one of our birds is sickly and needs to shut down. We'll be coming in with five lifts instead of six, over."

Adkins keyed his mike. "Roger, Rough-Rider, be advised that will leave us five men short unless we can fit an additional man into each of the other five birds, over."

"That's a negative, Alpha One-Six; we're pulling max torque getting off the ground as it is. We can split into two lifts for you, if you prefer, over."

Adkins looked down his line of exhausted men. "Bring in the whole lift, Rough-Rider, and then send a bird back for me and my headquarters group, over."

"Roger that, Alpha One-Six. We'll send a bird back for you pronto. ETA zero-five minutes, over."

Adkins keyed his mike twice in acknowledgement and sighed. "Shit, we can't get a break."

"That's kind of risky for us to stay out her all alone, isn't it, Sergeant?" Christen asked wearily.

"In the mood my men are in, it's a risk worth taking, Captain," Adkins replied. "Shift on over there with Sergeant Brooks' squad and have him send one of his men over to wait with me."

"I'll wait with you," Christen replied.

"You just said it was risky, Captain. You're beat and you'd just be in my way if the gooks come half-stepping around and we have to hightail it out of here."

Christen smiled grimly. "I'll wait with you, Sergeant."

Adkins nodded. "You've got the makings of an Infantry-man about you, Captain. It's a shame you're wasting away up there in the head-shed drawing on maps with crayons."

Christen grinned. "Us REMFs aren't all bad, Sergeant."

A few minutes later Christen watched the line of aircraft appear on the horizon and turn towards their LZ. As they slid down in front of them in a torrent of noise and flying debris, Adkins' men surged forward and clamored aboard. Seconds later they were climbing skyward, leaving him, Adkins, the RTO, and two other men standing in the eerie quiet of the deserted LZ.

"Let's move back into the wood line," Adkins ordered. "Keep your eyes peeled. We're sitting ducks for the next twenty minutes."

After an interminable wait, Adkins' radio crackled. "Mustang Alpha One-Six, Rough-Rider Six. I'm inbound to you now, zero-five out, over."

Adkins keyed his mike. "Roger, Rough-Rider, LZ cold, over. Okay, let's go get a cold one," he called as he led them out into the LZ.

As the chopper flared to land, a volley of automatic fire erupted across from them, sending them ducking for cover in near panic.

"*Shit! Breaking off! Taking fire! Taking hits!* Rough-Rider is breaking off, Alpha One-Six! I thought you said the LZ was cold, over!"

Adkins led them back into the trees in a mad scramble and reached for his handset from his RTO crouching beside him. "It *was* cold, Rough-Rider. I guess they decided to welcome you in style, over."

"Welcome, my ass! They shot the shit out of me. My gauges are fluctuating and I have a high-pitched vibration in my pedals. I hate to do this to you, buddy, but I've got to nurse this baby back to base."

"Roger, Rough-Rider. Good luck, over."

"Good luck to you, buddy. Rough-Rider, out."

"Fuck!" Adkins groaned. "I don't need this shit!"

Christen swiped the sweat from his face and tried to calm his pounding heart. "What do we do now, Sergeant?"

"We find an alternate LZ and call for another extraction." Adkins switched frequencies on his radio and keyed his mike. "Flat Iron, Mustang Alpha One-Six, over."

"Mustang Alpha One-Six, this is Flat Iron, over."

"Roger, Flat Iron, LZ hot, Rough-Rider returning to base with damage. Request alternate LZ for single bird emergency extraction, over."

"Roger, Alpha One-Six. Standby, over."

"Hold your fire!" Adkins hissed as an AK-47 spat a long burst at them from across the LZ. "The fuckers are probing. Don't give away our location."

"Mustang Alpha One-Six, Flat Iron, over."

Adkins keyed his mike. "Flat Iron, Alpha One-Six, over."

"Nearest alternate emergency LZ is Rosebud, coordinates Golf Zulu 184375, over."

Adkins shook his map open and plotted the coordinates. "Roger, Flat Iron. Estimate two-zero mikes to LZ Rosebud, over."

"Roger, Alpha One-Six. Wild Thing will be standing by for extraction in two-zero minutes. Contact this frequency, over."

"Roger, Flat Iron. Alpha One-Six, out."

Adkins took a compass reading against his map and folded it into his pocket. "Let's go, and keep your head out of your ass," he cautioned as he led them swiftly away from the LZ.

CHAPTER 67

Cai huddled in the corner of the safe hooch unable to sleep, her arms hugging her body as she shook. After her scouts reported the Americans were patrolling away from the tunnel entrances today, she sent only a light screen of her soldiers out to harass the Americans at the ambush site and grudgingly allowed the remainder of her force the day to recuperate after almost twenty-four hours of continuous combat operations.

She sat meditating, her thoughts wandering back to the devil man at the ambush site who she allowed to live because he filled her with such dreadful trepidation. The man who dragged her into the armored car had the same haunting eyes filled with flickering yellow light. This new demon's complete lack of fear for the hovering darkness unnerved her. The thought of him waiting for her there drove sharp spasms of alarm through her. She did not believe in heaven or hell in the conventional form the Catholic missionaries taught when she was an orphan. She did not accept that such a God as they portrayed would ever let one of his children experience what she had gone through. Therefore, if He did not exist in His bountiful garden, their Devil did not exist in his burning hell.

She did not like to revisit her past. There was little there she found pleasure in, but she did know the forbidding darkness existed because she had been there. She did not ever want to return. The thought of spending eternity with the demon man and his flashing yellow eyes who showed no dread of that sinister place terrified her. For him to have no fear must mean that he had been there as well—and longed to return there to await her. Surely, his promise to torment her for all of time was pointless now since she had not harmed him, and even stopped Le Loi from doing so.

She shuddered and switched her thoughts almost joyfully to Le Loi holding her in his arms as the waves of panic swept over her. She had eagerly sought the safety of his embrace. It was a sensation she once associated with her father, though she could not recapture the precise essence of his affection. Le Loi's arms served to ward off the evil around her. He did not hold her as her husband Pin and Colonel Chien held her. His arms were gentle and caring. He had been strong when she was weak, fearless when she was consumed with fear, calm when her emotions were in turmoil. The memory stirred currents within her that she did not understand, but longed to experience again.

On impulse, she stood and walked down into the bunker where Le Loi slept, a small room five feet below the surface built to provide protection from bombs and artillery, such as all peasant hooches in the embattled countryside employed. A small candle flickered in the corner spreading soft light as Le Loi slept on a straw mat on the floor, his breathing belying exhaustion. She sat beside him staring into his passive face for a time. Impetuously, she stretched out beside him and slid back against him. He turned in his sleep and draped his arm across her, hugging her to him. Delicious swirls of contentment coursed through her as his breath tickled her neck.

The encompassing security swept over her again as she pushed closer and closed her eyes, gratefully to sleep without dreams in his protective arms.

CHAPTER 68

Christen eased through the thick brush and paused behind Sergeant Adkins as he knelt on the edge of a small clearing scanning it with care against his map to ensure they were in the right location. The other men fanned out behind them facing outward, rifles poised, faces grim.

Adkins held his hand out and keyed the transmitter when his radioman handed him the handset. "*Wild Thang, Mustang Alpha One-Six, over*," he whispered.

"Mustang Alpha One-Six, this is Wild Thing, over," the static filled voice responded from the receiver at his ear.

Adkins winced and lowered the volume before pressing the transmit button. "*Wild Thang, we have arrived at LZ Rosebud. Verify coordinates, Golf Zulu 184375, over.*"

"Roger, Alpha One-Six, standby, over."

Adkins double-clicked his transmitter button in acknowledgement and handed the handset back to his RTO.

"This doesn't look like much of a pickup zone," the RTO whispered as he swiped at the ribbons of sweat draining down his cheek in the sweltering humidity.

"The rotor-heads pick the PZ's, not us," Adkins whispered back as he studied the dense foliage around them for signs of pursuit. "This is one of the emergency pickup zones for the long-range recon patrols. The Sneaky-Pete's are half-crazy anyway. Who the hell'd want to slip around and report on enemy locations without engaging them in combat? Screw that shit."

"Well, whoever selected this as a PZ was an idiot," the RTO argued as he studied the preplanned extraction point. "It ain't big enough to set a helicopter down in."

"Mustang Alpha One-Six, Wild Thing, over."

Adkins keyed his mike when the RTO handed him the handset. "*Wild Thang, Alpha One-Six, over*."

"Alpha One-Six, Wild Thing is inbound to extraction point Rosebud, ETA one-five mikes. Coordinates Golf Zulu 184375 confirmed, over."

"*Wild Thang, Alpha One-Six, roger, out*," Adkins whispered.

The minutes ticked by in the hush as they waited, their senses strained to the breaking point as they surveyed the tangled growth around them for sight or sound of the pursuing enemy. In the distance a muffled explosion, the product of a hand-grenade Adkins had hastily strung along their route with the pin attached to a small strand of wire at ankle height to slow the enemy advance and compel them to move with greater caution, announced their pursuers were still on their trail.

Adkins grinned. "Well what do ya know—we got one of the bastards!"

After an interminable wait, the receiver crackled. "Mustang Alpha One-Six, Wild Thing, over."

Adkins keyed his transmitter. "*Wild Thang, Alpha One-Six, over*."

"Roger, Alpha One-Six; SitRep, over."

"*Situation stable, LZ cold, over*."

"Uh, Alpha One-Six, if I may be so impolite as to inquire, *why are you whispering, over*?"

Adkins grimaced. "*Enemy in close pursuit, over.*"

"Alpha One-Six, are you going to get my tail feathers plucked out, per-chance?"

"*Sure hope not, Wild Thang.*"

"I sure hope not, too, old buddy. We're in vicinity of Rosebud now. Pop smoke, over."

"*Uh, I'd rather not throw smoke, if it's all the same to you, Wild Thang.*"

"Damn—just how close are those jokers to you, anyway?"

"*At least a couple hundred meters, over.*"

"Oh, shit! I've got a bad feeling about this. What's the deal, did I hit on your baby sister stateside of something?"

"*Not that I know of, Wild Thang, but if you'll pull our ass out of here, I might consider introducing you to her some-day.*"

"I'll hold you to that, buddy. I can't pick out the LZ. In fact, I don't see anything that even resembles an LZ. I need smoke, over."

"*I hear you to the south of us. Keep coming and I'll vector you. The LZ is tight, over.*"

"Roger, I'll continue north and do a fly by. Let me know when I'm overhead and I'll circle back around, over."

"*Roger. You're approaching Rosebud now. Turn right. You're getting closer, closer, you're overhead now, Wild Thang!*"

"That's not an *LZ*! You've got to be shitting me! I can't set down in there."

"*I didn't pick it—some other fool did. I told you it was tight.*"

"Roger that, Alpha One-Six, but it's not as tight as my puckered asshole. Sorry, buddy, but you're going to have to

295

move to an alternate LZ. We'll never make it in and out of there, over."

Firing erupted behind them as one of their men opened up on full automatic with his M-16. An enemy AK-47 returned fire, the rounds clipping leaves overhead. A second and third enemy weapon joined the first in a jarring roar.

"What going on down there, Alpha One-Six?"

Adkins turned up the volume in the carnage as his men returned fire. "We have enemy contact, Wild Thang! Looks like they've caught our scent! Abort the mission and return to base. We'll try to shake them off our tail and find another LZ, over."

"*Aw shit*! Hang on, buddy, we're coming down for you!"

Christen turned and fired into the brush behind them with the other men as the three enemy AKs barked back in a brisk exchange. Wild Thing's helicopter appeared overhead and sank down into the tiny clearing, the rotor wash whipping at the encircling jungle, blowing the undergrowth back in a swirling circle.

"Let's go!" Adkins yelled as he lay down a barrage of blistering covering fire for the others as they ran for the LZ.

Christen dropped his empty magazine from the bottom of his rifle and slammed another home as he backed into the LZ, spraying the jungle to cover their withdrawal. He dropped the second magazine, and dug for a third as he turned and ran for the chopper, leaping aboard as it lifted off the ground.

Adkins jumped up on the skid and tumbled in after him, bowling him over into a tangle. Two VC emerged from the jungle firing at them, the bullets slamming into the chopper with solid wallops as the Plexiglas windshield shattered. The door gunner on the right opened up on the two VC, sending them scrambling back into the tangle of green as the aircraft shook violently and the cargo bay filled with a tempest of flying leaves and debris.

Christen belatedly realized the limbs had swung back over the top of them when the aircraft set down, and now the blades were chopping through the overhead foliage like a giant lawn mower as they pulled straight up. He grabbed for anything he could hang on to in the violently lurching aircraft as the impact tossed them around in back like mannequins.

A VC rushed out into the clearing firing point-blank at them, the bullets punching jagged holes through the skin of the shuddering aircraft as it tore a path through the encircling limbs. The door gunner swung his muzzle around firing blindly at the man as leaves and chips of wood flew around their heads. They popped out of the top of the encroaching trees and the nose of the aircraft dropped as they accelerated rapidly away with their skids inches above the treetops, still shimmering severely as the pilot fought the controls.

"*Yeeehawwww!*" Adkins yelled as he swung his muzzle around and emptied the magazine on full automatic into the tops of the trees below them. "*What a fucking ride! Let's do it again!*"

Christen stared at him apprehensively as he untangled himself and stumbled up onto his knees behind the pilots, trying to control the quaking in his legs and the stutter of his thundering heart. He removed his helmet and jammed a headset hanging on the back of the pilot's seat over his ears.

"Are we okay?" he asked fearfully as the aircraft turned almost sideways.

"With all due respect, you're one bunch of crazy fuckers, Captain!" Wild Thing admonished hotly through the intercom as he fought the cyclic jutting up between his legs. "Brace yourself, we're losing power!"

They staggered through the air like a wounded duck in spite of the pilot's best efforts as Christen keyed the mike on his headset. "Are we going to crash?"

"We're losing our tail rotor!" the pilot panted as he fought the gyrating controls. A large rice paddy appeared to their front with a dirt road running through the middle of it. "I'm going to try and make a running landing! Prepare your team for impact! *Mayday*! *Mayday*! *Mayday*! *Wild Thing going down, Grid 4097*! Grid 4097, Wild Thing, going down! *Mayday*! *Mayday*! *Mayday*!"

"*We're going to crash*!" Christen yelled to Adkins beside him.

Adkins turned to his men. "*Grab hold, guys*! *We're going down*!"

Christen braced himself against the back of the pilot's armored seat as the aircraft drifted down in a slow descent and lined up with the dirt road.

The skids touched down in a whirl of dust and bounced back into the air as the pilot fought the controls. The helicopter steadied as they dropped back down and hit hard, bounced again, and then settled down in a grinding dust storm as it skidded down the road swaying from side to side. When it shuddered to a halt, the pilots frantically shut down electrical switches as the crew chief and door gunner ran to open the pilot's doors and grabbed the fire extinguishers.

"That wasn't much of a crash, Captain," Adkins complained. "I expected something a little more dramatic, didn't you?"

"You really worry me at times, Sergeant," Christen stuttered as he expelled his pent up breath.

Wild Thing removed his helmet and glared over his shoulder at them. "My commander is going to have a case of the red ass, for sure. Your baby sister better be worth all this."

Adkins grinned. "Actually, Wild Thang... I don't have a baby sister ..."

The pilot shook his head with a disgusted scowl on his face. "*That* figures!"

Adkins dispersed his men around the aircraft for security as the pilot called for a rescue team. Christen stumbled around the helicopter on trembling legs surveying the damage, finding the tail rotor missing from the tail boom, leaving only twisted metal in its original mount. Numerous dents and gouges from the limbs decorated the main rotor. He counted eleven bullet holes in the fuselage, with half of the windshield missing. Unable to restrain himself, he dropped to his knees and heaved up the C-rations he'd had for breakfast as the others pretended not to notice.

Soon, two Cobra gunships appeared overhead to fly cover for them. Ten minutes later, two Hueys flew out with Big Bird to recover the aircraft, the crew, and their team. As they circled down to them, Adkins turned to Warrant Officer Hubbard and offered his hand.

"Thanks, pal. Sorry about your little bird."

Hubbard scowled. "Do me a favor, Sergeant: the next time you guys overload you ass, lose my call sign. Okay?"

Adkins laughed and waved as he led his team to their waiting aircraft.

CHAPTER 69

Cai awoke in Le Loi's arms encased in contentment. She knew by his breathing he was awake. She shifted to face him. The hard maleness of his body poked through his thin silk underpants. His anxious eyes drifted down to watch her fingers at work as she deliberately unbuttoned her blouse to expose her breasts. She cupped his maleness in her hand as he stiffened, his breathing intensifying. She rolled him over on his back and slipped her bottoms off as she covered him, enjoying his moan of anticipation.

"Colonel Chien will ..."

"He is of no concern," she assured him.

Later she bathed in the stream near them and returned to the safe hooch at dusk to change into her tiger fatigues. As they ate the boiled rice and fish her staff prepared, Le Loi glanced at her cautiously. She looked boldly into his eyes. She had never wanted a man before, but she had enjoyed mating with him and regretted when he shuddered and rolled away at the end of their coupling. A stirring of desire filtered through her as she recalled the event, a sensation unknown to her until now. When she stood, he took up her rifle and handed it to her, his hand lingering over her own as she took the weapon from him.

"Assemble, Lieutenant," she ordered softly. "We go now."

"Yes, my Captain."

He turned to the door and her gathering soldiers as the dying sun dipped below the horizon.

CHAPTER 70

Christen sat in his bunker in a reasonably euphoric mood as the adrenaline seeped out of his still-frazzled body after their harrowing rescue. Life had never seemed sweeter than at this moment. Coffee had never tasted better. The C-ration pound cake he munched on from the can had never been as moist. He stifled the inclination to stand and dance a jig as Master Sergeant Pierce briefed them on the results of the battalion's search of the areas between the four sectors while they were away evading the enemy. He half listened, the vestiges of his numb mind vaguely registering that only one element drew fire in a brief engagement, and that the S-3 was certain nothing of importance was in any of the sectors after their through search. He poured himself a second cup of coffee and dumped a liberal dose of sugar in it, marveling that he was still alive, as Pierce concluded the briefing.

"Any questions, Cap'n?"

He shook his head absently, unable to focus his thoughts.

Adkins pulled off one of his boots and examined a blister. "So what the hell are we missing out there?"

Pierce shrugged. "Damn if I know."

Christen was certain their conversation had some relevance, but he couldn't quite grasp the issue at hand as he replayed the harrowing flight and improbable rescue through his mind over and over again in amazement.

"What do you think, Billy-Bob?" Adkins asked.

Billy scowled. "I think Devil woman very close."

"Are you okay, Cap'n?" Sergeant Pierce inquired, watching him pensively.

"His nerves are still a little on the frayed side," Adkins advised. "He'll come around with a good night's rest."

"Why did she leave that prisoner alive?" Howell asked. "Why tie him up and butcher everyone around him?"

Adkins slid his naked foot back into his boot. "Doesn't make sense to me either, but he wasn't much help to us with all his mumbling and carrying on about seeing somebody in hell."

"Do you think she's trying to tell us something by leaving him alive?"

Adkins scowled. "You guys give me a headache with all your analyzing bullshit. A gunship probably flew over them or something and she didn't have time to finish him off. There's no message."

"We're *supposed* to analyze everything," Pierce argued. "That's what we're trained to do. You seem to be doing a good bit of analyzing of your own lately."

Adkins grimaced. "You guys have got my mind all screwed up now too. In the good old days, I just stomped around out there and killed whatever I found. Now you've got me looking under bushes for a fucking banshee."

"Knock-knock," the battalion S-3 announced as he paused at the opening to the bunker.

"Come on in, Captain," Specialist Howell called. "We're having coffee and bitching about being stupid. Want to join in?"

"Thanks, but we're having a bitch session of our own over at Operations," the S-3 replied as he entered the bunker. "I have a strange message for you from one of my platoon leaders."

"A message?"

"A Vietnamese farmer approached one of our platoons here in this location." He pointed to a spot on their map. "He stated that his name was Tran Duc Thinh. He requests that you meet him at that same location in the morning. He said you were to bring him back here to the firebase for interrogation. He said you would understand. Do you know what he's talking about?"

Howell sat up quickly. "That's Cai's uncle!"

"Who the fuck is Cai?" Adkins asked.

"Tiger Woman," Pierce answered. "We offered him a reward for information on her."

"Why didn't your platoon leader bring the little fucker on back in with him?" Adkins demanded of the S-3.

"He insisted that he would only deal with Captain Christen," the S-3 replied.

"He *insisted*?" Adkins growled. "Who the fuck's running this god-damn war anyway? Fucking gooks don't *insist* on *anything*. Especially *Viet*-fucking-*Cong* gooks."

"Calm down, Sergeant," the S-3 ordered. "The platoon leader radioed back for instructions. I told him to leave him in place until I could figure out what this was all about."

"You did the right thing, Sir," Sergeant Pierce soothed. "This man could hold the key to finding her. You might have compromised him if you did it any other way than the way he wants it done."

The S-3 glared at Adkins. "Does that meet with *your* approval, Sergeant?"

Adkins sighed. "Sorry, Captain; guess I'm just a little frustrated."

"Apparently we all are," the S-3 snapped. "Let me know your operation plan." He stared at Christen for a moment. "What's wrong with him?"

"Oh, he's still a little frazzled after the helicopter crash today," Pierce replied.

The S-3 shook his head and hurried out of the bunker.

Pierce clapped his hands. "This could be big!"

Adkins rose and studied the location on the map. "Can we trust that jackass? He could be luring us into an ambush."

"I can't say if we can trust him or not—he's a Vietcong suspect, but I *know* he wants that reward," Pierce replied.

"A suspect?" Adkins glanced at Billy. "He's a slope ain't he? Of *course* he's VC."

"*I* not VC," Billy insisted.

Adkins smirked. "That's too bad—our body count is lagging."

"Knock it off, guys," Pierce urged. "We're *supposed* to be on the same team."

"*Are* we on the same team, Billy-Bob?" Adkins asked.

"We same team," Billy confirmed.

Howell studied the map. "We know Tiger Woman is in this area after last night. Thinh is fifteen clicks from his village. He has to have information for us to come this far to find us."

"How the hell did he know you were even here?" Adkins asked.

"Damn good question," Pierce replied. "Do you want a support platoon to accompany us to go get him?"

Adkins shook his head. "It's only a couple of clicks from here. We can move faster without them. But I'd like a standby reaction force in case Billy's little pal tries to pull a fast one on us."

"He not my pal," Billy objected.

"We need to make it look good," Adkins continued. "Once we locate and capture him, we should probably continue on to another objective and do a search. It'd look suspicious if we just marched out there, grabbed him, and headed straight on back here." He poured himself a cup of coffee and headed out of the bunker. "I need to see to my men. Put the Captain to bed and keep an eye on our pet gook here."

"I *not* pet gook," Billy admonished.

"Sergeant Adkins is just yanking your chain, Billy," Howell soothed. "He's only joking with you."

Billy sulked. "I *hope* it joke."

"Here you go, Cap'n." Sergeant Pierce took Christen by the arm and led him over to his bunk. "Let's get you all tucked in for the night."

Christen realized he was exhausted and meekly allowed himself to be put to bed, his eyes closing before his head hit the coarse fabric of the cot, still unsure of what had transpired on this most unforgettable day.

CHAPTER 71

Cai spent a long night picking their target and moving her force into position around the Americans. However, one of her new half-trained soldiers stumbled into a bush in the darkness and alerted them. They blew their claymore mines and a bitter fight ensued. With the surprise lost, they quickly withdrew in the face of the American's superior firepower and the artillery soon raining down on them. She lost five men killed and six wounded in the encounter. Though they inflicted casualties on the enemy as well, they could not determine the number. It did not matter, for in her mind, it was another abject defeat. Strangely, she felt no bitterness at the lost opportunity to punish potential captives, only rising warmth with the prospect of being alone with Le Loi as they dispersed back to their scattered day positions to rest.

Le Loi took her hand without comment and led her down into the tiny underground bunker. She slipped into his arms and lay back as he stroked and disrobed her, relishing the feel of his hands on her body, surprised by the pleasure it brought her. When he finally took her with tender ardor, she cried out as her body responded to his thrusts with a throbbing ecstasy such as she had never imagined possible. When

Le Loi collapsed on her in shuddering gratification, she held him as he lay on her gasping for breath, enjoying the feel of his maleness twitching inside her as she stroked his damp, matted hair, more content than she had ever been in her life.

CHAPTER 72

Adkins led them back to the firebase in the early afternoon after they collected two other detainees along with Thinh, one before they picked him up, and the other on their way back, blindfolding each man and tying their hands behind their back. They placed all three in the middle of the platoon perimeter and then led the first decoy inside the bunker to subject him to thirty minutes of questioning by Billy and Howell concerning local VC activity in the area. The man gave them no useful information and was led back out as Thinh was brought inside. They removed his blindfold and gathered around as he blinked his eyes to adjust to the dim light.

"Do you have information for us?" Christen asked.

Howell translated. "He says Cai is in the area," Howell reported and paused as Thinh continued to speak. "He says he plans to lure her to his hooch in the next few days."

"How does he plan to do that?" Adkins asked.

Howell and Thinh exchanged dialogue. "He says he will tell her that a messenger has come to meet with her from the North with information on her son."

"And what happens then?" Adkins persisted.

"He says we will need to lay a trap for her. He says she will not come alone and that we must be prepared for this."

"Ask the fucker how he knew you guys were here to begin with," Adkins demanded.

Howell translated and then turned back to them. "He says he saw Captain Christen in one of the aircraft the day we flew in to build the firebase. He says he expected to meet with Cai on that day, but that he was forced to return to his village because of all of the Americans. He asks why we are here in this place?"

"Tell him that's none of his damned business," Adkins replied. "Ask him how we're supposed to know when this Cai bitch is going to come to his hooch so we can trap her?"

Howell translated. "He says to look for his ox cart in front of his hooch each morning. When we see it gone, it will mean that she will come on that day."

Christen nodded. "We can fly a reconnaissance aircraft near his hooch each morning to look for the ox cart."

"Tell him we need to know exactly when she is there," Adkins continued. "We need another signal when she arrives." They waited while Howell and Thinh exchanged dialogue.

"He says Cai will come in his ox cart with others disguised as peasants. When the cart stops at his hooch, it will be Cai and her escort. He wants to know when he will get his reward."

"Tell him I will be with the force that comes for her," Christen replied. "I will make a positive identification. I will have the money with me and deliver it to him once we have captured her." After a brief exchange, Howell interpreted.

"He says she will die before capture. He says it is important that we leave none of her escorts alive."

"We will ensure no one is left behind," Christen replied.

"No. It important all die," Thinh replied directly to Christen. "No capture. All die."

"We can't kill them if they surrender," Christen argued.

Thinh turned to Howell and exchanged an extended dialogue. "Sir, he says that the VC have extensive intelligence gathering methods. He says that if we put her or one of her escorts in a POW camp the VC will know he betrayed them and they will execute him. He can not take that risk. He says that all must die or he can not do this even for the money we are offering to pay."

"There is no way I can guarantee him that all will die," Christen argued. "If they surrender or are wounded, we must take them prisoner."

Howell and Thinh again talked. "Sir, he insists we use only American soldiers in the operation. He says there are many spies in the ARVN forces and he does not want them involved. He also wants you to assure him that you will leave any prisoners you take with him. He says if you cannot guarantee him that you will kill them, then we must allow him to do so."

"This is not something we can agree to, Cap'n," Pierce advised. "That's against the Geneva Conventions and would be akin to murder. There's got to be another way."

"I kill prisoners for you," Billy volunteered.

"We'd still be a party to it," Pierce insisted.

"He's right, Billy-Bob," Adkins agreed. "Nobody likes killing gooks more than me, but I'd have to shoot you myself before I let you murder them in cold blood. Of course, I could do that *after* you dispose of them. That'd give us one more body count."

Billy shrugged. "No can do then. No profit in that."

"So what do we do if one of them surrenders or is captured?" Christen asked. "How do we insure Thinh's safety?"

"Sir, what if we take him into our protective custody if a prisoner is taken?" Howell suggested.

"That might be feasible," Christen agreed. "But then what would we do with him?"

Howell translated and then listened to Thinh's response. "He wants to go to America."

"*Shit!*" Adkins scoffed. "I'm ain't taking that little commie fucker home with me!"

"Tell Thinh we will place him in our custody if prisoners are taken until we can figure out what to do with him," Christen instructed.

Howell translated. "He says he wants your word that if a prisoner is taken he will go to America."

"I don't have the authority to make that decision," Christen argued. "But I can guarantee him a safe haven somewhere. That's the best I can do."

"I'll hide in Thinh's hooch and waylay her when she arrives," Adkins suggested. "Under the circumstances, I really don't foresee any prisoners being taken, so that ought to solve the problem."

"We don't know how many will escort her," Christen argued. "It's too risky."

"Our best chance at her will be with someone on the ground when she arrives," Adkins insisted. "We can't afford to blow this opportunity."

"I'll go with you too," Howell offered. "I speak the language and I'd be in a position to help identify her."

"No disrespect intended, Specialist," Adkins replied. "But you've never been under fire before. It's a different matter when you're faced with the reality of taking a life. There's a better than even chance you'd freeze up and not be able to pull the trigger. It happens all the time."

"I go with you," Billy offered grimly. "I pretend to be messenger from North."

"That might work," Adkins agreed. "The two of us ought to be able to handle up to six of them with surprise on our side."

Thinh jabbered and Howell translated. "He says he is agreeable to Sergeant Adkins and Billy accompanying him to meet Cai. He says it is time to return him to the other prisoners and for us to watch for the ox cart to leave the front of his hooch."

"Tell him that on the morning we see the ox cart missing, a small American patrol will sweep through the village and past his hooch," Adkins instructed. "Billy and I will drop off and hide in his hooch to wait for her to appear. The Captain here and other forces will fly in by helicopter once the shit starts."

Howell translated. "He says that is acceptable to him. He is concerned that the other Americans will shoot him by mistake."

Adkins nodded. "Tell him that I will protect him from the Americans as long as he's on the up and up, but that if he's not square with us, I'll be his worst fucking nightmare."

"He says we have a deal. If all are killed, he will get the reward of 50,000 piaster. If prisoners are taken, he will get the money *and* we will protect him."

"We have a deal," Christen confirmed.

"Get him back outside and bring the last guy in," Adkins ordered. "Let's make it look good."

They replaced Thinh's blindfold, led him outside, and brought in the third man for questioning. Forty minutes later, they released all three through the wire and watched them hurry away from the firebase.

"Let's go brief the battalion commander," Christen ordered when they were out of sight. Fifteen minutes later, he wrapped up his briefing to the small, select group in the battalion command bunker. "Are there any questions?"

The battalion commander turned to Adkins. "Son, you put one in that bitch's ass for me, you hear me?"

Adkins nodded. "It'll be my pleasure, Sir."

The battalion commander put his hand on his shoulder. "I wish it was me going in there instead of you. Do us proud."

Adkins nodded. "If she drives up to that hooch, it'll be the last ass-end of a water buffalo she'll ever see."

"I don't doubt that for one minute, Sergeant. Good luck and good hunting!"

"Thank you, Sir." Adkins led Christen, Pierce, and Howell out. When they settled in at their own bunker with cups of coffee Christen turned to Adkins.

"I've got to fly out and brief the CG. How do you visualize this operation from beginning to end, Sergeant?"

"I'll hide until the cart arrives. Thinh and Billy will be visible. She may even send scouts in first to check the area out. When Thinh greets her, I'll step out and blast her. From there it will degenerate into a dogfight. I'll hold on until you and the cavalry arrive."

"Do you intend to give her the opportunity to surrender first?" Howell asked.

Adkins shook his head. "Not a chance. Let's not fool ourselves. This is an assassination mission, pure and simple."

"That's pretty cold hearted," Howell observed.

"That's why I'm going to be there and not you," Adkins replied. "I'll hit them while they're still on the cart bunched together and unable to maneuver. My platoon bloodied her a few weeks ago, and the platoon last night gave her a stiff upper jab, but this time around, I'm going to put her down for keeps."

"You not say how much you pay me for this," Billy reminded them.

"The money thing is between you and the Captain," Adkins allowed. "But you coming out of this alive is between *you* and *me*. You bic?"

Billy grinned. "I bic. You not think I VC now?"

"Hell, I *know* you're VC. But for this mission, I'll consider you a mercenary."

"What mercenary mean?"

"A soldier for hire," Adkins said.

"You trust me now?"

"As long as I've got my rifle trained on your back."

"You funny, G.I."

"Do you trust me?"

"As long as my back not turned to you."

Adkins grinned. "Then we understand each other."

Pierce laughed. "You two make a lovely couple."

Billy grew sober. "Thinh very dangerous if things go wrong."

Adkins nodded. "I agree. Keep a close eye on him when the shit starts. If he even *looks* like he's going to betray us, don't hesitate to take him down."

"We'll be three minutes from the ground and another minute or two getting to you after we land," Christen reassured them.

"Five minutes can be a lifetime, Captain," Adkins warned.

Christen nodded. "I need to get back to Cu Chi and get this mission approved."

"I've got a chopper standing by, Cap'n," Pierce replied.

CHAPTER 73

O ne of her female soldiers awakened Cai shortly after noon from a sound sleep in Le Loi's arms. She washed her face and donned her black peasant's disguise before accompanying the woman up from the underground bunker into the safe hooch to meet with the courier waiting for her. The man bowed to her as she approached.

"What information do you bring me?" she asked as one of her soldiers handed her a cup of tea in a chipped china cup.

"I come from the village of Ly Van Manh. Your Uncle, Tran Duc Thinh, instructs me to arrange a meeting with him immediately if possible. Your Uncle has a visitor from the North who desires to meet with you in a matter concerning your male child."

"Why does this messenger from the North not travel here to meet with me?" Cai demanded.

"Your Uncle instructs me to inform you that it is deemed unsafe in this area due to the Americans. He will arrange for a cart to pick you up and return you back here. Your Uncle feels it is most urgent to arrange this meeting as soon as possible so that the messenger may continue his journey and complete his other duties."

"Inform my Uncle to send the cart for me in the morning," she instructed the courier in annoyance.

"I will obey," the courier replied. He bowed and departed.

She sipped her tea. This was most unusual. It could only mean that harm had come to her son, perhaps a disease, or the American bombing in the North. Her husband's parents lived on the outskirts of Hanoi. The Americans had recently stepped up their bombing in that area. Or perhaps her in-laws were ill and could no longer care for the child since they were growing old. If this was the case, her husband had many relatives in the area that could care for him. They knew she was a commander of distinction in the Southern Liberation Forces and surely would not expect her to return to the North to care for a child she had little empathy for and rarely thought of now. Surely, a simple return letter would suffice to deal with this troublesome issue.

Though she wished the child no harm, she did not feel any anxiety concerning his health or wellbeing. If some tragedy had befallen him, that would be unfortunate, but well outside of her scope to deal with here in the South. She experienced only annoyance for the time required to meet with the messenger, which would serve to dilute her energies in dealing with the American dogs here. It would have been simpler for the messenger to travel here to meet her. Thinh was most inconsiderate to waste her time instead of that of the lowly messenger.

She would reprimand him for this oversight when she met with him.

CHAPTER 74

"That pretty much sums up the situation, Sir," Christen finished his briefing to the general and his assembled staff.

The G-3 chortled as he clapped his hands. "By god, I never thought your little team could pull this off!"

"You have done a magnificent job, Chris," the general agreed.

"Thank you, Sir, but the hairy part is still to come. I'm really torn about putting Billy and Sergeant Adkins in that hooch with Thinh, who may or may not be on the up and up. I think this is for real, and I agree our best bet is to have someone on the ground in place when she appears, but I'm concerned that if anything goes wrong they will be on their own until we can ram an assault force in there to help them."

"This Sergeant Adkins has proven quite capable of handling himself in difficult situations, Captain," the G-2 argued. "He's the natural choice for this mission. This is too important to risk on chance."

"There's no question Sergeant Adkins is the best candidate," the G-3 concurred. "Under the circumstances, I don't think he would hesitate to strike first, and from all indications, he's cool as a cucumber under fire."

"He's very good, Sir," Christen agreed. "The Battalion Commander out there thinks he's officer material and would like to have him reassigned to his battalion when this operation is over."

The general arched his eyebrows. "From the way he operates, he'd be a credit to the officer's corps."

"We'll have a shooting war between our two battalions if Colonel Hawkins tries to steal him from Colonel Moore," the G-1 advised as the staff laughed. "He thinks highly of this sergeant as well. He won't even let me assign a new lieutenant down there because he's afraid I'll ruin his best platoon."

"Is this our best plan of action then, gentlemen?" the general asked as they settled down.

The G-3 frowned. "It's risky, Sir. But it would put one of our men in place to kill her, or at least to pin her down until our assault force can get there."

"How much exposure would this Sergeant Adkins face?" the general asked.

"Sir, he would face anywhere from an estimated four to six men, or more likely women, to include Tiger Woman. He would have her uncle, Thinh, with him, and the Kit Carson scout, Billy."

"One American soldier facing the most vicious small unit commander we've ever encountered in this war, and three to five of her handpicked bodyguards who would undoubtedly die for her," the G-2 mused. "And his backup is one VC suspect and one VC defector."

"Colonel Hawkins says he can land his whole battalion around them in minutes; five minutes at the outside," Christen advised.

The G-3 shook his head. "That's still a pretty gutsy call."

"I think it's worth the risk, Sir," the G-2 urged. "We can't afford to pass up this opportunity."

The general looked at Christen. "And this Sergeant volunteered for this mission, Chris?"

"Yes, Sir."

"Would we be better served to put several men in there with him?"

"Yes, Sir, we would. But he thinks we would also run the risk of tipping our hand if we put too many men in there, Sir."

"If this Sergeant survives this, I want to personally pin a medal to his chest," the general stated in the silence. "And I might even throw in some lieutenant's bars in the process."

"Then it's a go, Sir?" the G-3 asked.

"You tell Colonel Hawkins I said he better put his *whole damned* battalion on the *ground* in *three* minutes flat *or else!*" the general ordered. "Understand?"

The G-3 grinned. "Begging the General's pardon, Sir, but you don't cuss."

"*The hell I don't,*" the general insisted as his staff stifled their laughter.

CHAPTER 75

With the emerging morning light, Cai reluctantly left the warmth of Le Loi's arms to bathe in the nearby stream. She consumed a hurried breakfast of rice and fish, and then selected four of her female soldiers for escorts. They dressed as peasant women for the journey and hid their AK-47 rifles under the straw in the cart when it arrived an hour after sunrise. Le Loi appeared and insisted on driving the cart for her himself, and left Thinh's driver to await their return.

She settled down in the straw in the back and dozed blissfully as the cart bobbled along to the village of Ly Van Manh.

CHAPTER 76

"Captain, wake up!" Howell shook Christen's shoulder roughly.

Christen sat up to find the sun barely peeping over the eastern horizon.

"The cart is gone, Sir!"

Christen jumped to full awake with his nerves jangling. "Get Sergeant Adkins!"

Howell clapped his hands in anticipation. "He's on his way, Sir! Today's the day we bring that bitch down, Captain!"

"Things were quiet last night," Pierce said, handing Christen a cup of coffee. "She must be licking her wounds after that platoon caught her and her monkeys sneaking up on them the other night and gave her the worst of it for a change."

Christen placed his hands on Billy's shoulders and looked him in the eye. "Billy, you take care of yourself and our Sergeant out there."

"You never say how much you pay," Billy prompted.

"How much do you want?" Christen asked.

"I mercenary soldier today. I want 150 piaster."

Christen blinked. "A hundred and fifty—that's *nothing*."

"It enough for this mission. But you not tell Sergeant Adkins this. It just between us. Okay?"

Adkins entered the bunker and headed for the coffee pot. "What's just between you two?"

"Billy and I just set his fee for today's mission," Christen replied.

"Uh huh. About 5000 piaster is all he's worth, if you ask me," Adkins grumbled. "And that's only if I come back alive. By the way, on the off chance I don't and he does, one of you shoot him for me, will you?"

Billy faked a scowl. "You so funny, G.I."

Adkins sipped at his coffee and studied him. "Billy, Specialist Howell here got you some extra-small jungle fatigues you can wear so they'll think you're an American when we sweep through the village. You stand out like a sore thumb in that ARVN uniform. After we get in Thinh's hooch you can change into these so you'll look like a dink from the North." He held up a set of black peasant's garb. "Sergeant Pierce, once Billy and I fall out at Thinh's hooch, you and the platoon will continue on to the next checkpoint. Sergeant Handler will be in charge. They know how to handle themselves if you come under fire."

"I'm sure I'm in good hands, Sergeant," Pierce reassured him.

"The choppers are due in half an hour to lift us out. Let's get our shit together and get this show on the road. Good luck with your insertion, Captain. Billy and I'll be waiting for you to bail our ass out."

"We'll be there for you," Christen assured him. "You can count on it."

"Well, okey-dokey then, let's rock and roll!" Adkins allowed as he turned to the door. "Let's not keep this fucking little vixen waiting."

"Good luck!" Christen called after him.

"Luck only applies to horseshoes and amateurs," Adkins scoffed as he departed.

Forty-five minutes later, the choppers inserted Sergeant Adkins and his platoon on the outskirts of Ly Van Manh. They conducted a routine search of the hooches as they moved past the disgruntled men, women, and children huddled in the center, and continued on to Tran Duc Thinh's hooch on the outskirts of the village, where Sergeant Adkins and Billy slipped unnoticed down into his small underground bunker as the platoon, with Master Sergeant Pierce, continued on-ward. Billy changed into his peasant's garb and settled down with Thinh to sip tea near the entrance to the hooch as Adkins hid just inside the opening to the small underground bunker to their left, relinquishing the next move to Tiger Woman.

CHAPTER 77

Cai awoke when Le Loi stopped the ox cart, forcing her mind back to the present as she surveyed her surroundings, reluctantly shaking off the remnants of her of dream of lying in Le Loi's arms and basking in the warmth of his appealing embrace. Her escorts looked around warily as she stood and stretched, surveying the small wooded area located several hundred yards from Thinh's hooch, eagerly anticipating her meeting with the messenger so she could return to the safe hooch with Le Loi, relishing the pleasure he would give her upon their return.

"Captain, I will continue on with two of our guards," Le Loi prompted. "You and the others wait here until we ensure it is safe."

"There is no need," she replied impatiently. "My uncle would have sent a courier if he deemed it unsafe."

"A peasant informed me that an American patrol was in Ly Van Manh earlier this morning," Le Loi advised. "We should use caution."

"Let us continue," she ordered. "We waste unnecessary time."

"Then let us keep our weapons close at hand as a precaution," Le Loi insisted.

John W. Huffman

Le Loi placed his rifle at his side as she and the others propped their AKs against the rails of the cart within easy reach. When satisfied with their preparations, Le Loi prodded the ox forward. As they rounded a bend in the dirt road, they saw Thinh and one other man sitting at the entrance to his hooch drinking tea. The two men stood and watched their approach from the wide doorway. When their cart drew up in front of them, Thinh turned his head to his left and spoke. Instantly Cai realized this was all wrong because the man with Thinh was on his right

"*Prepare!*" she ordered in alarm.

Her soldiers swung their weapons up and outward. In the same instant, an American soldier materialized at the lower left edge of the wide door in a kneeling position with his rifle to his shoulder. A ripping roar accompanied the flashes sprouting from his rifle. The Viet man with Thinh stood and fired a pistol at them. A bullet tore at her arm even as her own rifle spit out a lethal answering burst. Her escort opened up in a roaring jar, each side firing point-blank into the other from thirty yards distance. Cai flinched as splinters flew into her face from the wooden rail in front of her. One of her escorts crumpled beside her and a second spun and collapsed. Two simultaneous punches caught her hard in her stomach, knocking the breath out of her with the force of their impact.

The American spun backwards as spurts of dirt kicked up around him. Thinh snatched up a rifle and fired upon the Viet man with the pistol, sending his body flying backward. The American rolled over and turned his rifle on Thinh, firing a burst into his back as Thinh attempted to flee. Blood and flesh spewed outward from Thinh's chest as he crumpled. The American swung his rifle back to them firing on full automatic. Another of her soldiers crumpled beside her.

A burst of fire from her remaining escort sent the American rolling for cover behind the thatched wall of the hooch as he attempted to reload a magazine into his rifle, the rounds kicking up dust around him. Le Loi prodded the ox frantically as they pulled away from the hooch. A line of helicopters descended near them as Cai's knees buckled under her. She collapsed against the splintered rail as Thinh crawled drunkenly towards the heavy brush at the side of his hooch. She tried to tell her remaining soldier to kill him for his treachery, but she could not summon the breath to speak. She looked down at the blood spreading across her stomach, and then at her three soldiers lying near her with blood seeping from their wounds. She looked back at the hooch as the cart jostled away and saw the American stumbling after them, dragging one leg behind him, shooting at them as they fled. Her last soldier fell across her as the American's bullets riddled the cart and pieces of wood splintered around her. Le Loi turned in his seat and fired a long burst. The American spun to the ground. She could no longer hear the discharge of the weapons above the roaring in her head. Her vision faded as a heavy fatigue engulfed her.

She briefly regained consciousness lying on her back in heavy jungle with Le Loi's palm over her mouth, his eyes inches from her own staring down at her fearfully. American voices shouted nearby as men crashed through the dense undergrowth around them. Burning pain throbbed in her stomach and arm. Le Loi placed his lips on hers, bringing warmth and security.

She closed her eyes blissfully.

CHAPTER 78

Christen stood behind the podium with a heavy heart as the general staff waited expectantly after he'd flown back to Cu Chi minutes before, bone tired and covered with grime after spending the day with the assault force.

"Sir, I can't tell you what went wrong." He looked the general in the eye as he spoke, tears brimming in his own. "Sergeant Adkins was barely conscious when we got there. He said something alerted them. We found the cart about two hundred yards from Thinh's hooch. It held four female bodies. We found some bloody bandages in the jungle near the cart, but the others got through us somehow, most likely by hiding in the brush as we ran past them in our haste to get to the hooch. I'm sorry to report that we failed, Sir... that *I* failed."

"Are you certain none of the four women you found in the cart was Tiger Woman?" the G-3 asked in the hush.

"There is no doubt in my mind that none of them were Tiger Woman," Christen replied. "Sergeant Adkins felt sure he hit her. There's a chance that she may have been seriously wounded due to the large amount of blood in the cart and the bandages found in our search of the surrounding area."

"What did Sergeant Adkins say happened?" the G-2 asked.

"Sir, he said he fired on the cart and struck several of the occupants as planned before one of them caught him flush with their counter fire. He said that when he went down, Thinh turned on our scout, Billy, and shot him. He said he then fired on Thinh as he attempted to run away. We found Thinh's body in the foliage beside the hooch."

"Did he say specifically that he hit Tiger Woman in the exchange?" the G-2 asked.

"He said he thinks he got her, but in all the confusion, he couldn't be sure. He took a round in the chest and two in his legs in the exchange. He died in my arms while we waited for a medevac. Sir, I bear the full responsibility for this failure."

"Don't carry the guilt of this operation on your shoulders alone, Chris," the general admonished quietly. "We knew it was a risky plan. We all carry the burden of its apparent failure. We owe a debt to that fine young man, who never flinched in his duty as he saw it. For all we know, he succeeded in killing her and they carried her body off to keep us from knowing."

"I pray that to be so, Sir." Christen struggled to regain his composure. "He was one of the best soldiers I've ever known."

"Ensure he is cited for his valor, Chris," the general ordered.

"Yes, Sir, and I would also like to write his parents. I owe them that much."

"You may correlate your letter with my own," the general approved.

"Thank you, Sir."

"What is our next move?" the G-3 asked in the silence.

"Sir, at this moment, I'm not thinking clearly enough to give you a recommendation," Christen replied. "I'm not a drinking man, but tonight I'm going to get drunk. Tomorrow I'll regroup and recommend a new course of action."

"I'm not much of a drinking man either," the general replied. "But on this occasion, I think I'll make an exception. I have a very old bottle of bourbon that somebody gave me that I have been waiting for the right occasion to open. I propose a farewell salute to Sergeant Adkins. Will you gentlemen join me?" The general retrieved the bottle from his desk as an aide produced paper cups and passed them around.

The general lifted his cup. "Gentlemen, I salute Sergeant Adkins! May we never forget his last full measure of devotion to our country!"

"*Here—here*! *To Sergeant Adkins*!" the staff saluted as they raised their cups and tossed the whisky back.

"Thank you, gentlemen." The general slumped back into his chair as the staff settled back around the conference table. "Chris, you may be excused now. Please take the bourbon with you and make good use of it."

Christen stumbled to his office and collapsed into his chair behind his desk, thankful Pierce and Howell were still out in the field, needing this time to himself. He pulled the cork on the bottle and poured himself a shot in his cup, which he lifted high.

"Here's to you, bitch. If you got away, I promise I will hunt you down and kill you or die trying in the process." He downed the shot and poured another, which he lifted high as the liquid burned its way down into the pit of his stomach. He focused on the coffee pot sitting cold on the burner, recalling the horrible brew Adkins had made and his complaint that he didn't have any bourbon to cut it with.

"Here's to you, Sergeant: a finer solder has never served our nation." He toasted the air as the tears trickled down his cheeks and downed the shot. He poured another.

"And here's to you, Billy. Regardless of what you were in the past, you were a true patriot to your country in the end." He downed the shot and poured another, which he lifted in toast.

"And here's to me: for I will carry the guilt of this day to my grave!"

CHAPTER 79

"Colonel, Lieutenant Le Loi requests to speak to you," the operator called from the table after the southern line buzzed. Chien sat his teacup down and stood as he surveyed the map before him on the wall. All was quiet. The Americans had flown out of their base early this morning to some unknown destination and returned several hours later. There had been no other activity in his sector during the day, which gave him comfort where Cai was concerned. He walked over to the operator's desk and picked up the receiver.

"Yes?"

"*Colonel, my Captain is wounded!*" Le Loi shouted. "*She is in grave danger! Please, we must get her inside the tunnel so she may receive proper medical attention!*"

Chien's stomach clutched as his mind reeled. "*How is this so, Lieutenant!*"

"*Please, Colonel! We have little time to help her!*"

"*I will open the entrance!*" Chien slammed the receiver down. "Open the south entrance immediately!"

Men rushed to the entrance to pull back the dirt as Chien hurried to watch, fighting the building nausea in his stomach.

CHAPTER 80

"You go to toilet now," Joe ordered as Allen and Bubba sat on their cots.

"I don't need to take a crap," Bubba retorted.

"You go now!" Joe insisted.

"*This is it, Bubba!*" Allen whispered as they crawled towards the small room that held the chamber pots. "*They must be opening the entrance.*"

"Oh, shit!" Bubba whispered back. "I think you're right, Bo!"

"I'm scared shitless," Allen warned. "But I'm ready to get out of this hole or die trying."

"There's no turning back, Bo! It all comes down to this, right here and now!"

"We've talked about it enough! Let's do it!"

"Good luck, Bo. I mean it."

"Same to you, Bubba. No hesitation, remember?"

"Yeah—we leave each other behind if we have to, right?"

When they crawled into the chamber room, Joe pulled two AK-47s from under some cloth in the corner. He handed them an extra clip of ammo and two grenades apiece.

"You wait here. Go to entrance tunnel when you sure it open. Good luck. If you no make it, no skin off my back.

You must not to be recaptured. It be bad for you. You understand this?"

"Thanks, Joe. If we make it, we won't forget you," Allen promised.

"No. You must to forget me now. It be very bad for me if you speak of me. That very important. You must to forget me now forever!"

After Joe left, they waited in tense silence for a sign that the tunnel was open, each knowing that their fate was now in the hands of divine intervention.

CHAPTER 81

Cai was faintly aware of the jostling stretcher under her and caught occasional glimpses of the stars overhead through the trees as brush plucked at her arms. She could make out Le Loi's indistinct outline beside her as they stumbled along and tried to speak to him, but only weak gasps escaped her lips. The ball of fire in her stomach throbbed in waves of intense heat. She gritted her teeth as they pulled her from the litter and lowered her body into the hole, where groping hands guided her downward. Le Loi's harsh voice ordered them to be careful with her as she cried out. She gasped in agony as they pushed her into the small horizontal tunnel at the bottom, the searing pain in her body intensifying as they drug her on her back through the narrow channel into the larger room, where they lifted her back onto a stretcher.

Le Loi hurried out of the entrance to the tunnel and rushed up to her side as Colonel Chien hovered over her and reached out to comfort her as she moaned.

"How did this happen?" he demanded of Le Loi as they hurried along with the litter bearers rushing her to the infirmary.

"She was summoned to her uncle's hooch to meet with a messenger from the North who brought news of her child.

An American soldier and a Viet male were waiting for us there. The American shot my Captain and killed four of our soldiers," Le Loi reported.

"And of the American and the Viet male who awaited her arrival?" Chien demanded.

"They were both killed during the attack. The American also killed Thinh as he attempted to escape, my Colonel."

"*You have failed me*!" Chien admonished him bitterly.

Cai attempted to defend Le Loi as he shrank back from Chien, but could only muster strangled gasps as intense pain again consumed her body in racking waves.

CHAPTER 82

Two men carrying a stretcher with a body on it rushed by with the Vietnamese colonel and another man hurrying after them.

"*That's it!*" Allen hissed. "*The tunnel's open!*"

"*Fuck it, Bo!*" Bubba hissed back. "*It's time to get the fuck outta this shit hole!*"

Bubba led him out of the toilet room into the narrow corridor, where they hurried along to what they thought to be the entrance tunnel without meeting anyone, and rushed into the small room where three men gaped at them in shock. Bubba opened fire without hesitation, the noise muffled by the damp earth surrounding them, crumpling the three in a tangle before they had time to recover.

"*Get in there, Bo!*" Bubba shoved him toward the small opening. "Come out the other end shooting! I'll cover you!"

Allen dropped to his knees and scurried forward. He reached the end of the horizontal tunnel and squeezed up into the vertical shaft as a muffled explosion sounded below him. He heaved himself up out of the vertical shaft and rolled to the side, startling several dark figures nearby. One of them called out to him in Vietnamese. He swung his AK around and fired in their direction on full automatic as they scattered in panic. Bubba's head popped up out of the hole behind him. Allen grabbed his arm and jerked him to the surface.

"*Let's get the fuck outta here, Bo!*" Bubba yelled.

Allen ran after him as the group he had fired on yelped in alarm. One man stepped in front of them and Bubba cut him down with a burst of fire without pausing in his head-long rush as the others cowered in confusion. Bubba paused, pulled the pin on a grenade, and heaved it into the foliage behind them.

"Give me your extra magazine and one of your gre-nades!" he panted, snatching one of Allen's grenades and the spare clip of ammo from him. "You go that way, Bo, and I'll go this way!"

"That's not the plan, Bubba!" Allen gasped. "We need to stay together!"

"*Don't have time to argue with you, Bo. Good luck!*"

The grenade behind them exploded, throwing leaves and dirt into the air as they ducked, the blast electing a cry of pain out of the darkness in the aftermath. When Allen turned back, Bubba was gone. He cursed under his breath and ran off in the direction Bubba indicated he was to go in.

"*Run, Bo, run! These gooks can't catch us,*" Bubba yelled from off to his right.

For a startled instant, Allen couldn't believe the idiot was shouting, then realized Bubba was playing the decoy to draw the VC in that direction in order to give him a bet-ter chance of escaping. A hot flush of anger engulfed him as he slammed through the encroaching vegetation whipping at him. He didn't slow his headlong rush until he collapsed in a wheezing heap, his shirtless chest heaving from the ef-fort and glistening with sweat. He sank back against a tree, choking off his gasps as he listened for sounds of pursuit.

He massaged his bare, bleeding feet, now mere painful orbs from the thorns and limbs that had cut into the flesh of his soles as he ran. When his senses steadied, he struggled up and staggered forward. To his right the brief roar of AKs firing disrupted the strangling silence. He threaded his way along in the opposite direction at a more subdued pace, picking his way through the clumps of vegetation instead of his previous headlong gallop, stopping every few meters to hold his breath and listen. Hearing nothing, he pushed on again. A muffled explosion off to his right, followed by more automatic weapons fire, confirmed Bubba was still in a running battle with his pursuers.

He cursed Bubba's stupid heroics as tears stung his eyes and pushed on through the dense jungle, his senses on full alert and his nerves jangling.

CHAPTER 83

Colonel Chien instinctively ducked as a barrage of gunfire broke out behind them. "Were you followed?" he demanded.

"No, Colonel," Le Loi yelled over the muffled den. "The firing is down here with us, not above ground!" An explosion shook the interior of the complex and dirt fell from the ceiling onto their heads as an aide rushed up.

"Colonel! The American prisoners are attempting to escape! They have armed themselves and are in the entrance tunnel!"

Colonel Chien turned to Le Loi. "There is nothing you can do here! You must stop these men before they reach their own forces and compromise our operations in this sector!"

Le Loi swallowed and nodded as he glanced down at Cai. "Yes, Colonel. I will obey." He hurried towards the entrance tunnel.

Chien continued on to the infirmary as the fight behind him grew more distant and men rushed for the entrance tunnel. He arrived to find the medics attempting to remove Cai's clothing as she struggled with them from where she lay on the operating table. He tried to soothe her as she cried and begged Le Loi to help her as the medical staff held her down and stripped her shirt away, exposing two small puncture wounds in her stomach oozing blood mixed with a vulgar green substance from her intestines. She screamed as the surgeon probed her abdomen. An assistant injected a needle into her arm and her struggles weakened until she lay with her eyes half-lidded, staring unseeing up at the ceiling.

"Can you help her?" Chien demanded as the surgeon examined her wounds.

"It is very serious, Colonel. Her intestines are ruptured. There is great danger of infection. I will do my best," the surgeon replied as he worked, his hands covered with gore. "Please, Colonel. You must go now and allow my staff to properly assist me!"

Chien backed out of the room and hovered at the door as the medical staff worked over her. A staff member hurried up to him.

"Colonel, the Americans have escaped through the tunnel. Five of our men are killed and three wounded."

"Seal the South entrance immediately," he instructed quietly as Cai lay completely still now, uncaring of the scalpel slicing into her stomach or the vile contents emptying out of the dreadful cavity.

CHAPTER 84

A llen stumbled blindly through the night, pausing often to listen for sounds of pursuit. As dawn emerged, he found a dense, briar-covered area and wallowed into the foliage, covering his bare chest and legs with dead leaves, too exhausted to continue. He slept sporadically through the morning, waking only once to brush at an insect crawling across his face. When he next awoke, he estimated it was noon from the height of the sun, which was blinding after the weeks of being underground. He held a palm up to shade his eyes as he watched a helicopter fly overhead, its thumping blades music to his ears, invoking a strong sense of home-sickness within him and a desperate desire to be back at the base camp with his fellow soldiers around him. He thought of home and his mother as a lump rose in his throat to choke him. He focused his thoughts on Bubba with deep-seated remorse. After the last round of firing and the grenade ex-plosion, he had heard nothing else from his escape attempt. He suffered a wave of consuming guilt at Bubba's incred-ibly brave gesture in sacrificing his own safety in order to increase his chance of survival, whispering a silent, urgent prayer that it was not in vain.

He sat up and surveyed his surroundings. For all he knew he could have run in circles in the dark and was back where

351

he started. He checked his AK-47, finding half a clip of ammo left to go with his one grenade.

He stood and listened, trying to decide which direction he should go in. Bubba thought they should go south. He studied the sun overhead trying to determine which way south would be. He marked a shadow on the ground and waited for it to move to tell him east from west. After a few moments, he selected what he thought would be south and hobbled through the jungle, pausing often to listen, avoiding trails completely. When he noticed his bare, shredded feet leaving bloody imprints on the leaves from the numerous cuts, he paused to rip his shorts off and tear them in half to bind his bleeding feet. Now wholly nude, he was able to travel faster, but was prone to make more noise with the clumsy padding in the dry leaves.

Hunger gnawed at his stomach and thirst clutched at his throat. He held the automatic weapon at the ready with the safety off. He was scared, but resolved to the fact that he would die before allowing them to recapture him. He paused to watch another helicopter fly overhead going in much the same direction as the previous one. He hesitated, trying to decide if it was going to their base camp at Cu Chi or flying away from it. He continued in the direction he thought was south, which was in the opposite direction of the flight of the aircraft, moving faster as the undergrowth thinned out. He hugged the shadows of the trees as he skirted around open fields and rice paddies. He hid once as an ox cart with a man and a woman plodded by on a rutted trail near him. On another occasion, he slipped deeper into the shrubbery to hide when he thought he heard voices, but no one came near him. He tried hard to remember terrain features, but nothing looked familiar. He estimated that he had covered two miles in the three hours he had been moving when another helicopter flew overhead, this time going the same way he was traveling in, which gave him some hope that he was moving in the right direction. His thirst became a severe problem, overriding his stomach rumbling from hunger.

His heart pounded in earnest when four VC carrying rifles appeared to his front moving from his left to his right. He froze in place and squatted down as he watched them pass. He stayed hidden for half an hour after they disappeared from view, waiting and watching, before he moved again, stopping often to turn in all directions to look and listen. From his front, the thumping of artillery firing brought hope to his glazed mind. He marked the direction, which was slightly to the left of the route he had been moving in, and increased his pace, hoping it was artillery from their main base at Cu Chi. He estimated the firing was several miles away and fought the urge to run in that direction, forcing himself to slow down and move with more caution. He worked his way around a deserted hooch as the artillery stopped firing, worrying in the resuming silence that he had lost the exact direction in the heavy foliage. He realized tears were sliding down his cheeks only when he licked at the bitter salt encrusting his lips.

CHAPTER 85

Terror gripped Cai as the five imperialists tore greedily at her frail body, their hands stripping her clothes away. She screamed and fought them until she collapsed, sobbing, devoid of strength to resist them, begging Le Loi to help her. But the demon man appeared instead with his flickering yellow eyes. His huge shaft tore into her, ripping her belly in blinding pain as the others pinned her back.

For the second time in her life, she sought the near darkness to escape the searing pain in her abdomen, welcoming the refuge as she descended in a lazy spiral down into the nothingness. She tried to control her descent, conscious that she must not drop too deeply into the pit, that she must eventually find her way back. Gradually the pace became more rapid and she could no longer control the plunge. She fought to slow the dive, thinking she must go no further. The pain in her stomach began to ease mercifully with the plummet and soon she felt no pain at all.

All around her was serene. She had gone far enough to escape now, but continued to spiral downward, finding the tranquility so welcoming she wondered why she had ever feared this place. Her resolve faded. Why return to the hell above? She would stay here forever. None could harm her here, not even the demon man with the flickering eyes. Soothing contentment encased her.

She relaxed, her thoughts of Le Loi, as she slid gently, eagerly to the bottom.

CHAPTER 86

"*Freeze jackass*!" a voice to his right called, not ten feet away.

Allen stopped with his heart in his throat before realizing an American voice had spoken. He turned his head and saw two American infantrymen staring at him with narrowed eyes, their rifles trained on him.

"*Don't shoot*!" he begged as waves of sheer relief washed over him. "*I'm an American*! *I need help*! *I'm lost*!"

Other men stood up from the bushes and circled around him cautiously. A lieutenant and his RTO moved forward and stopped a few feet away.

"Drop your weapon! Who are you?"

Allen dropped the AK-47 and the grenade to the ground. "Sir, I'm Private Allen Hayes, from Alpha Company, First of the Twenty-Seventh Infantry," he sobbed, wanting to hug the men around him. "I've been a prisoner. Bubba and I escaped last night. I need help to get back home. Please, I need some water. And I haven't eaten for a long time."

"Well kiss my ass," one of the men responded. "I think I know this man! Yeah, we were fucking new guys together in the Combat Orientation Classes when we first got over here! Hell, we drank beer almost every night at the Wolf's Den while we were waiting for our platoon assignments. Here man, have some of my water. Hey, somebody give him some C-rats!" he encouraged as he held out his canteen to Allen.

Another man stepped up and scooped his rifle and the grenade off the ground. "Easy, fellow," the soldier ordered as he edged back. "Where's your clothes and boots?"

"The VC took them. My underwear is all they left me with." He lifted his foot to show them the rags adorning his feet.

"You were really a POW?" the lieutenant asked.

"Yes, Sir. They wiped my platoon out on my first night ambush patrol and I was taken prisoner."

"You're one of Tiger Woman's prisoners?" the lieutenant asked as excitement swept through the men around him.

"I don't know who Tiger Woman is, Sir, but a woman led them."

"You're one lucky son of a bitch," another man offered, as the others edged closer mumbling in agreement.

"Where's the other man that escaped with you?" the lieutenant asked.

"I don't know, Sir. We split up last night. I heard a lot of shooting and a grenade explode as they chased him. I don't know if he made it or not. Please, Sir. I just want to get back home."

"Sergeant Haley, let's head to that clearing we passed a ways back," the lieutenant ordered as he turned to his RTO. "I'll call for a chopper to pick him up."

"Thank you, Sir. I saw four VC about an hour ago. They were heading in that direction," Allen pointed to his right. A man finished opening a can of peaches and handed it to him as another worked on a can of beans and franks.

"Alright, quit gawking and get your heads out of your ass!" Sergeant Haley ordered. "Let's get organized and moving."

Allen fell in behind the lieutenant and his RTO, eating from the cans as they moved towards the clearing. Fifteen minutes later a medevac chopper fishtailed down to the smoke grenade and he ran through the rotor wash to climb aboard. One of the medics on board knelt and unwrapped his bloody feet as they lifted off.

Allen stared down at the jungle below him as they streaked towards Cu Chi and safety, certain he had never seen such a beautiful sight as the rag tag bunkers and hooches of the base camp when they came into view. A stretcher team waiting for him at the hospital helipad rushed him to the emergency room. A tall captain with freckles and red hair hurried in a few minutes later, followed by a thin man with a silk scarf around his neck, and a heavyset master sergeant. The three of them questioned him as the doctors treated the wounds on his feet.

When they released him from the emergency room, the men produced a map and showed him where the platoon found him. He tried to help them guess where he had come from by picking out certain terrain features. They grew excited when he told them of the tunnel complex, and became even more animated by the approximate position he thought he had come from. They questioned him about the tunnels, which he described in as much detail as possible, and gave as much information on the entrance as he could remember. He described the attack on their platoon, weeping as he told of the torture and killing of the prisoners by the woman they called Tiger Woman. He described Colonel Nguyen Van Chien and the beatings he and Bubba had received, and gave them as much information on Bubba as he knew. They reassured him that other units were rushing into the area to look for Bubba as they talked.

When they left, a nurse put him in a wheelchair and pushed him to the hospital shower point. She tied plastic bags around his feet and waited while he enjoyed his first bath in seven weeks, standing under the hot spray scrubbing vigorously with a bar of medicated soap. From there, he dressed in a clean cotton hospital gown and she wheeled him into a ward where a steak dinner with baked potato and dessert of apple pie and ice cream awaited him. Afterwards he lay back in the softest bed he had ever imagined.

Before he drifted into sleep, he said a silent, fervent prayer for Bubba.

CHAPTER 87

Chien stood in the infirmary staring down at Cai, who was unconscious and covered with a fine film of perspiration. Her breathing was shallow, but her features were calm. His heart was heavy and filled with anxiety for this strange woman. If she recovered, she would thankfully not be able to serve in combat again due to her extensive injuries. Nor would she ever bear his children. But she would be his, and that was all that mattered.

"She has a high fever, Colonel," the surgeon advised. "We must move her to our hospital in Saigon. I had to remove most of her stomach. She will be many months recovering."

"I will arrange transportation," Chien replied. "This complex has been compromised by the escape of the Americans. We will leave tonight and relocate to our other tunnel system. We will seal this one after we evacuate. You will prepare your sick and wounded for movement."

"Yes, Colonel."

Chien returned to his operation's room where his staff was destroying maps and documents in preparation for the move. He arranged for an escort to carry Cai to the surface and transport her to the hospital in Saigon disguised as a peasant woman injured during a firefight between the Americans and the People's Liberation Army, one of many civilian casualties that frequently occurred in the crossfire between the two forces. No one in the hospitals in Saigon ever questioned this type of incident when they often sent their seriously wounded soldiers there.

Le Loi contacted him by the land phone later that afternoon to inform him that they had killed one of the Americans, but that the other evaded them. He directed Le Loi to continue the search in the hopes of finding the man before the Americans did, knowing the effort was futile.

That night the five hundred-plus men in the complex slipped to the surface. Guides led them in groups around the ambush sites of the Americans to another underground system. Others worked to fill in the four entrances to the old tunnel system to ground level and camouflage the area around them. Cai was transported by litter to a safe hooch. A Lambretta would take her the following morning to Saigon, accompanied by two medics. There was nothing more he could do for her.

The next afternoon Chien learned that the American's caught Le Loi and most of Cai's remaining force in a trap the previous night and destroyed them. He also learned that one of the females killed by the Americans had been drug to their base camp at Cu Chi and hung upside down from a tree. Later his intelligence network informed him that the Americans thought the woman was Cai, or Tiger Woman, as they called her. He received confirmation within the hour that Cai was safely in the ARVN hospital in Saigon, still unconscious.

At midnight of that day, a new commander assumed command of the Cu Chi district and ordered him north to face a board of inquiry for his negligence in allowing the Americans to escape.

He prepared for the long journey with a heavy heart, desiring to remain in the south near Cai, knowing but uncaring that he would never hold a command again.

CHAPTER 88

"General, I wish I could tell you it was a brilliant tactical operation on our part, but the fact of the matter is, we were damned lucky," the G-3 briefed the general and his staff as Christen sat at the table listening. "Tiger Woman and her force walked into one of our ambushes last night at this location here." The G-3 pointed to the map. "When the dust settled, they found her body among the dead."

The general turned to Christen. "Chris, have you confirmed her identity?"

"Sir, my staff and I visited the site this morning. Due to the mutilated state of the body, we were unable to make a positive identification."

"Sir, she was wearing her trademark tiger fatigues and was positively identified by our soldiers at the site who had photos of her," the G-2 argued.

"How was her body desecrated?" the general asked.

Christen cleared his throat. "Sir, they stripped her nude, cut her breasts off, and then scalped her. Afterwards, they drug her behind one of the mechanized tracks back to a spot just outside our perimeter and hung her up by her feet from a rubber tree."

The general glowered. "I am severely disappointed by our soldier's actions."

"Sir, what they did was disgraceful, but in a way, you can't blame them for their hatred of her," the G-3 defended. "Look at what she did to our men, dead and alive."

"That doesn't excuse our own barbaric actions," the general countered. "I would hope that we are above that ourselves, and I would have liked a positive identification. They ruined any chance of that."

"Yes, Sir, but I'm convinced we got her this time," the G-3 insisted.

"Under the circumstances, I guess only time will tell," the G-1 replied. "We'll just have to wait and see if she reappears again on some dark night."

"May God have mercy on our souls if she does," the general observed. "Now what of these tunnel complexes the young man who escaped told us about?"

"Sir, we've had three battalions in that area searching every square inch of it and found nothing," the G-3 replied. "Additionally, we've had experts out there from the Corps of Engineers. They estimate it would take several years to dig such a structure, and even then, it would be next to impossible to have such a tunnel complex in that soil. They consider the ground too porous and estimate the monsoons would fill them with water and collapse them since the soldier's description indicated there were very few reinforcing joists to shore up the ceilings. They consider it highly improbable that such a complex as he describes exists. I hate to suggest it, but his captivity may have made him delusional."

"I'm not an engineer, Sir, and certainly not qualified to argue the structural integrity of such a system," Christen said. "But I personally questioned Private Hayes and he did not appear delusional to me. The area fits in every way with what he described, and is directly in the vicinity of where we were searching for her base. Specialist Robert Andrews, the man Private Hayes claims escaped with him, is in fact one of our MIAs who we lost *after* Hayes was captured. He had no way of knowing that if he had not seen the man himself."

"Then why can't three thousand men find the tunnel complex or the soldier if either is out there?" the G-3 argued.

"Sir, Private Hayes said they covered the entrances up when our forces were in the area," Christen replied. "I believe that to be the case now."

"Have the battalions conduct another search tomorrow," the general directed. "If they don't find anything, bring them back in. Chris, you and your team have done an excellent job on this project. I'm placing you back in your regular assignments unless we get a further indication that this woman still exists."

Christen nodded. "Yes, Sir."

CHAPTER 89

A llen stepped out of the taxi early on a hot Sunday morning and adjusted his dress uniform as he wiped the perspiration off his forehead with his handkerchief. He walked
up to the small, white-framed house rehearsing his introduc-
tion and knocked on the door as a church bell tolled in the
distance. A slim, pristine woman wearing an apron opened
the door and looked up at him through the screen door with
curious eyes. Allen removed his cap and fought the sudden,
choking clog in his throat.

"Mrs. Andrews, I'm Private First Class Allen Hayes. I...
knew Bubba in Vietnam. He... saved my life, Ma'am." Tears
streamed down his cheeks as he sank to his knees in front
of her on the porch, sobbing. *"I promised him I'd come see
you... he said you make the best biscuits in the world..."*

"Who's at the door, Julia?" a male voice called from inside the house.

"It's a little lost soldier boy, Jessie. He's come from a
faraway place." She opened the screen door and wrapped
her arms around Allen's head, hugging him to her stomach
as he wept.

"He's hungry and... he's come to bring a piece of our
Bobby back home to us..."

PROLOGUE

Chien shuffled down the corridor of the sanitarium on the outskirts of Saigon with heavy steps after his long six years spent in the north working in the logistics branch overseeing the movement of supplies down the Ho Chi Minh Trail. When the Americans at long last withdrew their hated forces from his country, he applied for retirement and spent a month working his way south through the fast fading remnants of the South Vietnamese government. It took him a week of inquiries to find Cai. He left the office of the head psychiatrist with his heart beating rapidly and paused at her door to knock. When there was no answer, he stepped inside and found Cai seated in a chair with her hands in her lap staring out the window without expression.

"Cai? It is me, Chien," he whispered.

She made no movement, and her eyes were without focus in her expressionless face. He moved in front of her and blocked her view as he lifted his hand to stroke her long, unkempt, coarse hair.

"They tell me you do not talk," he pleaded. "Will you not acknowledge me?" He knelt before her. "I have come for you, Cai. I have come to take you home."

She made no move to resist when he took her hand. It plopped limply back into her lap when he released it. She remained impassive as he embraced her tiny body, hugging her to his chest as tears streamed down his cheeks. When he stepped back, she slumped back into her chair and leaned to the side without correcting her balance.

"You must come back to me, Cai. This place is not good for you. I will take care of you forever. You will become my wife. Can you hear me, Cai?" He wiped at his cheeks as the pain tore at his chest. "You cannot spend your life here in this place. You must raise your son. You must spend your days with me in our home. Please come back to me, Cai. *Please hear me!*"

He returned every day to talk to her, to soothe and plead with her as he held her in his arms for long periods, but received nothing from her but the unsettling, vague stare. He spent time with the staff in the sanatorium learning to care for her.

Two weeks after his arrival, he settled Cai into the back of an ox cart wrapped in blankets and set out on the lengthy voyage back to his ancestral home in the village of Muong-La, his heart aching with the unbearable pain of her being so close, yet so far away…

3392192

Made in the USA